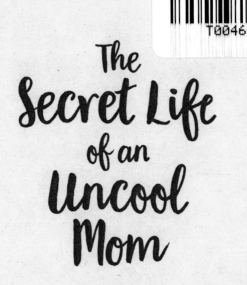

The Secret Life of an Uncool Mom

Comedian, writer and public speaker, Serena Terry, known as Mammy Banter, has taken the social media world by storm after her hilarious videos started going viral across TikTok, Instagram, Facebook and Twitter.

Serena's down-to-earth, 'tell it like it is' realness has resonated with fans around the world. She has over 1.5 million followers, with more than 28 million views across all platforms.

She lives in Derry with her husband and two kids.

The Secret Life of an Uncool Mom

SERENA TERRY

HarperCollins*Publishers*

HarperCollins*Publishers*
1 London Bridge Street
London SE1 9GF

www.harpercollins.co.uk

HarperCollins*Publishers*
1st Floor, Watermarque Building, Ringsend Road
Dublin 4, Ireland

Published by HarperCollins*Publishers* 2022
1

With thanks to Claire Allan

A catalogue record for this book
is available from the British Library

ISBN (US): 978-0-00-855329-6

Typeset in Berling LT Std by Palimpsest Book Production Ltd, Falkirk, Stirlingshire

Printed and Bound in the UK using 100% Renewable Electricity
at CPI Group (UK) Ltd

MIX
Paper | Supporting
responsible forestry
FSC™ C007454

This book is produced from independently certified FSC™ paper
to ensure responsible forest management.

For more information visit: www.harpercollins.co.uk/green

To Ava

'Flying might not be all plain sailing, but the fun of it is worth the price'

Amelia Earhart

1

That's not Nutella

Everything is perfect. My house is perfect. My life is perfect. My children are perfect. My heart is full and at peace. Which can only mean one thing: the shit is about to hit the fan.

As sure as night follows day, the moment I, Tara Gallagher – wife, mother, friend – so much as think, 'Ah, this is lovely. Everything is as it should be,' something big happens. Something big. And bad. And generally very messy.

On a good day, if you asked me to describe myself, I'd say I'm a thirty-six-year-old, happily married mum of three, and I'd stand by that, that's a nice description, right? On a bad day, I'd say I'm an emotionally exhausted mess of a woman, who is hanging on by a thin thread every single day trying to be a good mother, wife, friend, daughter and colleague with a social life of her own, a successful career and a body that I most definitely have 'let go'.

And today was supposed to be a good day.

In about twenty minutes' time my firstborn child – my princess – will walk through the front door with her best friend Mia in tow. It's her thirteenth birthday. A momentous day in the Gallagher house. We have successfully completed Level 12 parenting and Gemma is progressing to the big leagues and Level 13. I kept a child alive for thirteen years, can you believe it? Go me! (And Paul; I suppose it was a team effort.)

I take a deep breath. I am ready for this. I took a half-day from work and have spent the last three hours pinning photos of Gemma, from birth to now, on the walls of our kitchen. She asked for helium number balloons like the ones influencers use on Instagram when they get to a new milestone of followers. Eugh. But for her, I got them, and some retro Poundshop balloons for good measure.

I've dusted off my old disco lights, which were lying in the back of the garage, and have confettied the kitchen table to within an inch of its life (I'm a dick: I'm already thinking about the mess afterwards . . .). There are plastic Prosecco flutes, ready to be filled with sparkling apple juice. I bought her favourite pink icing cupcakes instead of a cake. There are crisps and sweets (foam shrimps and cola bottles) and a chocolate fountain with marshmallows and strawberries and bananas for dipping. It's all very Instagrammable. Teenagers love this shit, right? I get a pang of something between grief and nostalgia – it seems like only yesterday I was covering this kitchen in Disney Princess-themed decorations, and Gemma was dressed as Belle, her favourite princess at the time. And somehow now I'm hosting her thirteenth birthday party – how has time gone so fast!? Like, granted, I wake up every day with a new joint pain, but I often forget that I'm not still in my mid-twenties.

Before I get the chance to have a panic attack about the passage of time, I am dive-bombed by two small, very strong, very loud and – I can see – very, very hyper boys.

'Mammeeeee,' Nathan, my adorably manic five-year-old, shouts. 'Can we go to the trampoline? I want to jump! My legs feel fizzy, and my arms, and my hands and my face . . .'

Looking down, there's a sticky congealed mess of slabbers and sugar coating his lips and cheeks. His eyes are wide, pupils dilated. Shite. Classic sugar-rush symptoms. Behind him, my two-year-old Jax has done a mini Full Monty – all his clothes gone bar one sock, a drool-soaked vest and his nappy, staring at his own hands as if he has just discovered he owns them.

He is clattered, and I do mean absolutely clattered, in the same gooey sugar shite that Nathan is. At least I hope it's sugar. By the look of them both I wouldn't be surprised if they were off their shiny tits on cocaine. (Not that we have cocaine in the house, mind. The hardest drug we rock is Calpol for Over Sixes – aka The Hard Stuff.) With a deep sinking horror, I take my gaze from them to the kitchen table where I am at least two bowls of fizzy cola bottles down.

Sweet and gentle Jesus.

'Nathan, did you take some of the sweeties from the table?' I ask, hoping that my Cocomelon-esque sing-song voice is hiding the sense of mild hysteria clawing at my very soul.

He looks at me, his eyes wide as my new Primark support

knickers. 'Fizzy candy,' he says in a voice that sounds more Darth Vader than five-year-old boy. He also speaks in an American accent as we're deep in the age of YouTube parenting. Don't judge me, I'll bet my bottom dollar you've got a half-Yank child or grandchild running about.

Glancing over his head I spot a trail of destruction that makes my head spin. Toys and clothes are scattered as if there has been an explosion in a soft play centre. A lone sock dangles precariously from the light fitting. An abandoned, upturned Fruit Shoot is leaking its purple-coloured poison into my new cream rug. (Yes, my children drink Fruit Shoots. Yes, I am a mammy of young children and I bought a cream rug. Call me a silly cow later; I've bigger fish to fry.) The closing bars to the *Paw Patrol* theme tune blasts from the living room and God, I'm scared now but I must show no fear. These little shits can smell fear.

'Mammmmmeeeeee,' Nathan says as he follows me.

'Just a minute, pet,' I say through gritted teeth. 'Mammy's going to turn the sound down on the TV so I can hear you properly.'

When I walk into the living room I want to cry. I think I *might* actually cry. It was tidy and clean when I left it. All ready for Gemma and her friends to come have her party. It looked like something out of the Ikea catalogue. But now – sweet living lord! Now, it looks like a case for one of those hoarder cleaning crews in Hazmat suits. I'm pretty sure every toy my children have ever owned is strewn around the room; that definitely looks like permanent marker on the wall, my sofa cushions are upturned on the floor and in the middle of one of them there is a mass of wet, sticky, slimy cola bottles. And who in the name of my wee Granny Annie (rest her soul) smeared Nutella on the sofa? Christ on a bike.

'Mammeeeeee,' Nathan opines again as I wonder if he is too old to be put up for adoption.

'Nathan, pet, what happened here?' I ask, and really I deserve an award for my acting skills right now because he doesn't seem to have any idea whatsoever that I'm about to lose my actual shit.

He shrugs. 'Didn't like 'em so I spitted 'em out.'

'After sucking the sugar off?' I ask.

He nods. 'I only liked the sugar part.'

'Ahh you liked that?' I ask. 'Did you like making a big mess too?'

He nods enthusiastically, then, perhaps seeing my gritted teeth or my twitching eye and catching on that this might not be the response I was hoping for, he stops himself and starts to shake his head solemnly instead. The self-preservation is strong in this one.

'Right,' I say, to myself as much as anyone. 'We'd better try and tidy this up a bit.' I regretfully smell-test the Nutella on the sofa . . . Ah fuck, it's not Nutella.

'But mammmeeeeeee,' Nathan says, and the whine is back in his voice.

I take a deep breath. 'I know your head is fizzy and your hands are fizzy, but it's your big sister's birthday party and we need to tidy up. Will we sing the tidy-up song?' I don't have a tidy-up song, but I'm sure I can bastardize a Beyoncé song to suit the purpose. ('To the left, to the left, put all that plastic crap in a pile to the left.')

''S'not that, Mammy,' he says, shaking his head. 'Jax boked on the carpet.'

I can't speak. I am struck mute by the full horror of the situation unfolding in front of my eyes. How am I going to get shit off the sofa and vomit out of the carpet before the girls get home without the eau de puke permeating everything?

'And Mammy . . .' Nathan continues before I cut him off with what can only be considered a death glare, which I immediately regret when I see his bottom lip start to wobble.

'Sorry, pet,' I say in my best not-a-horrible-mammy voice. 'What is it?'

'Am gonny boke too.'

Woah there, crotch-goblin. Not on my watch.

Or more accurately, not on my cream carpet.

With lightning reflexes, I scoop him up in one seamless movement before hurtling at breakneck speed – past the baby who is now contently playing with a toy car beside a puddle of his own vomit and a shitty nappy he removed himself – into the downstairs toilet in the nick of time. As he manages to get almost all his regurgitated sugar and Fruit Shoot into the toilet bowl, and only a small amount is sprayed down the front of my lovely new white T-shirt, I remind myself that in days to come this will be a memory I will laugh about. I'll probably be in a nursing home, swigging from a bottle of vodka I asked them to smuggle me in, mind you, but I'll be having a wee giggle about it too, I'm sure.

His stomach emptied, Nathan rests his head against my soggy chest and it appears all the fizzy must be gone from his system because his eyes flutter closed and he falls asleep in my arms. At least, I hope it's sleep and not a diabetic coma.

In moments such as these, when my children are finally asleep, I often realize just how much I love them. And I love the very bones of Nathan. Even when he is a rascal – and this definitely falls into rascal territory – my heart can't help but swell with love for my blue-eyed boy.

Carefully, I carry him upstairs and lay him on top of his bed before pulling an old, battered grey T-shirt from my drawer to change into while I clean up. I'm halfway down the stairs, and halfway into my new T-shirt, hands over my head, face hidden, and an ill-fitting bra on full display when I hear the front door open, quickly followed by the perhaps the loudest intake of breath I have ever heard in my entire life.

Hauling my T-shirt down to make myself decent I see my beloved eldest child staring at me with a mixture of rage and humiliation. Beside her, the best of her BFFs, Mia, has her hand clamped over her mouth in shock. Mia has not only seen my tatty-bra-covered boobs, but is now also turning green at the sight of the vomit on the hall carpet.

I don't even have time to speak before Gemma does. 'Oh. My. God. Why do you have to ruin everything? You're so embarrassing!'

It's as if our roles have reversed but as I try to find a way to explain myself, she lifts Jax from the floor and stomps off upstairs muttering to Mia that she 'has to do everything in this house'.

'Offer it up for the Holy Souls,' I whisper to myself. It's her hormones. Or her age. Or maybe she's just turning into a really horrible child. The kind everyone whispers about in the car park after birthday parties . . .

No. No, she's mine, she can't be a dick, it's her age. Puberty is brutal. Seeing your mammy in her bra is brutal. Walking in on a scene that looks like it could be from an NSPCC ad is really brutal. I'll make it up to her, I tell myself. This will be the best birthday party of her life. I'll make sure of it.

Just as soon as I've figured out how to get permanent marker off the walls, vomit off the carpet and actual shit off my sofa.

FML.

2

Five, six, seven, eight

I'm impressed at how quickly I'm able to undo the damage the boys have done. By the time Paul – the Ross to my Rachel – arrives home from work, things are almost back to normal. The permanent-marker situation is still unresolved but I've been able to hide it behind a hastily shifted side table.

Yes, I might now look like a hella hot mess and, yes, I may have already poured myself a glass of wine purely for medicinal reasons, but I have won this battle. Thankfully, Paul and I know each other pretty well by now. For example, I know that when he comes in from work on a Friday night, he likes to crack open a bottle of his favourite beer while he fantasizes about what we will order from the Chinese after the kids are in bed. I know not to comment on this. I know not to ask him why he needs to study the menu when we both know he's going to order the banquet for one, with an extra portion of chicken balls – just like he does every week.

In return, he knows that if he arrives home to see me halfway down a glass of rosé and with a slight twitch in my right eye, then he's best to speak only to apologize for his role in impregnating me with whatever child has worked my last nerve that day.

'Are you ready to talk about it yet?' he asks, and I shake my head. I fear I'll punch him in the testicles.

'Which one was it this time?'

'The boys. Vomit, shit and permanent marker all made an appearance. It was bad, Paul. It was very bad.'

'As bad as the time they Sudocremed the sofa?'

I think for a moment. That was a nightmare, yes, but it didn't threaten to ruin a hormonal almost-teen's birthday party. 'Worse,' I say, taking a big drink of my wine. His eyes widen imperceptibly. 'It was full-on code red, or should I say code brown, and Gemma managed to arrive home with Mia right in the middle of it. I may have also flashed my breasts.'

'Oh,' he says, and I nod. Neither of us need to say more. We are both aware of how volatile our precious firstborn has become. 'The place looks well though,' he says, looking around the kitchen, which retains its party-central feel. 'Does she love it?'

'She hasn't seen it yet. Stormed upstairs as soon as she came in. I left some cold drinks and crisps outside her room and I've heard her and Mia doing TikToks, so hopefully her mood will be better by the time her other friends arrive.' Which, I see from looking at the clock on the wall, will be any time now. Desperate not to do anything else

10

to bring the wrath of Gemma down on my shoulders, I ask Paul to mind the boys and get them ready for bed while I run upstairs and have a quick shower. I remind myself that I'm one very lucky girl – Paul has arrived home sweaty, with engine oil smudged on his face and hands. With his dark hair and tall physique he could've stepped out of a Lynx poster in the nineties. If the models had dad bods instead of washboard stomachs. But hey, do not knock a dad bod: my husband, to me, is an absolute ride.

By the time Gemma's besties arrive I will have shed my sweaty, stressed-out appearance and will have transformed into the kind of cool mammy every teenager wants. I have to make it quick though, so it's more of a trailer-park wash than a proper shower. Tying my damp hair up into a messy bun, I slip on the very trendy new PJs I bought to get onboard with the sleepover theme. Glancing at myself in the mirror, I think I look OK. Cute even. Yeah, let's go with cute.

I can put the carnage of the last few hours behind me and get in the zone to help my big girl have a truly unforgettable night. I've got this. I can boss this in my sleep. When I was a teenager, my birthday parties were the place to be. We would have sleepovers with karaoke and dance routines. We'd laugh so much that our sides would ache and if we were lucky we'd get an hour or two of sleep at most – but everyone would be talking about how amazing it all was for weeks after.

This is my comfort zone. I wrote the book on this party shiz.

A ring of the doorbell and thunderous clatter of feet on the stairs, followed by screaming so high-pitched I fear for my wine glass, lets me know that the girls have arrived. Feeling a little shiver of excitement at seeing how Gemma will react to the balloons, cupcakes and disco lights, I head downstairs.

My daughter doesn't mention my pyjamas but there is an expression on her face that I can't quite read. She's in a new pair of *Friends* PJs and has applied make-up with a confidence and talent I've not mastered in my thirty-six years on this planet. How do teenagers do it? How do they figure out contouring and cut creases and winged eyeliner so young? When I was a teen, it was a matter of covering as much of your face in Pan Stik or Elizabeth Arden, dark lip-liner over concealed lips and Aunt Sally amounts of blusher. We thought we were the shit, but these girls are all self-taught MUAs. I'm jealous, but I'm also immediately emotional. Gemma looks so grown up. I want to keep her this age forever. To stop the clock before midnight and her official thirteenth birthday. I want to keep her as a child. My child.

'C'mon upstairs,' she tells her friends. 'You lot need to get ready.'

'Do you not want to see what I've done in the kitchen?' I ask. 'I've got all your favourites, Gemma. And I even got some Rocky Road ice cream for later!'

'We were going to have pizza,' she says, with a coolness that wounds me. Last year she had my head melted for a full six weeks before her birthday to make sure I got the stupid damn pink cupcakes. When I went to get the groceries, she'd come with me and throw extra treats in, 'just for the party and not for you and Daddy to eat when we're in bed'. She planned that Little Mix-themed party like a pro, but now she wants to get offside as quickly as she can and just have pizza.

Paul pops his head around the door. 'Hi girls,' he says. 'Are youse all ready to party?' He does a funny little dance and even I have to cringe a bit. But Gemma and her friends? They laugh as if it is the most hilarious thing they've ever seen. Daddies can get away with it. Dads are supposed to be a bit cringey, and Gemma would forgive Paul anything anyway. They have always adored each other.

'Gemma, your mammy has gone to a lot of trouble to set everything up in the kitchen. Maybe it wouldn't hurt to have a wee look before you and your pals go and finish getting ready?'

Gemma, of course, doesn't roll her eyes at him. She smiles sweetly and says, 'OK, Daddy,' and leads her friends through to party central.

I'm so relieved when I hear squeals of delight and exclamations of how 'class' everything is. I even hear Gemma's voice in the mix. 'Guys,' she says, 'you have to try these cupcakes. They're the best thing in the world, ever!'

As tears of relief prick at my eyes I look at Paul, who is smiling a broad told-you-so smile back at me. 'You've got this,' he says with a wink, and I think right in that moment I fall in love with him all over again. His faith in me is unwavering. It always has been.

'I don't think the boys are anywhere near sleeping. Did Nathan have a nap earlier?'

I give him a look which lets him know that the answer to his question lies at the root of my traumatizing afternoon and he nods. 'Right, well I'll set them up with a DVD in our room. You just focus on enjoying Gemma's party.'

'Thanks, pet,' I tell him. He's a good spud, when push comes to shove.

'By the way,' he says with a smile. 'You are looking so hot in those pyjamas. Is that real flannelette?'

'Only the best for me,' I say with a grin. 'Primark's finest. Who needs Victoria and her secrets?'

'Not me anyway,' he says, looking me up and down. 'Give me high-neck, flame-retardant material, and a nice tartan pattern any day of the week.'

'I'm thinking I might even wear my dressing gown later,' I say with a wink.

'The big fluffy one?' he asks, widening his eyes with fake lust.

'Well, it is a Friday night,' I purr back at him. 'And you know what always happens on a Friday night.' I run my hand down his chest and look deep into his pale blue eyes. He moves his face closer to mine so I can feel his breath hot on my skin. 'I didn't think we'd be doing that tonight. Not with all those girls here for a sleepover,' he says breathlessly.

14

'Oh Paul, nothing – and I do mean nothing – gets in the way of our Friday-night routine.'

He groans a little. 'I can't wait,' he says, and he moves to kiss me.

'But we have to,' I tell him, putting one finger against his lips and very gently pushing him away. '*Gogglebox* doesn't start until nine.'

He laughs and I do too, allowing myself a moment of pink-cheeked pleasure. Whatever else I have done in my life I know that when I chose Paul, I chose a good one. There aren't too many men who would tolerate my sense of humour. And while our Friday nights are no longer the wild events they once were, our time together on the sofa watching *Gogglebox* is a sacred time for us. It's when we switch off from everything else around us, kids included.

Perhaps unsurprisingly, Gemma doesn't seem to want me to help her enjoy her party. When I pop my head through the kitchen door to see if they need anything I'm immediately shooed away. I offer to help them with their make-up – which they're all still insistent on slapping on even though they aren't going out and are in fact planning to sleep – but I'm quickly told the girls have brought their own.

Looking at the palettes and glosses, brushes and powders strewn on the worktop I am shocked to see they all seem to have higher quality and higher priced cosmetics than I ever owned in my life.

They don't even allow me to order the pizza in. Gemma is

only too keen to do so on the iPhone she got for Christmas and which has already become a permanent fixture in her hand. She taps at the screen with ease, placing her order before I can say 'get me a garlic bread with that'.

Feeling a little dejected, I sit in the conservatory and listen to their excited chatter. When the music starts up, I can't help but think back once again to my own younger years. Pop music had been my raison d'être – and there wasn't a Steps dance routine or a Backstreet Boys song that I couldn't throw shapes to with both passion and style. As I listen to them sing along to Ariana Grande and talk over each other, seemingly never taking a breath, something a wee bit like envy creeps over me. Yes, turning thirteen is a difficult time. Puberty is an absolute shitshow, I wouldn't go through it again for all the money in the world, especially not in the current world of social media – but those innocent times? Singing at the top of your lungs to some cool tune with your friends? I'd do it in a heartbeat.

I think that's what spurs me on when I hear the opening strains of 'Tragedy' by Steps ring out. Are they really listening to this absolute banger of a tune? I lost so many hours to perfecting that dance routine when I was around Gemma's age. I dreamt of marrying H (yeah, I wasn't too quick on the uptake then) and dancing to this in my wedding dress on our wedding in a totally non-ironic way. Funnily enough I was also convinced I'd marry Stephen from Boyzone, and Mark from Westlife . . .

I still have much to offer the younger generation and,

delighted to have a reason to show off my dance moves, I barrel into the kitchen with a smile plastered wide on my face.

'Girls, did you know that there was a dance routine to this one and all? It was the best fun. Here, let me show you.'

I begin to raise my hands towards my head in short, staccato movements as the chorus builds to its glorious crescendo, accompanied with the wee shimmy of a shoulder. Who needs those emotionless, complicated routines on TikTok when we, the older generation, had this covered years ago? I'm launching into the second half of the chorus, I'm killing it – well, I think I am – when I see my daughter's face.

She is horrified.

HORRIFIED.

More horrified than when I exposed my bra to her and her friend earlier. More mortified than I have ever seen her in my life. My hands drop slowly to my side. God love Mia, because she is at least trying to mimic my moves but hasn't realized the dropping of my hands in defeat isn't part of the official routine.

'Oh. My. God. Mammy! Why do you have to do this? Pretending you're cool and all. You're so . . . you're so . . . you're so OLD!' The word *old* cuts through me like a knife. 'Why do you have to keep embarrassing me? You're ruining my life!' Her friends look to the ground, awkwardness descending around us.

'Gemma, it's just . . . you were listening to this song and I thought . . .'

'I don't even know what this song is,' she yells. 'Mia's mammy saved it into the wrong playlist on Spotify.'

Right. OK. I muster what very, very little of my dignity I have left and apologize. I shouldn't let her talk to me like that but giving out to her in front of her friends will cause a blow-up that no amount of chatting will repair. I'll deal with it later.

My face blazing, I take my 'so not cool, old AF' self out of the kitchen and traipse into the living room biting back the urge to cry.

Tragedy, indeed.

3

Bonnie Tyler has entered the building

My mother loved to do things on a big scale. She still loves to do things on a big scale, if the truth be told, but age has calmed her down a little bit. However, when I was the same age as my beloved Gemma, my mother could only be described as a liability when it came to earning cool points in front of my friends.

Big earrings. Big hair. Big personality. And she loved to sing. As the old saying goes, what she lacked in talent she more than made up for in enthusiasm. Being a Derry woman – where music and song are drummed into us from the earliest of ages and even the most weak-voiced child will be forced to compete in the Feis Doire Colmcille at least once – she believed she had a God-given right to sing as often as she wanted.

As with all Derry people, she had what she referred to as her 'party piece' ready to bring out at a moment's notice. Everyone in Derry has to have one, or you risk being forever exiled from the banks of the Foyle.

My mother's party piece was – and the thought still gives me the cringe – 'Could It Be Magic' by Barry Manilow. If I close my eyes, I can see my aunties and uncles sitting around my granny's living room, clapping in time to the music while my mother stood in front of the fireplace and performed her song with a passion and volume that no one within a ten-mile radius could escape.

But while it was bad enough that she performed this song in front of family members, it was unforgivable when she got up to sing it at my fourteenth birthday party. The haunted looks on the faces of my friends as they tried to stifle their giggles because they knew laughing would be considered impolite! I can still feel the heat of embarrassment rise on my face and I swore that I would never, ever subject my own children to such an experience. There would be no Barry Manilow moments from me. Not a one.

And yet, there it is, burned into my brain: the same look of horror on my daughter's face. Jesus, was I now Barry Manilow? But . . . but I'm supposed to be Beyoncé. Was I now officially the most embarrassing mammy in the entire world???

'Are you OK, pet?' Paul asks, patting the space on the sofa beside him, signalling for me to sit down.

I shake my head.

'Still the PTSD from earlier?' he asks. 'I think the boys might be asleep now, if that helps. I'm going to leave it a wee while to be sure, and then I'll shift them into their own beds.'

''S'not the PTSD,' I say, and to my shock and surprise my

voice cracks when I speak. 'Or maybe it's a new PTSD,' I sniff, sitting down beside him.

He puts his arm around me and I curl up into the soft, familiar comfort of him. 'Do you want to talk about it?' he asks, kissing the top of my head.

While I shake my head as if it's the very last thing I want to talk about, I start talking anyway. 'Am I embarrassing?' I ask him. I feel him pull back and I look up to see he is staring at me as if I've lost the run of myself.

'Aye but in a funny way,' he says.

'In a funny way?'

'Well, you're not afraid to take the mick out of yourself. You don't care if you come across as a bit silly as long as you get a laugh. It's one of the things I love about you. Most of the time,' he adds with a wink.

'But I don't mean when I'm acting the eejit being embarrassing on purpose. I think . . . Am I not cool any more? Gemma seems mortified to spend more than five minutes in my company these days and just now, when I tried to join in her fun . . . Well, the look on her face said it all.'

'You tried to join in her fun?' he asks, his tone incredulous.

'Yeah, well it's her birthday party and she normally likes me getting involved. Or she did. Even last year she did.'

'There's a big difference between turning twelve and turning thirteen,' he says, as if he has more experience of child-rearing than I do. 'And thirteen these days is a bit like it was when we turned fifteen or sixteen in our day. Now, bring yourself back to those days – all those years ago.'

21

I give him a playful slap on the arm. 'Hang on one wee minute,' I say. 'It's not all that many years ago.'

'If you say so,' he says, with a hint of a smile. 'But anyway, cast your mind back a couple of years to when we were fifteen or sixteen. If our ma's had tried to "join in the fun" with us, we'd have wanted to hide under the bed until our teenage years were long gone and everyone had forgotten the shame of it all.'

He has a point. My own mother in full 'Copacabana' mode springs to my mind again. As does her backcombing and teasing my hair into a bird's nest of a style she swore was the height of fashion, when all my friends were using GHDs and getting blonde streaks put in. 'The bigger the hair, the closer to heaven,' she'd told me, but the only way in which I was closer to heaven was due to the high flammability of my hair with three quarters of a can of Elnett holding it in place. Christ, I remember panicking if anyone came near me with a cigarette.

But I wasn't that bad . . . Was I?

'I was only trying to show them the dance routine to—'

'I'm gonna stop you there,' he says. 'You, my obviously very youthful and beautiful wife, were trying to show a group of hormonal twelve- and thirteen-year-olds how to do a dance routine?'

I nod.

'Dare I ask, what song?'

I feel my face flush. 'That's not really important,' I tell him.

'Oh, I think it very much is important,' he says, and I can tell that he is enjoying this, very much.

'OK, OK. It was "Tragedy" by Steps, but I thought they must

have liked the song. Why else would it be on their playlist? And I thought I was being a bit retro, you know. They do say the Nineties are making a comeback.'

'Aye, but I think they mean the grunge and fashion scene, not the stick your hands in the air and wave them like you just don't care scene,' he says. 'But go on. You were trying to teach them the dance routine to "Tragedy" and . . .'

'Well, it didn't end well,' I tell him. 'In fact, you could say it ended in tragedy. Gemma was, no is, mortified. She told me I ruined everything. And I swear her friends were laughing at me, and now I have to come to terms with the fact that I'm Barry Manilow.'

'Whoa there! Stall the ball. How have we segued from Steps into Barry Manilow?' he asks.

'Because of my mammy,' I say, as if that should explain everything.

'Your mum. Who is currently on her holidays in Donegal with her sisters?'

'My mammy who, do you not remember, sang not one but two Barry Manilow songs at our wedding but saved the big perform-ance for a heartfelt rendition of "Total Eclipse of the Heart", roping Auntie Bernadette into singing the "turn arounds".'

'Right,' he says, the penny dropping. 'But I think, on balance, Steps are marginally less embarrassing than Eighties rock. And Gemma will get over it. In time. With therapy.'

His teasing is gentle and I am reminded once again why we make a good partnership. Everything about what we share is comfortable and secure. We rub together nicely almost all the time. We know each other's routines. Our hopes and fears. Our quirks and hates and most of each other's embarrassing stories. Albeit I've already won in the embarrassing stories stakes and I feel like he'll never catch me at the rate I'm going.

But it strikes me, sitting across from him in my new pyjamas, getting ready to watch *Gogglebox* and waiting for our Chinese to arrive, that maybe we have become too comfortable with each other? Maybe we are too set in our ways. Too boring. So boring that I don't know what the young ones are up to these days. My cultural references still largely live in the later Nineties and early Noughties. Those were the days when I was still learning who I was and who I was going to be. I'd been so very sure that I was going to be famous, and back then famous meant having a talent. I wanted to be a singer and an actor. I wanted to tread the boards, but not just local boards: the West End or Wembley Stadium. I wanted to stand in front of a crowd of fans and hear them sing my own song back at me.

Damn it, I wanted to be Claire from Steps and I wanted to teach the world the routine to 'Tragedy'. I wanted to be Beyoncé, Britney, Christina; hell, I'd have even settled for being in a girl band like the Sugababes. And there was a serious chance there, because one was always leaving.

But here I am, thirty-six years old, in my pyjamas on a Friday night with not so much as a scrap of make-up on. Beneath my pyjamas I am wearing my most comfortable knickers and not even a bra: I can't hack one in the evening; titty jail is too much as it is during the day. So no lingerie or seduction for me. It's all about comfort and the feel of that knicker elastic above my belly-button line. It's a habit I got into when I was pregnant – swapping out my sexy pants for 'full briefs' – and it's a hard habit to break. I honestly get thrush these days if I even think of wearing a thong.

I have no plans for a world tour in the offing. I'm not learning my lines for the next blockbuster movie. I haven't had the photographers round for my OK! magazine shoot. I'm just here, my titties free as a bird, embarrassing the life out of my daughter, sitting on the sofa with my husband, doing the same thing we do every Friday night.

Gemma has been right all along. I am not cool. I can't even pretend to be cool right.

'I want to show her I'm still cool,' I say, in almost a whisper.

'Pet, you don't have to be cool. Sure, don't you have me, and don't we have our nice life together? Coolness is overrated!'

'Is it though?' I ask. 'Do you not think about it yourself? Do you not ever sit there and wonder when we got so sensible? What happened to partying into the wee hours and then doing it all over again the following night? What happened to going to gigs, and wearing insanely high heels?'

'Well, those high heels were always murder on my calf muscles,' he says with a wink. I don't smile back. 'Look, yes there are things I'd like to be different too. There are moments from our younger years I'd absolutely love to relive, but it's not so bad now, is it? The kids are brilliant. Most of the time. We have a nice house and enough money in the bank to be able to afford our takeaways and bottles of wine. We get our wee holiday once a year and . . .'

'But shouldn't we want more? Shouldn't we be cooler and do cooler things?'

Paul shrugs and takes a slug of his beer before looking deep into my eyes. 'When do you think we'd get the time for more? You're flat out with work. I'm chasing my tail half the time. The kids are full on – and we're about to start potty-training Jax. There's rarely a night when you're still awake after ten thirty, and when was the last time we had sex?'

His words are like a slap to the face. Is he unhappy with our sex life? Admittedly it's a pretty non-existent sex life these days, but still, when we get round to it, we always enjoy it. Don't we? I mean, it's not the wild, all-night sessions we used to have when we were younger, but it's still good. We still enjoy it. We've just honed it to make it, well, more efficient . . .

'It's not my fault we don't get peace and quiet for sex,' I say defensively. Paul has never mentioned being dissatisfied in any way before. I feel my stomach knot with anxiety. This is not a conversational road I want to go down but my face is giving away my shock right now.

'I know it isn't. I'm only saying, you're always too tired and I don't blame you. You work hard. The children are exhausting. But maybe we should look at making things in our actual life a little easier before we start planning trips to concerts, or nights out in a club. I mean, God . . . remember the struggle to get a taxi home? The queuing for food after the clubs kicked us out? Someone always puking everywhere? And the hangovers? Jesus, naw. A quiet night in with you, with the hope of a quick shag at the end of the evening and I'm a happy man.'

26

I don't quite know how to tell him that part of me does miss those nights – the craic in the taxi queue, and there was always a sing-song starting up in the chippy. And the hangovers – sure, they were proof of a good night. They were proof you'd done something fun.

So I don't tell him. Instead I nod in agreement and he gives me a kiss on the cheek just as the doorbell rings signalling the arrival of our Chinese. The banquet for one for him, with extra chicken balls. And a chicken chow mein for me. The usual.

4

The fuck-it list

I can't shake the feeling that I have let Paul down. And Gemma. And probably the boys too by not supervising them enough the previous day. What is it with mammy guilt anyway? Why do we feel we never do enough? Sure there are days when I feel like my efforts are wasted as I never get any thanks from the wee shits, but then I think, they are my kids, I need to do everything I can to ensure they're happy. But am I doing too much? What is too much? I don't know these days. All I know is that mom-guilt rides my ass as much as these shapewear pants I insist on wearing to work every day.

If I thought teenagers (and now it's official: midnight has been and gone and my little Cinderella has turned into an absolutely disgusted pumpkin) were tough to handle, I was sorely mistaken. Compared to Jax and Nathan, now in the full thrall of a comedown from their sugar binge, dealing with Gemma and her abject mortification seems like a walk in the

park. If anyone, and I mean anyone, tells you that the newborn phase is the hardest, they are either lying to you or they partake in smoking crack every day.

A five-year-old, deep in the fear brought on by a sugar crash, is quite an experience. Nathan has been clinging to me all morning as if he can't bear for us not to be joined at the hip for more than a second. Everywhere I have turned he has been there, looking up at me with those big soulful eyes of his and asking for hugs, and for me to play with him, and saying he 'feels sad in his tummy'. I haven't quite managed to work out if that means his tummy is sick (no more boke, please!) or he feels sad. Or maybe both.

I have tried offering him his tablet to watch YouTube, and to my utter shock he refuses. This may be a first. 'But look, Nathan, here are your videos of cats doing silly things! Look, you like this one! The cat gets scared and look, whoops! It does a poo.' Normally this is enough to bring on near hysterical laughter from my son, but today he looks glumly at it, like a nineteenth-century poet. 'But Mammy, the wee cat is scared.' His lip trembles and I have to lie and tell him the wee cat is only acting, before offering him a cupcake to try and balance his sugar levels. Hair of the dog and all that.

Jax, meanwhile, is what you would call a crabbit wee shite. He is stomping around chatting, half in English and half in his own special two-year-old language, and to the outside observer he looks like a very small, very drunk old man. I keep my distance. I am not emotionally strong enough to be berated by my two-year-old today.

Things between Paul and I feel a little off too. We've always sung from the same hymn sheet when it comes to our relationship, but now it's as if we're not only singing from different sheets but in different languages. I crave a bit of the old, cool me back. I want to feel more like myself. Paul? He's happy with the status quo – or he would be if we were at it like newly-weds, shagging in every room of the house. (Every room except the children's rooms, obviously. We're not total beasts.)

I look at myself – and at Nathan, as he's currently sitting on my left foot with his arms and legs wrapped tightly around me – in the mirror. Nathan has managed to pull my joggers – the comfortable ones I wear for Saturday-morning cleaning – down off my left hip and there's a daring glimpse (OK, expanse) of white (OK, grey) cotton knicker exposed to the world. My T-shirt is wrinkled and has a jammy handprint on my right boob (that was Jax) and my hair . . . Well, I'm trying and failing to ignore the grey hairs I've spotted at my temples. They're not grey, I kid myself. They're platinum blonde. There are people who spend an absolute bloody fortune to get this colour in their hair.

But my overall look is best described as haggard. The folks behind the *Real Housewives* franchise better not come looking here. There are no fake boobs, false nails and micro-bladed eyebrows. No, the *Real Housewives* of Derry would be all about the comfortable slippers, the practical cleaning clothes, hair in a messy bun, a bra on if you're lucky and the frequent shout of 'Jesus, Mary and the wee donkey!'

How on earth can Paul still want to have sex with me? Can

he really find me sexy? Even without a child attached to my leg, I'm not exuding even an ounce of sex appeal. If I was him, I wouldn't fancy me. Not really. Not in a 'have to have you right now, right here' way. Is it bad that I'd love it if he looked at me that way from time to time? God knows he can still make me feel a little bit weak at the knees, but his body hasn't been ravaged by pregnancy and childbirth. He doesn't have stretch marks or have to worry when Nathan asks him to bounce on the trampoline, afraid he might piss himself. (It happened twice, OK?)

'Hi love,' I hear him say, and I spin to look him with as much elegance as I can muster with Nathan still clinging to me, claiming to be stuck.

He must see the desperation on my face because he looks at me with sympathy in his eyes. 'Why don't you call the girls?' he says. 'Go out for brunch, or lunch, or afternoon drinks or whatever you want to call it? I'll bribe the boys into submission with *Toy Story* 1, 2 and 3 if necessary. Gemma's gone into town with Mia. You go and enjoy yourself. It might give you a wee lift in your mood. You can remind yourself you're still cool.'

I look at him closely, trying to gauge whether or not his comments are heavily laced with sarcasm, but he seems genuine. His smile is genuine anyway. And I would like to see the 'girls' – meaning my two oldest school friends, Cat and Amanda. Life has gotten in the way of us catching up for much too long.

I allow Paul to peel Nathan from my leg and send out a

quick text hoping against hope that they are both free. They are busy ladies in different ways. Amanda is mum to six-year-old twin girls, Rosie and Lily. They are her entire life, and she measures her success entirely around their happiness and their achievements. I'd never known her to be a competitive sort until motherhood addled her brain, but now she's one of *those* mothers: devotes her life to ferrying her offspring between singing lessons, drama lessons, horse-riding lessons, swimming lessons and art club. And she feeds her kids only vegan foods and limits their screen time. What type of psychopath limits a child's screen time, and how does she have a pee in peace? Or a poo – does she know what most mothers would give for an uninterrupted shit!? All the screen time in the world, that's what. If I hadn't known her most of my life, I would probably hate her. Well, maybe hate is a strong word. I would admire her stamina but hate that it can make me feel woefully inadequate as a mother. It's a long shot that she will be available.

Cat, on the other hand, is the anti-mother. The kind of woman who comes out with quips like, 'Oh yes, I love children. I just couldn't eat a whole one.' She's 'childfree by choice' and perfectly happy with that. She's not waiting for the right time to be a mother – that's never been in her plan. Cat is so cool that even Gemma thinks she cool. She may well be on a city break or disgustingly hungover and not available, but I feel, really feel, that some time spent with these two women today could help me work through my crisis of cool confidence.

I offer up a prayer to the Holy Souls as I hit send and I

actually squeak with delight when both reply within minutes to say they are free for lunch. Of course Amanda is only free for an hour, then she has promised the twins they will bake organic cookies, but an hour is good. An hour is enough to talk it through, isn't it?

As it turns out, an hour is not enough to talk it through. I meet the girls at Primrose on the Quay, a lovely little eatery that just happens to sell alcohol. Cat immediately orders a bottle of Prosecco, declaring that we are celebrating.

'What are we celebrating?' Amanda asks, as she places her own order for fizzy water.

'It's Tara's mammyversary,' Cat declares. 'Thirteen years since she became a mammy. Since she expelled a human being from her body through her vagina and shit herself during it.'

I snort laughing but I notice Amanda has flushed red. 'Can you keep it down?' she whispers. 'You can't say vagina in a café!' (She mouths the word 'vagina' because she seems to believe that you really, really can't say that word in a café.)

'Absolute crap,' Cat says. 'It's a part of the female anatomy and not something taboo. You know what I think?' she says, and although I'm amused, I start to worry what's coming next. Cat lives life on a strict 'no filters' basis.

'No,' sighs Amanda. 'I have no idea what's going on in that head of yours ninety-nine per cent of the time.'

'Well,' Cat says, 'I'm thinking vagina, vagina, VA-GI-NA!'

Credit where it is due, her enunciation is perfect. It's the kind of enunciation that Amanda spends a small fortune trying to get her girls to perfect in their speech and drama classes. With less vagina, obviously.

Amanda has now gone through the colour spectrum and is pale. I'm trying not to laugh and Cat looks as proud as punch. In the rest of the café, there is silence. All eyes are momentarily on us, until a child's voice cuts through the quiet. 'Mammy, what's a vagina?'

'Jesus Christ,' Amanda mutters.

'Language!' Cat admonishes her. 'Thou shalt not take the name of the Lord your God in vain.'

To my surprise, Amanda looks Cat straight in the eye. 'Oh away and fuck off,' she says. Thankfully she says it quietly enough that the small child doesn't tell his mammy to 'away and fuck off' too.

There is a moment of tension before our drinks arrive and then, as if nothing has happened, everything goes back to normal. That's how it's always been between the three of us. Spats never last; we've long realized that not sweating the small stuff is a very valid life choice.

'Happy Mammyversary!' Amanda says, her glass of fizzy water held aloft. 'How is the birthday girl anyway? I'd have thought you'd be spending the day with her?'

'It seems the birthday girl has reached the stage where she'd rather shit in her own hands and clap than spend the big day with her mammy. I've become an embarrassment to her.'

'Wise up!' Cat says. 'She's mad about you. You have the perfect mammy–daughter bond.'

34

Amanda coughs, subtly reminding Cat that she too is a mammy and has daughters and their bond is pretty special too.

'Yes, you and your girls are brilliant too,' Cat tells her in a conciliatory voice before turning her attention back to me. 'Is it maybe just her age?'

'I think it's maybe just my age,' I say sadly, before I regale them with the tragedy (see what I did there?) of last night's party, and the spiral it set off into a sense of deep unease about myself.

'Balls that you aren't cool!' Cat declares. 'You're a total MILF. If I was that way inclined, I'd ride you.'

'Jesus Christ,' Amanda mutters again, but Cat is past caring. She's two glasses of Prosecco down and has only been picking at her lunch.

'Seriously, Tara. You're class, and if Gemma can't see that right now, it's no reflection on you. It's her. You have to remember how puberty sends you a bit mad in the head,' Cat says.

'But the thing is,' I tell her, 'I don't think I *am* cool any more. We don't go out very often. I'm either at work, where I'm now one of the oldest staff members, or I'm in my joggers and T-shirt cleaning the house or trying to stop Nathan and Jax from wrecking the place. I love them, and I know this stage of childhood is fleeting, but where are all those things I used to enjoy doing on my own? Or with Paul even. We used to be fun. We used to be the "great craic" couple. Now we sit on the sofa in the evening and compare war stories about our day with the boys.'

'Well,' Amanda says, spearing a piece of grilled chicken onto her fork and eating it. 'I hate to say it, but stop being such a snowflake, Tara. And I mean that with all the love in my heart. You're a mammy now. To three real-life human beings. They rely on you for everything.'

I kid you not, that last sentence makes my blood run cold. She's right. They rely on ME for everything. I am enslaved by a stroppy teenager, a clingy five-year-old and a two-year-old demolition expert. And it's MY job to get them safely through to adulthood. OK, Paul more than pulls his weight too, but in the eyes of the world (thanks, patriarchy) it's mostly the mammy who shoulders the burden.

Amanda is still talking. 'Life changes, you know. That's part of the deal when we become parents. You put your own needs to one side and focus on what's important, which is putting those wains of yours front and centre.'

'I do put them first,' I protest. 'But I don't put me second. Or third. I don't bloody know where I put me any more, and it shows. My own daughter is mortified of me!'

'It's a mother's role to mortify their children,' Amanda says soothingly.

'Nah,' Cat butts in. 'I don't buy it. That's a lot of oul' crap. You don't have to set yourself on fire to keep other people warm, you know. You do so much for your family, it's perfectly OK to want to do something for yourself. The kids will cope. Paul will cope. If you want to go to a concert, let's go to a concert. Or on a weekend break. I'm going to Prague next month – book yourself a ticket and come with me.'

'I couldn't,' I say, while mentally calculating if I actually could.

'With respect,' Amanda says, 'Cat, you don't really under-stand. You're not a mammy. If you had children yourself, you'd get it. Yes, sometimes you feel frustrated that your life has changed, but you are doing the most important job in the entire world and that is reward in itself.'

'Your hole it is,' Cat says. 'Imagine we took that attitude with every other job in the world! "The more important it is, the more we should be happy to sacrifice ourselves to it. No salary for me, Mr Boss, doing this job is reward enough!" And no, I'm not a mother, but I am a woman and I think we as a gender have to prioritize our needs more. I've so many friends who lose their . . . I don't know . . . their inner Beyoncé as soon as they get knocked up.'

That's it. She's hit the nail directly and solidly on the head. I have lost my inner Beyoncé. The fierce and fabulous part of me that sings about being a survivor, and independent and kicking a sorry-ass loser to the kerb. I miss her. I miss when I felt glam. I didn't even need an air machine blowing my hair back in big tousled waves: I had an inner confidence.

And that's what's gone. My confidence. My ability to have the craic. To be both a cool mammy and a cool me. On my own. Free from the needs of the fruit of my loins. And I do want it back. I really, really want it back.

Amanda left after an hour, looking as if she might cry. She's happy in her life and I'm happy for her. I'm happy that she finds her kids enough and I hope she always does. I'm happy that she doesn't mind getting older, that she doesn't miss her old social life. I'm glad for her. Truly I am.

But I can't deny what I'm feeling.

We're halfway down a second bottle of Prosecco when I tell Cat that I want to be Beyoncé again.

'Then what's stopping you?' she asks. 'If you want to change it up, then change it up. What will make you feel with it again? Let's make a list.' She fumbles in her handbag and brings out a pen and an envelope which she flips over and starts to write on.

'I dunno,' I mutter.

'Do you really not know or are you just too scared to say?' she asks.

Snookered. I steel myself, swig back the rest of my glass of Prosecco, top it up and take a deep breath.

'I want to lose my mummy tummy,' I say. She looks at me as if I'm crazy.

'What mummy tummy? You're an absolute ride.'

'If we weren't in a public place, I'd show you how my tummy flops over the top of my knickers now. I can balance my glass of wine on it and everything. Nathan calls me "chunky monkey". It's not sexy, Cat. It's not cool. I want a flat tummy, or a semi-flat tummy at least.'

'OK,' she says and starts to write it down.

'And I want to get my belly button pierced,' I say. 'Maybe even get a wee tattoo or something?'

'That's a start,' Cat says.

'And get my hair done. Something a bit out there, ye know.'

She mouths the words 'out there' as she writes and looks up at me. 'By "out there" do you mean a Mohican or something? Because I'm not sure that's a look that will work for you.'

I shake my head, laughing. 'You eejit! Naw, maybe a wee colour. Something funky. Pink or blue or something.'

'I like it,' Cat says. 'And . . .'

'Get rid of the dootsy mammy clothes.'

'How are we spelling "dootsy"?' Cat asks. While it's a word often used in Derry to describe something old fashioned and ugly, I can't remember the last time I wrote it down.

'D-O-O-T-S-Y,' I spell out. 'Oh, and join a gym. Do a body-pump class or something. Spin, maybe? Should I get one of those bikes you have in the house and you can connect to online classes?' I'm suddenly quite loving the idea.

'Do you think your children, and in particular your younger children, would wreck it within a fortnight?' she asks.

'Fair point,' I concede. 'So I'll join a gym and this time I'll actually go to it and not just feel guilty when I see the direct debit come out of my account each month.'

'That's the spirit!' Cat says. 'Anything else?'

A thought crosses my mind and before I've even said the words I'm turning beetroot. I lean in. 'Spice things up a bit, with Paul. Maybe get some fancy lingerie. A toy or two.'

Cat's eyes widen. 'You're on a roll, girl. I love it! If you need any advice, I'm your gal. I can definitely give you a few pointers.'

I'm not entirely sure how comfortable I am with that, but I nod in agreement anyway.

'And finally,' I say, throwing back the rest of my Prosecco, 'I want to do a dance class.'

Cat writes it down, scribbles another few lines and then turns the envelope so that it faces me. 'Sign that,' she says, handing over a pen.

'Sign what?'

'It's a contract from you to you, to get your Beyoncé back. And I know, if you get this right, everything else will fall into place. The most important thing is for you to be happy, and then you'll exude that sunshine to everyone around you. Even exceptionally grumpy teenagers.'

I take the pen from her hand and after casting my eyes down her list I sign it, sure that now I have a plan, I can get to work.

I'm feeling positive, young and vital, as if I can actually do this. I can be the star I always wanted to be. Well, maybe not the star I always wanted to be. I don't see any world tour in my future. I don't expect to be papped while I'm mooching about in Tesco to see what rosé wine is on special offer. But I do think that maybe I can show Paul and my daughter that I'm still young, dynamic and full of vigour.

But first, I need to pee. That Prosecco has gone through and my pelvic floor just isn't what it used to be.

5

I'm not cursing, I'm praying

Today is the first day of the rest of my life. I will start as I mean to go on – with a positive mental attitude. Surely happy mammy equals happy family, right?

We will eat better. I will become the kind of mother who batch-cooks. I'll buy a slow cooker and become the queen of soups and stews. I'll smugly tell people that I've the dinner on and cooking from eight in the morning. I'm super fecking excited about getting an air fryer. What's that about?

I'll start to exercise. Properly. I'll rope everyone into going on long, bracing family walks that will tire the children, help tone my saggy arse and rein in these bingo wings that I've gotten quite comfortable with. The kind of woman who can confidently dance to a Beyoncé song without needing a defibrillator, and wear leggings without having to pull my oversized tee down round my arse to cover the pothole-sized cellulite I'm currently sporting. Paul will be unable to keep his hands off me and my new vitamin-powered self won't mind one bit. Hi there, libido, long time, no see! I might, just might, get on top some night! Oh Jesus, phone the fire brigade 'cos this mamma is gonna be smokin' hot!

But first, I have to get back in Gemma's good books (assuming that thirteen-year-olds have good books and aren't simply programmed to hate everything and everyone). She's been at me for a while to let her get the top of her ear pierced. I can do that; I got mine done when I was thirteen, and YES, maybe I can even get my belly button re-done at the same time. Hopefully I can find my belly button, it's more of a downward line now, like a wee sad smile. Might as well kill two birds with the one stone. Nothing says mammy–daughter bonding better than sticking needles through parts of your body, right?

I'll take her shopping too, let her have free-run in Primark. (Well, maybe not free-run, I'm not a total mug.)

Will it earn me cool mammy points if I offer to help her do one of those godawful 'haul' videos for her Instagram, without judgement? Would she do one with me? Maybe we could be a mammy–daughter Instagram sensation? That could be my key to mid-thirties success. I see loads on Momstagram, and none of them are half as cool as me. We could be like Reese Witherspoon and her daughter Ava, but, y'know, the Primark version.

Yes, and I'll definitely ask Gemma for advice in choosing new clothes for me too. My work wardrobe is looking so tired it's almost comatose. It doesn't help that they are judged against the flawlessly fabulous outfits my younger, skinnier colleagues get away with. I play it safe in soft and loose tailoring, two-inch heels and freshly pressed (well, tumble-dried) blouses. My Gen-Z colleagues seem to be able to throw the most random combinations of clothes together and look like they've tumbled out of a *Vogue* photoshoot. Frilly blouse with camouflage utility trousers, sparkly heels and a flat cap like my granda used to have? Not a problem – it's fashion, darling. If I tried the same, I'd look like I fell into the discount rack at the local charity shop and came out looking like the pigeon lady from *Home Alone 2*. They'd think I was having a midlife crisis and as I'm nowhere near midlife, that's not happening. Not so much mutton dressed as lamb as mutton dressed like a complete dick.

I'm mulling all this over, snuggled down in bed and enjoying the peace and quiet of our Sunday morning. If I can only manage to stay here, in this position, for another wee while, the hangover I feel nipping at the back of my head might go away. It was a mistake to order the third bottle of Prosecco with Cat yesterday. Drunk me is an absolute hero who always seems to forget she can't drink as much as she used to without serious consequences.

Drunk me also thought heroically ahead, though. I drank a pint of water before bed and took two paracetamol. A bacon sandwich and a tin of something fizzy and sugar-filled should sort me out. But first of all, I'll lie here a while and think positive. Breathing in and out slowly, I try to ignore the snores coming from Paul beside me. I am zen. I am evolving. I am a butterfly getting ready to break free from my cocoon . . .

'Maaaaammmmeeeeeee!' Nathan screams directly into my ear. 'Wake up, maaaaaammmeeeee!'

I startle, narrowly avoiding head-butting my own child. 'Jesus, Mary and the wee donkey,' I stutter, any hope of a zen start to the day evaporating and taking with it any chance of staving off my hangover.

'What? What is it?' I ask, opening my eyes, afraid of what scene will greet me.

'I went to the toilet and did a big poo and cleaned my own bum, Mammy – did I do a good job?' It is worse than I feared. My first visual of the day is a close-up of my five-year-old's bum, cheeks spread so I can get a really, really detailed look at how good a job he's done. (As it happens, he hasn't done that great a job, and my stomach lurches. When did he have sweetcorn?)

'Well, that was a very good try,' I say, trying not to gag. 'But let's go and make extra sure it's all super-duper clean.'

'Thank you, Mammy,' he says, and runs from the room, bare, shit-stained arse waggling, towards the bathroom. I glance at the clock. It's only seven. On a Sunday morning. This is going to be one long, painful day. I take a deep breath and prepare myself for what lies ahead but not before 'accidentally' jabbing Paul in the ribs. As usual, he sleeps on. He, like most men, has mastered the art of ignoring almost all child-related incidents before the hour of eight in the morning. I can't really complain when he kept them amused all yesterday and didn't even pass comment when I arrived home from my lunch with the girls three sheets to the wind. I just have to, as we say in Derry, take my oil, which is another way of saying 'suck it up'.

I will not let the 'new me' fall at the first hurdle. I will not be bested by a hangover – even if it does feel like the Orange Order are marching through my head banging their drums and twirling their batons. Yes, another few hours' sleep would have been ideal, but sadly I've no chloroform to knock the boys out for the morning. Caffeine will help.

Lots of caffeine.

And maybe carbs.

Lots of carbs. One last time, for medicinal reasons, obvs.

Tomorrow I will move on to fruit and yoghurt, maybe a smoothie. But today, if I'm to make it through the morning and set myself up for an afternoon of shopping with Gemma, I need all the sustenance I can get. This is survival mode, pure and simple.

'Maaaaammmmeeeee!' Nathan's voice rings out, and I wonder, has he always been so loud? Has the pitch of his voice always been this whiny? Or has the Prosecco I drank yesterday completely altered my brain chemistry to make every noise louder and sharper?

'Yes, pet,' I answer, my own voice sounding too loud to me.

'Jax has done a poo and he's taking his nappy off again.'

Dear, sweet, Jesus. Not today.

The boys are, predictably, exceptionally demanding this morning. I swear they smell the fear (or the alcohol) and thrive on it. They have ramped up their 'wee boy-ness' by about a million per cent and, I'm not gonna lie, I feel like weeping as I watch my living room transform from fairly respectable to bomb-site in record time.

I'm trying to keep my cool but I swear, my darling children have even started to breathe too loud and my poor, thumping head is aching with the loud suck of air in and whoosh of air out in every breath. Jesus, am I the worst mammy in the world that I want to tear my hair out at the sound of my own children just doing the bare minimum to stay alive?

Why don't I have the kind of children who take themselves off to the corner of a room to read a book? They even shun my suggestion that they sit peacefully on the sofa watching a movie so I can close my eyes for one wee minute. They exist in a world of shouting, farting, burping, crying, whingeing, jumping from chair to chair, dive-bombing each other and competitive willy-flashing. And if I hear 'YEET' one more time . . .

When I find myself explaining, once again, that willies are private and not for being waved around in front of others, I feel a part of my soul die and leave my body.

I bring out the big guns.

'Right, lads, enough! You can have a wee bit more time on your iPads later if – and I mean only if – you sit very quietly and watch the movie I put on for youse for at least half an hour.' I flick on *Moana* as I speak, and I'll give them this much: they do seem to be trying. I have a brief five-minute window of hope that I've cracked it, but then they start wriggling around as if they have ants in their pants and it is causing them actual physical pain to sit still.

Maybe if I let them burn off some excess energy it will help. I switch off the TV.

'OK, boys, time for a wee bit of exercise, I think. C'mon with me, why don't you see who can jump highest on the trampoline?'

'Are you coming too, Mammy?' Nathan asks. 'I want you in the garden to play too!' Wearily, I pull on my battered but oh-so-comfy cardigan and follow my boys outside, recoiling like a vampire as the light hits my eyes.

'Mammy, Mammy, watch how fast I can run!' Nathan squeals, and I applaud his efforts while acknowledging inwardly that Usain Bolt won't be losing any sleep over my son's athletic prowess.

'Watch me jump, Mammy.'

'Watch me try to whistle, Mammy.'

'Watch this hand-stand, Mammy.'

Watch me, watch me, watch me, aghhhhhhhhhhh.

I can't believe that I find myself, on the brink of tears, begging them to come back inside and use their iPads instead. By the puzzled looks on their faces, they can't quite believe me either. Nathan gives me a long look up and down. I can hear the cogs whirring (noisily, of course) in his little brain. I imagine he's asking himself what happened to his real mammy and who is this technology-wielding alien in her place.

'Just come on in,' I say. 'Do you want a snack? I can get you something? Here, take your iPads, and yes, YouTube is fine. Work away. Put your wee headphones on though, dotes, OK?'

For a child who isn't long two, Jax is shockingly good at

navigating to his favourite videos. There are mammies out there who would have me burned at the stake for such crimes against acceptable parenting.

Within seconds Nathan is howling laughing at a video of some squeaky-voiced child unboxing a toy, his headphones on as requested but not actually attached to his iPad.

Escaping to the kitchen, I try to limit my mammy guilt by preparing them some healthy snacks. See, I can do this. I might not go as far as crudites and hummus, but I can chop a banana like a pro.

Naturally, an ordinary chopped banana is not OK for Jax. He wants one that isn't 'broken'. It takes me a full ten minutes, a Google search and a very loud tantrum (him, not me, but it was a close call) to realize that 'not broken' means complete with the skin on. Nathan asks for an apple: I'm impressed, healthy choice, son, but the apple I give him is 'spicy', and not like the apples in school. We try another two apples, they're spicy too. Cue meltdown (him not me, but again . . . it was close).

On another day, a day when I was stronger, I'd have cut those meltdowns off at the pass – well, I like to think I would have – but today I'm tired and weak and my hangover has migrated from my head to the pit of my stomach. All I want to do is lie down on the floor and have someone rub my back (but not Paul; that's how two of my kids were conceived), medicate me with Tayto Cheese & Onion crisps and full-fat Coke until I feel better.

But knowing that isn't going to happen, I decide to bring out the extra-big guns. We're talking cannons now: it's time to take my beautiful children to the park. It's a brisk, still-much-too-early spring morning and the sun is shining, the dewdrops glistening in its glow. A walk in the fresh air will, I reckon, either kill or cure me. Hoping for the latter, I herd the boys into jeans and jumpers, socks and welly boots, and wrap them in their big coats. By this stage the hangover sweats have kicked in big time and I'm low-key worried I'm going to give off a hum of alcohol, as well as a sort of oily-faced, exhausted, scummy-mummy vibe.

Bravely, I don't give into my hangxiety and we go out anyway. It's hard to give in to a wave of nausea with fresh air in your lungs. And it's breezy enough that the alcohol aroma might just waft upstream away from me. I'll let the boys run themselves ragged in the playground while I sit and nurse a medicinal coffee and maybe go on my phone, or engage in my other favourite thing: people-watching.

That's not how it works out, of course. The boys, who had been practically bouncing off the walls at home, take a fit of laziness halfway through the walk between the car park and the play area. I've brought the buggy for Jax, thank God, but Nathan seems enraged that he is now a big boy and has to walk. It matters not one jot that he has not sat in a buggy for the guts of three years; this morning he yells with the passion of a drunken old man that it isn't fair and he still has little legs and they are tired.

Meanwhile Jax has decided to shout 'swings!' over and over again in different pitches and tones but with an ever-increasing urgency.

'C'mon,' I plead with Nathan in the sweetest voice I can manage. 'You love the park. I'll push you on the swings!'

'I don't like the swings,' he says, scuffing his welly boots along the path.

'You do, Nathan. You love the swings.'

'No. I do not. Not one tiny bit, they're stupid!'

'OK, so the slide then? You love the slide.'

He looks at me as if I have suggested we go home and start the unholy task of cleaning his bedroom.

'I do not like the slide,' he says, with a stomp of his foot.

This at least prompts Jax to stop shouting 'Sving! Sving! Sving!' Instead he switches to shouting 'Swide! Swide! Swide!'

'Dear Jesus, give me strength,' I mutter under my breath, forgetting for a moment that my children have the ears of bats and there is no mis-chosen word or taking of the Lord's name in vain that they do not hear.

'My teacher says you don't say Jesus unless you are saying a prayer!' Nathan says, his expression pious. I can't help but feel his teacher might feel differently if she were in my shoes right now.

'Well, maybe I am saying a prayer,' I say through gritted teeth. 'That you'll be a good boy and come and play nicely on the slides?'

'I think you were just saying a bad word,' he says. 'And my teacher says that's wrong.'

I'm teetering on the very edge of telling him exactly what his teacher can do with her views on bad words when the first spots of rain start to fall.

'OK,' I say. 'You win, Nathan. We'll go back to the car and

go home and watch some YouTube.' I can deal with Jax and his meltdowns. He can be bribed with half a packet of chocolate buttons. I don't have the strength to deal with Nathan when he is in one of these moods. Most of the time my middle child is a grade-A dote. The rest of the time, like now, he is a wee ass, and I can see from the expression on his face that he is about to transition to absolute wee asshole.

'But Mammy,' he whines, 'I don't want to go back to the car. I want to go to the slide.'

'You said you didn't want to go,' I remind him, and hear my voice crack. This is a fatal error. I've shown fear. That's all Nathan in asshole mode needs to ramp up to the next level.

'Jesus, Mammy! I changed my mind!'

'Nathan!' I say, suddenly aware that another perfectly groomed and well-behaved family are close enough to hear us. 'Language!' I'm secretly impressed that he got the context right though.

'But I was only saying my prayers,' he says, and I swear there's a hint of evil genius in his eyes as he turns and skips away from me, through the rain, to the shout of 'Cheesus, Cheesus, Cheesus' from Jax.

Cheesus indeed. And Mary. And the wee donkey.

I am determined that, traumatic morning aside, I will still make the most of this first day of the rest of my life. I've changed into dry, warm clothes and even put on a wee touch of make-up. I have been planning this conversation with Gemma all day – especially during the bleak hour where the boys ran me ragged around the playpark in the rain, determined to give me not one single solitary second to myself. But good times are coming and now, as she throws herself onto the sofa, her gaze never leaving her phone, I decide this is my time.

'Gemz,' I say.

'Wha?' It's a gruff greeting but there is no eye-rolling, so I take that as a win.

'I was thinking, as it's been your birthday weekend, maybe you and I could take a wee run into town later? Do a bit of shopping? You can choose some new threads and help me choose something funky for work.'

'Funky?' she says, looking at me as if I have fallen out of a bad Seventies movie.

'Aye, funky. Or cool or whatever you young ones say these days.' I try not to cringe to death with embarrassment. Did I really just say 'you young ones'? *Christ.*

'You want *me* to help *you* do some clothes shopping?' She raises one perfectly threaded (yup, no plucking for these dolls) eyebrow, and once again I think it grossly unfair that teenagers these days don't seem to have to endure the ugly duckling years before they blossom into beautiful swans. When I was thirteen my eyebrows were like tadpoles; underfed and deprived tadpoles.

I nod.

'For clothes?'

I nod again.

She examines me as if she's setting eyes on me for the very first time. 'Clothes for you? For your work?'

'Aye,' I tell her. 'I want to dress a bit cooler.'

'Oh God,' she groans. 'Is this about that dance routine again? Because, Mammy, can you not.'

'Can I not what?' I ask, and my hackles are starting to rise, even though I'm not entirely sure what hackles are and whether or not I have them.

'Not try to be cool! You're old!' She says the word 'old' as though it has the power to age her in a heartbeat.

'I'm thirty-six!' I bark. 'That's not old. Not a bit. I'm still young.'

'Mammy,' she says, and I see a smile playing on her lips. 'Wise up! There's nothing wrong with being old, you know. All the other mammies just get on with it instead of trying to embarrass the life out of their children. You don't have to try to be cool any more, let it go.' She seems genuinely amused at the thought I don't consider thirty-six particularly advanced in years.

'There's nothing wrong with being older, Gemma. I can dress in cool clothes. Skinny jeans aren't just for you young ones, you know!' Urgh, I said 'you young ones' again. I'm turning into *my* mammy.

'Mammy,' she says, and her tone has changed. She is using the voice I use when I'm trying to explain to the boys why they can't have a chocolate biscuit after brushing their teeth. 'Skinny jeans are so last year.'

I am stuck somewhere between wanting to cry and wanting to wring her beautiful little teenage neck. Old! I'll give her old! And how in the *High School Musical* are skinny jeans 'so last year'? They're jeans, a staple!

'Fair enough,' I say. 'I'll go by myself. Drag my aged and

decrepit arse into Primark. Maybe I can save my tired, old bones by hiring one of those mobility scooters to help me get around the place. I wonder, do Primark do orthopaedic shoes? Something comfortable?'

My acting is top-notch, if I say so myself, but Gemma is unimpressed. 'I'm not saying you're ancient. But Mammy, come on! No one wants their mammy dressing the same as them! Can you not dress like other mammies instead of trying to dress like a teenager?'

I try to drag my mind back to when I was her age – and find the image of my lovely mother at the height of her Bonnie Tyler phase, buying us matching tracksuits for our family holiday. I'd wanted to die of shame.

'OK,' I say, the wind pulled from my sails and my heart sinking deep to the pit of my stomach. 'Never mind. It was only an idea and clearly a shitty one at that.' I sound not unlike a petulant teen myself, but if I expect my hurt feelings to register with my firstborn, I am living in cloud cuckoo land.

Within seconds Gemma is back to having her eyes fixed on her phone. I have to leave the room before I shame myself entirely by crying or giving her the sneaky finger when she's not looking.

I'm starting to wash up from lunch (do the dishes, Cinderelly!) when Paul comes in from outside where he has been tinkering with his car. I feel his cold arms slide around my waist but I'm too annoyed to give in to his embrace.

'Do you think I'm old?' I ask, turning to face him.

'Have you been drinking again?' he asks with a laugh. 'What are you on about?'

'Gemma says I'm old and I should stop trying so hard to be cool.'

He laughs again, before pulling me into a big hug, 'Gemma's thirteen. She thinks everyone over the age of twenty is ancient. But no, I don't think you're old,' he whispers in my ear. 'I think you're in the prime of your life.' He kisses my neck and I lean into him, enjoying the warmth of his body against mine. 'A total MILF, as it happens. Ignore our darling daughter! Go shopping anyway. Treat yourself if it makes you feel better. I mean, maybe stay away from the polyester slacks and twin-sets, but why not spruce yourself up?'

At any other time, I might have heard this as nothing more than a loving husband urging his lovely wife to treat herself. I might have seen that he could tell I was upset and that some retail therapy might help. I might have focused on the fact that he considered me a MILF. At any other time, I might have turned around and given him a big kiss and told him I love him very much.

But right now, in this moment, all I hear is a husband telling a wife she needs to spruce herself up.

My pride isn't so much dented as broken in two.

6

What about my muffin top?

I was born to shop. I'm never happier than when I'm rummaging through the rails for a bargain. The dizzy heights of designer stores with their eye-watering price tags are not for me, no ma'am. I'm a 'give me a basket, two elbows and point in me in the direction of the sale rail' kind of a gal. There isn't a branch of TK Maxx I can't clear of all quality bargains in under thirty minutes.

With the skill and passion of a world-class rugby player, I can barrel through a queue of dithering grannies and pretentious teenagers, knocking them sideways with some deft jabs of my elbows, or tripping them up over my size-8 DMs, before reaching the sale rail and stripping that baby bare within seconds.

I am so good at it that friends have tasked me with getting them their dream items in any sale. I do not baulk at standing at three in the morning on Boxing Day outside Next waiting for the sale to start. I approach shopping in the same way a general would plan a military operation and I very, very rarely pick up a dud purchase. I am to shopping what Liam Neeson is to kidnappers. My very particular set of skills will find the item I want and will get it.

And yet today, my magic Liam Neeson-esque powers seem to be on the blink. It would appear that having a complete crisis of self-confidence is like Kryptonite to my ability to sort the chaff from the wheat, or the cheap polyester from the bargain cotton-rich buys.

I am standing, basket empty, looking at the rails, the dresses, the cropped tops, the cropped jeans, the oversized jumpers and hoodies. The kind of things the foetuses at work wear. Have clothing companies just stopped halfway through garment production or what? What if I want the entire top, or the entire pair of jeans? Why the f*$k is everything cropped? My muffin top is shrieking at the thought of these tops exposing it. And if I want a complete top, it must be oversized; apparently shops don't sell normal length tops any more. I don't want to rock up to work looking like Vanilla Ice, for God's sake! Is this what cool is? To look like you've put your outfit through a guillotine or to look like it's your first day at secondary school and your mammy bought you two sizes up in your uniform. I can't tell what's nice. Or if anything will suit me. Or if they are pure rotten or dootsy or whatever damn word Gemma and her gang use now.

I am frozen to the spot, vaguely aware that there are people now pushing past me. People I would easily have felled on any other occasion. There is a wee old lady with a walking frame who has just bagged a gorgeous leather jacket! God knows I wanted it, but now what I actually want is to see what she looks like wearing it. Go granny! Meanwhile, I stand there, like an absolute lemon. A hungover lemon at that. A hungover, tired, old, haggard, uncool lemon.

''Scuse me, missus,' a voice to my right chimes. 'Can I get past ye there?'

I look across to a whippet of a thing, five foot nothing, six stone if anything but with the beady-eyed stare of a seasoned shopper about her. I should pull myself together, I think. Grab a load of these clothes and buy them, bring them home and hide them under the bed until I feel brave enough to try them on. I could wait until Gemma and Paul were out of the house and I could risk looking like a complete eejit all my own.

But I can't do it. I just can't bring myself to take a chance on that dress or those platform trainers; as much as I was a die-hard Spice Girls fan, I don't want to be a try-hard fashion disaster. That oversized denim jacket will probably make me look as though I've borrowed my da's coat. And that sweater? The powder blue one? Will I end up looking like I'm on day release from pre-school?

I can't let this day beat me. I just can't. I can't go home empty-handed. I can't fail at this. So I grab a multipack of big knickers, a hoodie with #YOLO printed on the front for Gemma, and a couple of pairs of Paw Patrol pyjamas for the boys.

I'm not proud of myself. I feel as if I've let myself and my people down, but I know when I'm defeated. My mood deflated, I go home wondering if I should have opted for full brief rather than high leg. Maybe it's time to give in to comfort completely. I can still be a MILF in belly-warming knickers, can't I?

Thankfully my daughter is the worst liar in the world. I say thankfully as I'm doing my very best to hang on to whatever shred of positivity I can, and still being able to read my daughter is a positive. Before I even hand her the hoodie I bought for her, I know it's not going to cut it. I'm cool enough to know that, like skinny jeans, #YOLO is so last year. If not last decade. Still, God loves a trier and a small part of me hopes she will be delighted with her new top all the same.

I need a win, you see. Dear God, but I need a win today.

Gemma, for all her teenage moodiness, must be aware of this. It's entirely possible that Paul has had a word with her in my absence, or maybe it's because I look like a big enough picture of misery to prick her conscience. She gives me a weak smile.

'It's lovely, Mammy,' she says, and even though she will never win an Oscar for this particular performance, I'm warmed by her willingness to lie to protect my feelings instead of using my poor choice as another thing to beat me over the head with.

'Do you really think so?' I ask, neediness written across my face.

She smiles and nods, but I notice she slips it back in the shopping bag and says she'll put it away upstairs. Probably never to be seen again.

The boys, at least, are genuinely delighted with their pyjamas and for a moment I can forget the trauma of our morning expedition to the park. Seeing Nathan in raptures over a pair of pyjamas is enough to remind me that he isn't an asshole all of the time and that he can actually be quite cute and lovely.

'Love, did you not get yourself anything?' Paul asks, sitting down beside me on the sofa.

'Nah, didn't see anything I liked,' I say.

'But is there not something still in that bag?' Paul misses NOTHING.

'Ah, it's only some new underwear,' I say, and immediately regret my honesty. His eyebrows shoot straight up and he gives me a cheeky wink. I don't know where he thinks I've been shopping but he should know by now that I'm more Bridget Jones comfort than Cindy Crawford sexy ensemble.

'Oooh, can I see?' he asks.

I think of the multipack of high-legged cotton floral briefs – built for comfort not style – and I shake my head. 'No, darling. I don't think that's a great idea,' I say.

'A woman of mystery?' he says. 'I like the sound of that.'

'Oh my God,' Gemma groans from the sofa. 'You two are so embarrassing. Get. A. Room.'

'I'm totally up for getting a room,' Paul says, grinning at me, and I cringe almost as much as Gemma does. The last thing I'm in the mood for now is getting a room. All I want to get are my biggest, comfiest, old lady pyjamas. I want to put them on with a pair of fluffy bedsocks and my dressing gown. I want to eat the bag of Wispa Bites I have hidden in the back of the wardrobe and then I want to get an early night so that I can wallow in my own self-pity for as long as possible before Monday morning arrives and the real madness begins. Because if I think Gemma is hard going, she is nothing compared to the cohort of new recruits at work. Give me a teenager in a strop, or a five-year-old on a sugar rush any day over a team of over-eager, over-confident twenty-somethings who think they've nothing to learn.

'Not a chance,' I smile at Paul. 'I'm taking to bed with this hangover. Do not disturb!'

'Message received,' he says, and I can't help but feel guilty at the look of disappointment on his face. 'You'll feel better after a good sleep,' he says. 'Maybe your mood will be better.'

Great. So now he thinks I'm moody as well as in need of sprucing up. I grab my plastic bag of comfy pants and leave my family to their own devices.

I've run myself a bath, warned my husband and my children if any of them even think about disturbing me they will be risking their lives. I've lit some candles and poured myself a glass of wine – which I think shows remarkable fortitude, given that I am still being murdered by my own liver after yesterday's escapades. I've rescued the biggest, fluffiest towels I own from the back of the airing cupboard and yes, I have even taken out a pair of my new comfy pants to slip on when I get out of the bath, along with my fluffy pyjamas.

I sink under the bubbles. Tomorrow will be a new day. The

first day of the rest of my life, take two. The key to success is persistence and, quite possibly, comfy knickers. No one said I had to get it right the first time. Tomorrow is not only a new day but a whole new week – one that is filled with possibilities. All I need to do is grab on tightly to them.

'Mammmmmmmeeeeee,' shouts Jax at the door. 'Me awake! Nathan did boogers in my bed!'

And that's the end of my three-minute relaxing bathtime.

7

Away and take your face for a shite

ToteTech beckons me on Monday morning with its sweet siren call. Which is another way of saying, if I want to pay the mortgage I need to shift my arse, and fast, into work.

Thankfully, for all its many faults, the project management company I have worked for over the course of the last twelve years does at least offer some flexibility to my starting hours. This morning I needed that more than ever when Jax decided to spew Weetabix down the front of his coat and a little bit on my hair as I strapped him into his car seat.

That of course led to Nathan being late for school – and boy does that receptionist know how to do resting judgey face – and me now 'late' for work. On an ordinary day I should be on my computer and working by 9.15 a.m. at the latest. Today, I have dipped into my flexitime to deal with Weetabix-gate and have landed at my desk half an hour late, with my hair still damp from a quick sponge wash, and what looks like congealed cereal (at least I hope that's what it is) in a clump on my jacket.

For eleven of the twelve years I have worked at ToteTech this would've prompted a rueful smile from my boss, a lovely older man called Pat Doherty who was surprisingly accommodating for a man when it came to parenting crises.

But that was all before the merger. When our small but perfectly formed start-up company was bought out by a bigger and definitely messier company, things changed fast, with new-age processes and TEDx-inspired approaches to business management. It was, to be frank, a shitshow wrapped in a corporate bow.

The first of those changes was Pat's early retirement and the appointment of a new senior manager to oversee my department. I say 'senior' but Tony Handley (not to be confused with Tony Hadley of eighties pop sensation Spandau Ballet) is only twenty-nine. I'd worked out on the first day that I was already at primary school and learning my times tables when he was born. I'm a Nineties kid and he's a Y2K kid. There's a world of difference in that.

Plus, he's a dick.

And what's worse, he has absolutely no qualms about skating on thin ice when it comes to appropriate office behaviour. He doesn't ever cross the line but he gets close enough to it that one very slight move could land him in a tribunal.

He exudes the kind of creepy vibes that make my skin crawl as soon as he enters the room, I swear the temperature of the office drops a few degrees whenever he arrives. He does not walk, he glides, like some pale-faced vampire, from desk to desk, making not a sound until he is almost, almost right on top of you. Quite often the first you know of his presence beside you is feeling his cold, jelly-soft hand on your shoulder or hearing his overly loud mouth-breathing. I hate, and I mean HATE, him touching my skin. Mr Handley? More like Mr Handsy, amiright?

He calls me 'darlin'' even though he's seven years younger than I am and I am very definitely not his darling. It's nauseating, and there have been times when he has been talking to me that I've caught myself pulling a face which does little to hide the fact I'm fighting an internal battle to keep my food down or not punch him right in the middle of his chauvinistic face.

That's how I feel right now, as he glides to my desk and pointedly looks at his watch, then stands in silence as my computer whirs to life.

'Let me guess,' he says, 'another parenting emergency?' I see his eyes drop to the Weetabix stain on my jacket.

'Well, not quite an emergency, but it was definitely an occasion when I'm delighted this company has such a forward-thinking flexible working policy,' I smile. I know never to make it personal and restrict myself to reminding him there are HR directives on how this place should work.

'Hmmmm,' he says. 'I suppose. It must be hard, trying to juggle it all. You must feel as if you can't ever give anything your full and undivided attention. What's that saying? Jack of all trades and master of none?'

I force a smile that looks more like a grimace onto my face. Mr Handley is not sympathizing with me. He is, in his usual passive-aggressive manner, letting me know that he thinks less of me because I am a mother and that sometimes has a knock-on effect on my work life. It doesn't matter that I have never missed a deadline, or dropped the ball on any project I've worked on. I may have to take a more flexible approach from time to time, and my clothes may occasionally bear the markings of a mucky child, but I am damn good at my job. I've worked my way up the ranks and given them twelve years of my life. I may not be drowning in the posh degrees of some of my colleagues, but I have learned on the job how to be the best at the job.

And I've done it all while raising three children. I'm a bloody legend, if I say so myself.

But Mr Handley will never see that. He hasn't seen my growth from vaguely terrified twenty-four-year-old working part-time while her baby was at creche, to a full-time, confident, kick-ass asset to his company.

That's why I've been planning an exit strategy in the form of a promotion that's about to come up that I am more than deserving of.

A promotion to senior account manager will not only see me escape from Mr Handley's creepy domain to the nicer upstairs office, but it will also give me the safety net to feel I can whistleblow on his creepy, sleazy, chauvinistic behaviour. Imma bout to bring #MeToo to ToteTech mothatruckers.

It might even earn me some respect from the members of Gen Z who have joined the company since the takeover. I seem to be incapable of winning their favour with hard work alone, but maybe if I bring about the downfall of our very own Mr Burns, I might be welcomed into their gang.

'Oh I think I'm quite good at both you know,' I say. 'Us women – we're well used to multitasking. We do it with ease.'

He looks at me with what I can only describe as a sneer on his face – one he reserves for when he knows he has been bested but doesn't want to lose face. I can't help but smile as he walks away, moving on to flirt outrageously with one of my younger colleagues.

I can see he makes them uncomfortable. Yes, they may be hungry for success, disgustingly stylish and know a lexicon of industry buzzwords, but what they don't have yet is the life experience or confidence that comes with it that makes them sit up and say they've had enough of this shit and aren't going to put up with it any more.

And the sad fact is, I do have the confidence and life experience but I'm constantly at a disadvantage here. I have to work twice as hard to get half the respect because, of course, none of them have kids.

They are unfortunately also the type of dicks that send emails at 8 p.m. with an 'Ooooh look at me, I'm working after hours' subtext.

If – no, when – I get the promotion, they will realize I'm more than the old woman at the back of the office who sometimes has to dive out to deal with a child-related emergency.

As I scan this morning's emails, it occurs to me that I need to be less passive and more aggressive in proving my worth to them, and to the powers that be. I think I also need to be more aggressive in proving my own worth to myself.

Checking there is no one near to me, I take the 'fuck-it' list from my bag and look over it again. I'm sure I can devise some sort of strategy to make this all come together.

The time for thinking and talking is over. It's time to take action.

Not only will I smash it at work today, I'll smash it at home later too.

The list says I need to channel my inner Beyoncé. Would Beyoncé sit around in tired grey pants from a Primark multi-pack? No, she would not. I make a note to nip out at lunchtime and buy some properly fancy underwear. Something satin and lace. It will help me feel like a proper boss bish. All badass suited and booted to the casual observer, but a complete vixen underneath it all. They call it power dressing, don't they? And when I'm done pulling off some power moves in work, maybe I can pull off some power moves in the bedroom? I'm sure Paul won't mind seeing me in something other than baggy, saggy comfy underbags. He might die of shock, to be fair.

But I need to work on my queen energy from the inside out. I need to take baby steps and, while I know I can't expect to transform my entire life overnight, I can start by putting ToteTech and their forward-thinking, outside-the-box-but-definitely-still-sexist attitudes in their place.

Damn it, I'll even wear the sexy underwear to my interview for the promotion. Up yours, Mr Handsy, you'll never know my sexy secret because I'm not planning on sleeping my way to the top. (The very thought of it!)

I decide to ask Cat what she would wear to a job interview. I know my current look isn't going to cut it. There is nothing kick-ass about one of my well-washed tailored skirt suits, or my day-to-day work style of a non-messy bun. I'm a comfortable shoe away from looking like a dusty librarian, before the sexy makeover. And the worst bit is that I know if I were to let my hair down and take my glasses off I'd look more Sloth from the *Goonies* than sultry office siren.

I'm relaying these feelings to Cat via text as I drink my morning coffee at my desk and asking if she is available to meet me at lunchtime for a quick dive around the shops. I can't repeat yesterday's disaster. I need Cat and her ruthlessness on my side.

You should never have trusted me to do this on my own, I type. I can't seem to get anything right at the moment.

Don't talk shite, she texts back. You get loads right. You're obviously having a bad day. Is your period due?

I do a little mental maths and think, well, yes, she might well be onto something. But I also think it's so much more than that. This is not just the kind of existential crisis that comes from a hormonal fluctuation. This is next-level crisis.

That's beside the point, I tell her. I need help and you are my only hope. You're the most stylish person I know. Even Gemma thinks you're cool. I need you to share that with me. I can't be trusted on my own.

I will never let down a friend in need, Cat replies. Consider it a date.

8

I can tout on my five-year-old, right?

Cat takes no prisoners and tolerates no cowardice in the face of fashion and although I try to steer her towards shops I consider sensible and appropriate for a thirty-something mum of three looking for an important promotion, it's like trying to put a two-year-old in a car seat, one who's arching their back and suddenly gained strength sent straight from Odin.

'For the love of all that is pure and holy,' she says, pulling me away from a window display where impossibly thin and tall mannequins wear a selection of school-uniform-coloured suits, 'you said you wanted to step outside your comfort zone. This is not outside your comfort zone. This is slap bang in the middle of it. There's nothing in that window that you don't already own.'

'Cat, come on, I do want to shift things up a gear, but it would be nice to be sort of comfort-zone adjacent. Wouldn't it?'

'Tara. Do you want my help or not? Do you think that those wee skinny Amys and Lucys in your work would turn up wearing a suit like that? There is no current fashion trend that is "history teacher, circa 1997",' Cat says. 'We're going to find you a new look. There's cottagecore, or street-wear, or boho, or dark academia or art ho.'

'Art hoe? Hoe? As in . . .'

'Well not the garden utensil type of hoe,' she says, but her face is serious.

'There are people who dress like actual prostitutes as a fashion statement, and you think I should consider that for my work because . . . ? Seriously, Cat, are you on something?'

'I'm not suggesting you go down the art ho road as such – but there is so much choice now. You don't have to stick to the same old, same old.' She takes her phone from her bag and starts typing before thrusting it under my nose. It's an article highlighting the top ten current aesthetic trends and I'm a little comforted to see that the Nineties seem to be making a comeback. Grunge makes the list. As does the kind of preppy look Rachel Green sported in *Friends*. Sadly, for me, there is no Britney Spears in the 'Hit Me Baby One More Time' aesthetic. No return of orange streaks of blonde applied to hair with Sun In, super-shiny lip gloss, skirts over trousers and pastel-coloured eyeshadow. Clearly, it's not time for my version of the Nineties to come back yet.

'You don't have to go all out, but take some of the elements from each and make your own style,' she says. 'Here, this would suit you . . .' She thrusts her phone under my nose again and shows me a sage green midi-dress which skims the model's impossibly non-existent curves and is styled with a pair of white trainers.

It's not a bad look – but is it suitable for work? Does it scream "senior account manager"? 'I don't think we're quite there,' I tell her.

'Well, we won't get there standing here. Trust me on this, Tara. I'm not going to let you make a complete and total eejit of yourself.'

Half an hour, and a mini-breakdown in the changing rooms of a small designer boutique later, I have purchased a dress which I'm not sure will ever see the light of day. It's tailored, asymmetrical and in a selection of bright coloured stripes. When I saw myself in the mirror, I honestly couldn't tell if I looked great in it or like a very old, very stressed rainbow.

Cat assures me I look great. She even persuades me to buy a pair of four-inch nude heels to complete the look, and then she kisses me on the cheek before I stumble off to Primark, a mere ten minutes of my lunch break left, to pick up the first sexy bra and knickers set that I find, scurrying to the checkout before I bump into anyone I know and they see the size label.

I get back to the office just as Mr Handsy – ahem, Hand*ley* – returns from his lunch break and I find myself holding the door open for him.

'Thanks, darlin',' he says, with a cheeky wink, and yes, my skin crawls so much I half expect to find that my belly button has migrated far enough north to be seen over the top of my blouse. 'Have you been treating yourself?' He looks at my bags and I'm suddenly paranoid he has X-ray vision and is able to see straight into the Primark bag filled with cheap, vaguely sexy underwear.

My face colours.

'Just a couple of things to update my look. Nothing exciting,' I tell him without making eye contact. It's very important to make as little eye contact as possible with Tony Handley. He's like a dirtier version of Medusa. He doesn't turn you to stone with his glassy-eyed gaze, but he does make you feel as if you need a good wash after.

'Always nice to treat yourself,' he says. 'I know what you mum-types are like, forever treating your kids before yourselves.'

Mum-types!? Hold me back, Lord, hold me back! I will not rise to this fuck-wittery. We are not a type. We are individuals.

'Aye,' I nod in reply, keen to disengage as quickly as possible.

'Oh, you'll get an email about it this afternoon,' Mr Handley says, 'but your interview for the account manager position? It's scheduled for Monday. I think you're at 10 a.m. I hope that suits?'

'It will,' I say with a weak smile. 'Thanks.'

'No problem,' he says. 'Very competitive this time round. But you're so experienced and I'm sure that will go in your favour.'

I nod again. I don't know what else to say to him. All I want is to get away, tuck my fancy knickers under my desk and get on with my work.

As we're walking past the reception desk, Molly (all my female co-workers' names seem to end in a y) stops me.

'Tara,' she trills. 'Your son's teacher called while you were out. She wanted to check if you were attending the parent-teacher meeting later? She said you hadn't signed the confirmation slip.'

I hadn't signed the slip because I didn't know about the slip. Or the meeting. I blink at Molly while my brain tries to come up with a suitable response that makes her and Mr Handley think I'm completely in charge of the situation and am not the kind of person to forget about important meetings.

'It's all in hand,' I say. 'I'll call her when I get to my desk. Kids, eh? Nathan obviously forgot to give her the slip. That's five-year-olds for you. You can't trust them with anything . . .'

I realize I'm talking to myself, both Molly and Mr Handley having gone back to their own business, the reality of my parenting requirements not holding their attention – and I am totes OK with that. Anything that gets me away from Mr Handley and his grotty X-ray vision.

But now I know that he knows I'll be skipping out early, I'll have to make sure to work twice as hard to get twice as much work done before I leave. I don't want anyone to think I'm slacking because I have kids. Hell, I'm just as productive as the Gen Zs, if not more. I take a deep breath, wishing I'd found time to eat some lunch during my break instead of shopping for fashion-forward dresses. Vowing to grab a sandwich on the drive to the school, I send Paul a quick message to remind him about the parent-teacher meeting, deciding on this occasion not to tell him that I knew absolutely nothing about it myself.

My phone beeps seconds later. *I'm floored here. Will try and make it but you might have to go it alone.*

Shit.

Paul knows that parent-teacher meetings are my idea of hell on earth. Despite my advancing years, I invariably revert to scared pupil at the back of the classroom who is worried she might get sent to the principal's office. I feel the heavy weight of judgement from teachers who speak to me about my children as if they are complete strangers to me, and find myself apologizing for almost everything, suddenly losing the ability to form clear and coherent sentences in response.

That's without even bringing in the very uncomfortable logistics of attending a parent-teacher meeting in a classroom where everything is sized appropriately for very small people, with very short legs and very small arses. I feel like Will Ferrell at the start of *Elf*, and every time, I laugh at that thought and then have to stifle it to avoid looking like the mom who's just smoked a joint.

There's no way to look dignified perched on one of those wee seats. I wish I had read the note my son allegedly brought home, because then I'd have known to wear trousers and not a skirt that bunches awkwardly as I try to fold myself behind a desk meant for a five-year-old.

I've met Nathan's teacher before, and can I only say that she is *unnaturally* youthful. You'd be forgiven for thinking she was the same age as my Gemma; she certainly doesn't look old enough to hold a class of primary school children in thrall for six hours a day. Especially a class that includes Nathan, who changes his mind about what he wants to do approximately six times a minute and runs about like a blue-arsed fly on speed.

And yet, Miss Rose (because of course her name is a pretty floral name) is much beloved by pupils and parents alike. She, like so many of her generation (and that includes the specimens at work) oozes a confidence and capability I can only dream of and even though I reckon she is at least thirteen or fourteen years younger than I am, I am still intimidated by her.

'Mrs Gallagher, thanks for coming in. I hope it wasn't any trouble. Nathan said you didn't give him the signed note back.'

How appropriate is it to rat my own son out to his teacher? The reason I didn't give him the note back is that he didn't give it to me to sign in the first place. I'll let the lying little rascal away with it this time. One free pass down.

'It was no trouble at all, Miss Rose. I'm sorry for not returning the note. You know how busy life can be. Some things do get overlooked from time to time.'

Miss Rose tilts her perfectly symmetrical head slightly to one side, her doe eyes widening in what looks like understanding or sympathy. 'Oh, I know. Don't get stressed out. Nathan tells me all about what life can be like at home. It sounds . . .' (yes, she actually pauses for dramatic effect) '. . . very interesting.' She laughs, one of those tinkling laughs that sounds like wind chimes on a breezy day.

Sweet Jesus, what has he said?

'Well, life with young children is always interesting, that's for sure,' I say, thinking about how I'm going to wring his wee neck later.

'I imagine it is,' she says, as if she doesn't spend a considerable amount of her life in the company of young children. 'I suppose I'll learn some day when I have a family of my own.'

The cruel mammy in me could launch into telling her exactly how interesting her life will become once she has little darlings all of her own, but I want to keep her on side. At least for the next ten minutes or so, until she's delivered her verdict on Nathan and I can leave either suitably proud of myself or deeply ashamed.

'Well, it will probably come as no surprise to you that Nathan is a lovely wee boy. So enthusiastic in his learning. He always has a question or ten to ask.' The tinkling laugh is back.

'Yes, we have found him to be very inquisitive and we encourage him to ask questions,' I say proudly.

'Which is absolutely brilliant.' Miss Rose's smile begins to lose its width. 'But going forward, I think we could benefit from working to help Nathan realize the importance of taking turns and sharing time and toys with other boys and girls. Some of my more reserved pupils can struggle to get a word in when he's on one of his *inquisitive* rolls.'

The way she says inquisitive makes it sound like it's a very bad thing indeed. I shift uncomfortably on the tiny chair and try to straighten up. Miss Rose must read my discomfort as embarrassment. 'I don't mean to upset you by pointing this out. It's a very positive thing. It shows he's a confident little boy who is secure in his learning environment. We do find that reinforcing the message of taking turns and giving others the chance to ask questions is a very important life skill. If we can work on it in school and at home, he's likely to adjust his behaviour more quickly.'

To my shame, a little bubble of emotion catches in my throat. Is this it? Is this where Miss Rose will send me to the principal's office with a note saying I must do better as a mammy? I nod because I don't trust myself to speak right now. I don't want to make an absolute tit of myself by bawling all over Miss Rose and her shiny, happy demeanour.

'Now, let's look at his schoolwork,' Miss Rose says, and starts to lay out some of his exercise books in front of me. My heart swells with pride when I see where he has written his own name. OK, he has left the T out of the middle, but *Nahan* scrawled in impossibly big and slightly wonky letters is enough to make my heart melt. My baby. My beautiful, inquisitive, sometimes annoying, but always wonderful baby.

'He does normally write his name correctly,' Miss Rose tinkles. 'But he can rush ahead when he is excited about something, and mistakes do happen. Nevertheless, he is working within the class average and I have no concerns about his literacy.'

She proceeds to show me his numeracy work and I'm delighted to see he has a basic grasp of the numbers between one and ten. He seems to have mastered simple addition, which I know isn't really a big deal, but to me in this moment it feels like he is an actual child genius. I beam with pride.

'Now, art,' she says. 'I have to say he's a very talented little artist and he really enjoys it when we get the paints out. Is there anyone particularly artistic at home?'

I shake my head. I couldn't draw water from a well, never mind create a piece of artwork. And Paul? Well, as much as I love my husband, art is not where his strength lies. He hasn't quite yet mastered colouring between the lines, if his ability to pee solidly into the toilet without splashback is anything to go by.

Miss Rose takes a number of pictures from a folder and sets them out in front of me. I see where Nathan has painted what I'm fairly sure is meant to represent him and Jax playing in the park.

'Och, lovely! That's him and his wee brother: they love the park and Nathan loves being in nature!'

'Of course. Now this one,' she says, as she slides an A2 sheet in front of me, 'this one is just so precious.'

My darling son has painted five figures in bright primary colours on the large white sheet. There is clearly a 'daddy' figure – a smiling man with short brown hair. Then there's a tall girl, who I'll guess is Gemma, because the figure he has painted appears to be holding a small rectangular device that could easily be mistaken for a phone. Two small boys, both with wide red-painted grins, beam out at me from the page and I smile. But then I cop on to the 'mammy' figure.

Mammy has a slightly round tummy. She's blonde with black roots painted in, and spirals leap from her head as if her hair is exploding all over the place in abandon. It's the expression on her face that ends me, though. While the other four figures – even the creature with the phone who never actually smiles in real life – all look happy, 'Mammy' is scowling. Her eyebrows are painted in heavy and furrowed. Her mouth tight. She looks old and angry.

'Jesus!' I exclaim.

'Oh,' says Miss Rose. 'That was something else I wanted to talk to you about: the swearing.'

9

Le dinosaur de turkey . . . oui oui

I am, as we say in Derry, pure scunnered. I am disgusted and mortified. Not only have I been lectured on appropriate use of the Lord's name by a twinkle-voiced child masquerading as an adult, but I also have, in my handbag, the folded-up depiction of my family in which I look like a witch with crappy roots.

Is this how my child sees me? Do I always walk around with a face on me like a slapped arse? Does my hair look that bad? Sitting in my car in the school car park, I examine my face in the rear-view mirror. Is it a case of resting bitch face or is my resting face actually quite nice and I just happen to be one of those really crabbit mammies who rules her roost through fear and intimidation? (Not that I am averse to a little fear and intimidation, especially when it comes to my tornado twosome.)

I pull at my skin. Try out a couple of smiles. Tilt my head forward to see how bad my roots look from the top down.

OK, I should probably make the time for a hair appointment. My roots have definitely grown beyond socially acceptable levels and, hang on . . . calm the ham . . . is that a cluster of grey hair? An actual cluster? Like fecking Anna in *Frozen* after Elsa zaps her with the cold? I'm thirty-six. That IS still young. It's certainly not grey streaks and, if I'm not mistaken, crow's feet old.

And yet, there they are. Those signs of ageing and grumpiness across my face. Shit. It's possible that Nathan's depiction of me was in fact quite flattering, given the haggard scarecrow that is looking back at me in the car mirror.

This is not what I expected at my age. This is not who I am. I'm not someone who has let it go (bloody Elsa), so Jesus Christ, how *have* I let it – and by *it*, I mean me – get to the point where I didn't realize I looked this bad? Feck's sake.

I allow myself a wee ugly cry. In truth, it's a big ugly cry: not a dry-eyed Kim Kardashian one but snots and all, and then I start to drive – my fancy knickers and new dress mocking me, the portrait of my family painted by my lovely son burned into my brain. Stopping off at the wee Tesco, I buy a couple of bags of Cadbury's chocolate and a bottle of rosé wine. I might as well go all in with the tired, wine-o'clock, chocolate-addicted, middle-aged mammy vibe. If the roots fit!

Throwing Wispa Bites into my mouth a handful at a time, I am sufficiently self-medicated with chocolate by the time I arrive home to not fall through the front door and sob in a heap on the hall carpet. I allow myself a minute to listen to the sounds around me – the sounds of my home and of my family. I can hear Paul singing some nonsense made-up song in the kitchen – a ballad to the best dinner ever of turkey dinosaurs and potato waffles. I hear Jax laugh – it is probably the purest sound in the world, and even though he is in the middle of the terrible twos and definitely responsible for more than one of the grey hairs on my head, I remind myself there are some perks to being older and having children to come home to. Jax is, most of the time, a perk.

As I'm hanging my coat up, I'm clothes lined from the side by a very exuberant and tomato-sauce-covered Nathan. 'Mammy!!! You're home. You're my best mammy. Daddy made turkey dinosaurs and tayto wobbles for tea and says we can have ice cream after and said you were seeing Miss Rose and she was going to tell you I was a great wee boy and then maybe you'd get me a treat for being a great wee boy and can we go to the toy shop? Can Jax come too? He's too little for school but I think he's still a good boy and he should get a toy too. There's a *Paw Patrol* boat and . . .'

He is rambling on without breathing and his eyes are wide with excitement. So wide with excitement that I wonder if he's been at the sugar already, or perhaps mainlining hard drugs out the back of the primary school. Although surely if he had, Miss Rose might have mentioned that ahead of the swearing.

'Mammy! C'mon. Dinner's ready!' I feel his small, chubby and squidgy hand take mine. I love how it fits. I love the warmth of it. I love how his hand in mine makes me feel the world is a less shitty place even if only for a moment. I allow him to drag me through to the kitchen where my absolute eejit of a husband is wearing a chef's hat and apron, has dusted flour on his nose and is prancing around with a fish slice. He sees me and raises his eyebrow in a 'Well? Did he get expelled?' kind of way.

'They're allowing him to stay in school,' I say with a wry smile. I'll tell him about the swearing, and the portrait of me as Ursula the Sea Witch later.

'Ah, very good,' he says, in the worst French accent I have ever heard in my entire life.

'Sit down, Mammy,' Nathan says as he drags my chair, its legs screeching against the floor, out from the table. 'You are in a fancy café now.'

'Indeed, madame,' Paul says with a grin. 'And tonight's special is, how do you say, le dinosaur de turkey, oven baked with the finest waffle de potato and a tomato ketchup jus.'

'It's really yummy, Mammy,' Nathan nods enthusiastically. I look to Jax, who seems to have the better part of an entire potato waffle mushed into his hair and face, with a liberal helping of tomato ketchup 'jus'. My baby grins at me, his pearly white baby teeth so perfect and his smile so broad.

'I think I'll have the special, if you don't mind,' I say.

'Excellent choice, madame!' Paul says.

'And will there be another customer joining us for dinner tonight?' I ask, wondering where my precious firstborn is.

'I believe she is running late,' Paul says, his accent now definitely more Derry than Paris.

'Daddy said if she doesn't get her arse down the stairs, her dinner is going in the bin,' Nathan says solemnly.

I look to Paul.

'Her dinner is under the grill,' he says. 'But she's only up there watching TikTok videos and I told her I really will yeet it in the bin if she doesn't come and get it.'

'Yeet?' I ask.

'Oh aye. I learned it today. It's means to throw something. All the young ones are saying it. I thought if I said it, it might get through to Gemma, you know, via the cool kids' lingo?'

'Good luck with that,' I say with a smile as he places a plate of finest convenience food in front of me. I can't help but laugh when I see he has arranged the dinosaurs into a tableau of a dinosaur orgy.

'Mammy, why is the big dinosaur climbing on top of the wee dinosaur?' Nathan asks. Miss Rose was right: he does have a question for every occasion.

'To climb up to get the red sauce,' Paul says. 'Did you not know that red sauce is dinosaurs' most favourite food in the whole world?'

'Is it really?' Nathan asks, his eyes wide.

'Oh aye, one hundred per cent,' Paul tells him.

'I'm going to ask Miss Rose about that tomorrow,' Nathan says, and I'm about to say something but I don't. Let her explain it. It's her job after all.

A thunderous clatter on the stairs announces the imminent arrival of Gemma, who, eyes still firmly locked on her phone, earbuds in, bustles into the kitchen and fetches her plate from under the grill before attempting to beat a hasty retreat to her room.

'Ah, here. Hang on a wee minute,' Paul says. 'You can come and sit at the table and eat with the rest of us.'

Gemma glances at Nathan's T-shirt stained with sauce, at Jax who is now spitting masticated turkey onto his plate. The look of horror on her face is less than subtle, but it is nothing compared to the look she gives both Paul and me when she spots that the big dinosaur is mounting the smaller dinosaur from behind.

'Oh. My. God. Youse are so disgustin',' she says. 'Can I not just go to my room and do my homework?'

'Watching TikTok videos doesn't count as homework,' Paul says, and she tuts and rolls her eyes so dramatically it's a wonder they don't roll right out of her head. With the grace of a baby elephant, she sits down at the table and starts to eat, taking time between mouthfuls to sigh in an exaggerated manner.

'Gemma,' Nathan says, and I'm relieved that she doesn't bark a response to him. 'Miss Rose says I'm a good boy so Mammy and Daddy are going to take me to the toy shop for a treat and maybe do you want a treat too? 'Cos you're a weally good girl.'

He says it with such a straight face and such sincerity that he almost convinces me.

To my surprise, her face softens. 'I don't think the toy shop has any toys for my age,' she says. 'But well done, Nathan. Miss Rose is right.' She smiles warmly at her brother, and Paul and I look at each other with a mixture of relief and alarm. Where did nice Gemma materialize from so quickly and, more importantly perhaps, what is she looking for?

'I don't mind sharing my toys with you,' Nathan says. 'And with Jax.'

'Maybe I'll come with you and help you choose,' Gemma says. 'Do you think I could go too, Mammy?' she asks.

I open my mouth to answer but Paul gets in there before I do. 'Of course you can come,' he says. 'If you don't mind being seen with a couple of oldies.'

'Course I don't. You're my mammy and daddy and I love you,' she says, all trace of the murderous teen of five minutes ago gone. Paul and I glance at each other again. This is almost scarier than when she is in full hormone overload. This is a stealth attack in progress.

'Are you feeling OK, love?' I ask her, putting my hand to her forehead in case she has a rapid onset fever.

'Aye,' she says, shifting in her seat. 'Can I not just want to do something with my wee brother?'

We are walking on a tightrope here. One false move and it could all come tumbling down.

'Sure you can, pet,' Paul says. 'Always.'

Gemma smiles and it appears genuine. Nathan whoops with delight. I feel Paul's hand on mine, and I glance at him again. We share a moment of smug coupledom. Here we are, at our kitchen table, with our beautiful if very ketchup-covered family and, for the moment, no one is killing anyone else.

He squeezes my hand and I smile at him. I take in how silly he looks in his chef's hat with the flour dusted across his face. I love that he isn't afraid to act the eejit to make our children laugh. I think of how Nathan painted him as a happy, smiley daddy and my lip wobbles a wee bit as I think of how our son painted me.

'Are you OK?' Paul asks.

'A bit tired is all. Mondays, you know. Total pain in the arse.'

'Here's an idea,' he says as he gets up to start clearing the table. 'I'll take the kids to the toy shop – it's open late this evening. Gemma can help me herd them in the right direction. You get a bath and relax. I'll even clean up here first.'

'But,' I protest, 'I have a wash to put in the machine.'

'I can put a wash in the machine,' he says. 'Go. Relax. You've earned it.'

He is giving me the same beatific smile Nathan did, and speaking in the same soft tone that Gemma used. I can't help but feel I'm being hoodwinked without my knowledge.

'Okaaaay,' I say slowly. 'If, you're sure?'

'Sure I'm sure. Go. Light some candles. I'll bring you a wee glass of wine. Treat yourself!'

As I get to my feet, I wonder if it is me who has developed the sudden onset fever or maybe my fit of crying brought on a stroke. Something is off.

'Pet,' Paul says as I make to leave the room. 'You don't mind if I go out for a pint with the lads after I get back from the toy shop, do you? It won't be a mad one. Only a couple.'

And the penny drops – clanging directly onto my head. He wants to go to the pub, which will leave me to do the bedtime routine with the boys single-handed. But . . . it would be shitty of me to say no, given that I came home to the kids being fed and that I disappeared out for a boozy lunch which turned into a bit of a session on Saturday.

'OK, fine,' I say, trying to hide the level of gritted teeth I'm currently sporting.

'Brilliant,' he says with a grin. 'Right boys, and Gemma. Let's get tidied up here and go and hit the toy shop.' There is a collective whooping, except from Gemma, who simply nods.

I leave them to it. If I'm on a timer until they return and I have to read them *Guess How Much I Love You* for the eleventy-billionth time, I'm going to make the absolute most of it. I'm not going to look a gift horse in the mouth.

10

If Beyoncé did it, so can I

The plan is simple. I will soak in this bath and I will then shave my legs *and* my armpits. I will tidy my coochie so that it's less 1970s porn star, but not quite 2021 porn star, i.e. bald. I will slather on my most expensive body lotion and do a conditioning hair mask. Then, instead of going to bed with wet hair so that I wake up looking as though I spent the night plugged into an electrical socket, I will dry it with an actual hairdryer.

I won't slip into my very comfy pyjamas and pull on my dressing gown for warmth and comfort. I'll wear my less comfy but mildly alluring pyjamas instead. But I'll wait until the children have gone to bed, obviously. I don't want Gemma to completely lose her shit after seeing me glide into the living room in a little satin number.

I can allow myself comfy pyjamas for story time – easy as that. I listen to the rise and fall of my family's voices as they get ready to go out and I relax properly under the bubbles when I hear the slam of the car door and hear the engine turn and the car drive off.

They say your life can change in a heartbeat and I'm midway through my pampering session when it happens. I wonder now what it would be like to go back to the before-times. Will everything in my life from this moment on be defined as 'before' and 'after'?

I fear it will.

Because as much as I disliked the Anna from *Frozen* cluster of grey hair on my head, or the crow's feet which clearly belonged to some big-ass crow, or even the slightly wrinkly look of my cleavage, nothing has prepared me for the lone grey pubic hair which is staring back at me as I start to tend my lady garden.

Tall and mighty, it stands – bizarrely longer than any other hair in my pubic area. It's almost as if it is waving at me. Does this really happen? Do our pubes turn grey too? I suppose it makes sense but I've never thought about it before. Holy shit. Is my coochie now officially a geriatric coochie? What can I do to fix this? There's no pubic equivalent of Nice'n Easy, is there? (Is there?) Are we supposed to accept the white hairs of our nether regions as we trundle towards old age? Is the only alternative the wax strip or the razor? Do I have to go full 2021 porn star?

Horrified, I reach for my tweezers and rip that little bastard out, because I know that I am so not ready to have old-lady pubes. Nope. No grangina for me today.

That's it, I decide. I'm booking in for the works. If I'm

really going to work my new frock, and my new fancy undies, I'm going to make sure the body underneath it all adds up. I climb out of the bath and pull the 'fuck-it' list I made with Cat out of my handbag.

On the bottom of it I scrawl, *Get rid of rogue grey hairs down under.*

Then I add: *Inject whatever the hell it takes to get rid of my wrinkles* and sit back, satisfied to have a plan.

As I sit with the deep conditioner working its magic on my hair, I pop off messages to my hairdresser, a local beautician and to the Facebook page of a nearby gym. If I tell people I'm going to do this, then damn right I'm going to go through with it.

I sign the 'fuck-it list' again, message Cat to see if she wants to come to early-morning spin with me at 6 a.m., and then fold both the list and the portrait of horror and slip them into the drawer of my bedside locker.

Cat texts back in minutes. She thinks I'm 'fucking mad' but agrees to join me for spin. **Might as well do it in the morning before breakfast. Less to throw up,** she replies with a smiley emoji. She knows me well.

That's probably the first clue that I'm getting in above my head, but look – don't they always say no pain, no gain? I must suffer to get my old body back. Beyoncé did it for Coachella after having twins . . . so I can do it too.

I pack a bag for the morning so I'm good to go. What I haven't really considered is my lack of sportswear. Or at least my lack of sportswear which isn't years old, saggy and only comes out when I'm doing the big clean at the weekend. Joggers without bleach stains don't factor much in my wardrobe. I dig through what little I have and pull out the least offensive leggings (no holes and not the kind to stretch so much that people will be able to spot my floral comfy knickers through them – or another grey pube, FFS) and an oversized T-shirt. Or at least it was oversized the last time I wore it. Now it has a slightly more tight-fit feel to it. I throw a guilty look at the bag of Wispa Bites open on the bed. I vow that once I have finished that particular packet I will not buy any more. My body will be a temple. A chiselled temple . . . Well, maybe a toned temple . . . Or . . . OK, just a fucking temple.

I pull my battered Converse out from under the bed and throw them into my bag before I raid Gemma's room to steal a scrunchie for my hair. The temptation to have a good nosy through her things is high, but no; I must trust my daughter. The new me will be a cool mum who is 'totally chill' with her teenager – but sweet Jesus, I've counted six plates and three cups already. Why can't she ever bring them downstairs? I breathe deeply, find my zen. It's OK, it's OK, I'm chill, no biggy.

As I'm zipping my bag closed I hear the front door open and the excited voices of my children returning with shouts of 'Mammy! Mammy! Come and see!'

Smiling at my bag and slipping a couple of Wispa Bites into my mouth (well, I do have to finish the packet!), I go downstairs to bask in the glory of my beautiful family.

Nathan's in hyper mode, while Jax has the kind of fifty-yard stare on his face that lets me know he must go directly to bed or risk us hitting the very dangerous 'past his sleep' stage of the evening.

I reach out and take him from Paul, pausing for a moment as I feel his body sink against mine. My beautiful baby boy. Kissing the top of his head, I sneak away and get him changed and into his cot without incident. Success!

I'm about to go get Nathan ready for bed when I hear his voice coming from the direction of Gemma's room. This is highly unusual. Especially as I can also hear Gemma's voice, and she is not screaming at him at the top of her lungs to get out of her room and never to come back unless he wants his tiny ass handed to him on a plate.

It's possible I may be hallucinating. Standing outside her door, I press my ear as close to it as I can and listen in.

'Look, you have to be a good boy for Mammy, right, and go to bed. Do you want me to read you your story instead?'

Crossing my fingers, I hold my breath until I hear Nathan answer. 'Yes, please, Gemma. I'll be good, I pwomise. Can I bring my new Among Us plushie to bed with me?'

'Of course you can,' she says, and I feel tears prick at my eyes. My children, communicating with each other as if they are friends and not mortal enemies. An image of an idyllic future flashes before my eyes. The boys hero-worshipping Gemma who, despite her teenager years, has developed a sense of maturity and altruism. She's the kind of young woman I can be best pals with. I must be doing something right after all. This weekend has been a blip and all it needed was for me to take ownership of my life.

My heart light, I skip down the stairs to see Paul putting away the last of the dishes. It's amazing how a very stressful day has turned into the perfect evening. I slide my arms around his waist and rest my head on his back. He turns to face me.

'Hugs and all? What have I done to deserve this?' he says with a smile.

'Just being yourself,' I say, and stand up on my tiptoes to plant a quick kiss on his lips. I'm shocked to find that even that most gentle of kisses ignites something in me that I've not felt in a while. I've always, always fancied Paul. I still do. Sure, he's not as toned as he was when we first met but there's a lot to be said for a dad bod. He can still make me weak at the knees with one look. Unfortunately, I'm usually too exhausted to do anything about it. But right now, right here in our kitchen, I could absolutely do something about it. I kiss him again, a little more deeply this time but he pulls away.

'Are you feeling OK?' he asks, looking at me quizzically.

'Aye,' I tell him. 'I'm feeling better than OK. Jax is asleep, Gemma is putting Nathan to bed and I've just shaved my legs.'

'Shaved your legs, on a Monday night?' he asks.

'Yes,' I wink. 'I am clearly putting the moves on here.'

A pained expression crosses his face. 'Tara, pet. I promised the lads I'd go out for a couple of pints. They've been giving me a hard time for not getting out much recently and I—I'd rather stay here. God knows, I'd rather stay here,' he says and his eyes are so dark as he looks at me that I shiver: he is as eager to scratch the same sexy itch as I am.

But that can wait. Cool wife can make it worth his while later. I unpeel my arms from around his waist.

'Go on out,' I tell him. 'Enjoy yourself. I'll still be here when you get home and my legs will still be silky smooth.'

He pulls me back in and kisses me. 'I love you,' he says. 'Like, really, really love you.'

'I love you too,' I tell him and reach up for one more kiss. But as I'm leaning into the snog – a proper tongues-and-all snog – I hear a loud, 'Oh. My. God. You two are so embarrassing!' It's Gemma. Seems the new her didn't last for long.

I pull back and turn to look at her.

'We are married you know, love. We're allowed to snog,' I say.

'Oh my God, you did not just use the word snog. You are *so* uncool.'

'Maybe,' I say. 'But I'm uncool and enjoying a snog with the man I love.'

I watch as our daughter wrestles between utter disgust and a snappy comeback. I can sense Paul is both embarrassed and amused at her reaction.

'Your daddy is going out with his friends,' I tell her. 'If you can stand to be in the same room as horribly-embarrassing-me, then why don't we watch a couple of episodes of *Derry Girls* together and eat some ice cream? I picked up some Ben & Jerry's earlier.'

It is a truth universally acknowledged that my eldest child can be bought with Cookie Dough ice cream.

'Ach, can we?' she asks, her eyes bright. 'You're not all bad, bestie.'

Hmm. She only calls me this when I give her food, money or both. I'll take it though.

'Even though I used the word "snog"?'

'Eughhhhh! Can we not talk about that any more? I've put Nathan to bed, so can we go and watch *Derry Girls* now?' Her voice is sweet and kind again. Her mood swings are more extreme than mine. Oh God, I'm due my period soon. Maybe she's due hers too? Maybe we are syncing up? I almost feel sorry for Paul.

She scuttles off and I turn to see Paul laughing. 'You are the best mammy, you know. A total MILF.'

Despite myself, I blush. 'OK, love,' I say. 'Go and enjoy yourself. I'll be here when you get home.' I wink seductively.

'Have you got something stuck in your eye?' he asks.

11

Am I dead, is this how it ends for me?

I ache in places I forgot I had. I can maintain a level of pain management if I do not move. Or breathe. I cannot turn my head to the left and my lower back feels as if someone has dismantled my spine and all those wee bones are rattling about and poking me every two seconds.

The alarm I'd set on my phone has just woken me and it's taken a good thirty seconds for me to work out where I am, and why under God my phone was screaming at me when it was clearly too dark outside for good Christian people to be awake. As I sit up, the price of sleeping squidged on a sofa makes itself abundantly clear – what was I thinking?

I haven't even endured spin class yet and I am dying.

I'm paying for the exploits of the previous night – and they weren't even fun exploits. My intention to wait up and seduce Paul when he came home from the pub was ruined by my stupid inability to stay awake.

It's entirely possible that the ice cream and the three glasses of wine I had while watching *Derry Girls* with Gemma may have contributed to me not staying awake. But whatever the reason, not only was I not in an alluring position, ready to bat my eyelids and welcome my man to pleasure town, I was flat on my back, mouth open, snoring like a drunk on the sofa with slobber running down my chin. Sexy right?

Paul says he tried to wake me. I have absolutely no memory of this. I certainly have no memory of telling him to 'go away and shite' and then farting twice, which is the version of events he regaled me with this morning when I stumbled into our bedroom at 5.30 a.m.

My muscles scream as I bend down to put my sports socks on; I have clearly not given myself even half enough time to come up with a decent excuse to send to Cat as to why I'd rather dye all my pubes grey than go to a spin class. To try to force myself into going, I explain my plans to Paul as he gets dressed across the room from me.

To give him his dues, he does his very best to sound sympathetic and not laugh. 'Are you sure you're fit for spin?' he asks as I wince taking off my pyjama top.

'Sure it's only riding a bike,' I tell him. 'Face forward. Gotta keep pedalling towards the new me!' There is such bravado in my voice you'd be forgiven for thinking I believe what I'm saying, where in actual fact I'm mentally working out where my upstairs ibuprofen is.

'The current you is fine, you know,' he says softly, and maybe it's because I'm in pain or maybe it's because life has been telling me over and over again these the last few days that I am very much not fine, that I want to scream.

Fine. Fucking 'fine'. It's one of the most offensive words in the English language. Such a nothing, boring, beige, bland word. It's almost as bad as nice. Everyone knows when you use the words fine or nice it's so completely 'blah' that you might as well not bother. I do not strive for fine or nice. Would Queen Beyoncé of Knowles settle for fine or nice? Indeed, I think not.

So as I wince, stand up and groan as if I may die, then let out the smallest of farts as I bend over to pick up my cursed gym bag, my primary thought is 'fuck you, fine'.

I'm off to spin some shit.

I figure this class will be OK. I mean, I'm not stupid. I know it will be hard work – especially given my banty neck and back after my cock-blocking sofa sleep. But I'm hardcore. I've birthed three babies. I can carry all the shopping in from the car in one go. I'm pretty sure I've even broken the land speed record for getting the wash in from the line at the first spot of rain. So I'm feeling OK about spin as I drive to the gym, replacing key lyrics in Britney Spears's 'Hit Me Baby, One More Time' with 'my lower back is killing me'.

Cycling will in all likelihood work the kinks out of my muscles, warm me up and set me on my way for a productive day. All those endorphins will have me strutting about like Nikki Minaj.

But from the moment I walk into the fitness studio, I realize it's not going to go down like that. I don't consider myself a particularly large lady. I can stand to lose a few pounds (OK, like maybe twenty pounds or so . . .), but I'm passable, you know. I'm 'normal'. And yet, normal is most certainly not how I'm feeling, walking into the torture chamber and seeing a group of toned young stunners chatting and stretching as they prepare for class.

They're all wearing cropped Lycra leggings and those sports bra/crop top combos. It's going to be traumatic for them to see me do this in my saggy Primark bra and leggings which have definitely seen better days; they'll probably think I'm the cleaner joining in.

At least, my midriff is well covered. I don't need my poor wee tummy to be in direct competition with those of ladies who have clearly never gestated a nine-pound baby or had chocolate for breakfast for the last six months.

I turn to share a sisterly bitchy moment with Cat only to see her unzip her jacket and reveal her own perfectly flat and, to add to the insult, tanned midriff. She smiles at me and gives me an encouraging thumbs up while I resist the urge to put a different finger up at her in return.

I don't have much time to think about my lack of gym-bunny grace however as Connor (our instructor and not some child who wandered in on his way to school) announces it is time to get started.

Why does everyone in the world look so young these days? Where are all my old bitches at? Probably at home, eating toast, drinking coffee and wearing a nice, warm fluffy dressing gown, if they've any sense.

Connor assigns me a torture device in the middle row. I'd prefer to be in the very back row, or indeed to find they have run out of bikes, in which case I'd be prepared to sacrifice my need for exercise in the name of the greater good. But no, there are enough bikes and Connor helpfully asks if this was anyone's first time. I raise my hand – a gesture I immediately regret.

'OK then,' he says, pointing to the bike. 'You take that one. I want to keep an eye on you.'

Fuck! I want to cry. I want to tell him he's a sweet, sweet boy but he is so wrong. He does not want to keep an eye on me. Really, he'd be so much better off if I was anywhere but in front of his eyes. I don't tell him that, though. I remember how Paul said I looked 'fine' and decide I'll show Connor and the flat-tummy brigade, and myself for that matter, how it's done.

There are three things in this world that are particularly cruel to the coochie. The first is, of course, childbirth. No two ways about it, childbirth is not a friend to your genitals. There's the stretching, and the tearing, and the stitches. Not to mention the itching as your stitches knit together. All those days of sitting on the loo, pouring a jug of warm water on your battered nethers to stop your own pee from stinging you to death, when all you can think is 'Thank you Lord Jesus for not making me have to see what my downstairs looks like right now.'

The second thing is thong underwear. I do not care what you are wearing. I do not give one shiny shit about a visible panty line. Give me a visible panty line any day over the feeling of a permanent fanny-flossing; the fine strings of a thong cutting into me like cheese wire. Show the whole entire world my floral knickers but do not give me the yeast infection that will arise from me wearing such invasive pants.

The third thing I'm learning – and it is the worst of all these things – is the saddle on a spin bike. Clearly, they are designed for people who have never birthed a human being, but is there any need for them to be quite as uncomfortable as they are? Is it to encourage us to do that standy-up-and-cycle thing? Is it to bring a pain so intense that you sort of mentally transition and leave your body for a while and watch from the ceiling as a sweating, panicked, pained you struggles on below?

Whatever the reason, by the time we are doing those evil little bastard moves of standing for five seconds and sitting for five seconds I am ready to beg for an epidural. Not to mention the sweat is lashing off me. This is no dewy glow. This is water coursing in rivulets from my hairline, between my boobs and down the crack of my arse. I am soaked in so much sweat that I fear my hands will slip from the handlebars, or worse still, my arse will slip from the saddle of doom. I don't want to have to try and explain that one at A&E. *Well, my sweaty arse slid off a spin bike and the rest is history . . .*

I'm not a crier. I have a relatively high pain threshold. Yesterday, I stood on Lego three times, and I only took the Lord's name in vain twice. I am one hardcore bish, yo.

But not today. Today I get off that bike and I can't feel my legs. It's a bit like that one time I drank the better part of a bottle of sambuca on a hen night and cried the whole way home in a taxi, convinced I'd never walk again. I expect to splat on the ground only to look up and see my legs and my undercarriage now at one with the bike while the rest of me crawls to freedom.

'That was brilliant,' Cat says, her voice crossing the great void of blackness that's threatening to wash over me. I blink hard and look at her. Slowly she comes into focus. Serene. A dusky pink glow on her cheeks. The faintest hint of a sheen of sweat at her hairline but mostly she just looks sated. Is it possible she really enjoyed herself, like *really* enjoyed herself, as I prayed for death while resembling Mr Blobby?

'I feel so energized. Don't you feel energized, Tara? I'm ready to kick this day right in the dick and make it mine. This was a class idea of yours. I feel like superwoman!' She grins at me widely.

I nod and try to stay focused on her, but the room's gone a bit fuzzy and I feel a weird tingle at the back of my neck and my stomach suddenly does not feel at all good.

Making a beeline for the loos, I'm violently ill. The noises coming from my throat are inhuman as my stomach contracts again and again until I feel a hand rubbing my back gently. Cat must've followed me in, and I'm about to tell her that I'm never fecking coming to fecking spin fecking class again when I hear a voice I don't know reassure me that everything is going to be OK.

I turn, tears streaming from my eyes, slabbers caught at the side of my mouth, to see one of the stunningly beautiful Lyrca-clad ladies from earlier. There's not even a rock I can crawl under.

Is there a positive in all of this? Perhaps it's just that I didn't pee myself at the same time I threw up. That has happened before. Once. I'm still traumatized.

'I'm so embarrassed,' I manage to stutter while my new-found friend folds some paper towel and dampens it under the cold tap.

'Hold that to the back of your neck,' she says. 'Your friend will be back with some water in a minute. And don't be embarrassed, not at all. It's quite common to puke after your first spin class.'

I blink up at her. 'Did you?' I ask, knowing that if this vision in purple and black says yes, then maybe there is hope for me after all.

She nods with a smile. 'And the second. But then it started to get easier. I really enjoy it now.'

'But do you not find those seats really uncomfortable?' I ask.

'Let me tell you a secret,' she says with a conspiratorial smile. 'Padded cycling shorts.' She points to her crotch area and while I obviously had not studied her groin in any great detail before I can see the very slight bulge of cushioning. 'If spin is going to be your thing, they might well be the best investment you'll ever make.'

Could spin be 'my thing'? I mean, I'm not sure I can still walk, and I'm fairly certain that when I do, sweat will drip from my clothes. I hated every single painful second of it, but I did it. Didn't I? I didn't wimp out halfway through. I didn't climb into bed this morning even though I was in pain and I really would've loved another hour or two of sleep.

I did it. I am doing it. I am changing things, one exercise class at a time.

'Thank you,' I say as Cat comes into the ladies' bathroom with a glass of cold water. Behind her I can see Connor, with a concerned look on his face. 'Are you OK?' he shouts through the doorway.

I think about it for a moment. 'Yes,' I say. 'I'm OK. Thank you.'

'Attagirl,' Cat says as she hands the glass over. 'That's the toughest it will ever be. I promise.'

'Do you really?' I ask her.

'Cross my heart and hope to die,' she says. 'Wait and see. I've us booked in for Friday morning too.'

12

Hashtag LadyBoss

By Wednesday my legs finally feel as if they belong to my body and not Michael Flatley's. The thought of Friday's spin class sends prickles of anxiety up and down my spine, but I have to admit I've enjoyed a certain level of smuggery at dropping my 6 a.m. exercise class into conversation whenever possible.

'Yeah,' I tell Molly and Amy and Lucy at work. 'I think it's the best way to start the day you know. It really gets the blood pumping.'

'Wow!' Molly drawls with what I choose to believe is sincerity. 'And you have children to get up and ready, too. You're some sort of supermom.'

'Yeah,' Amy chimes in. 'Hashtag LadyBoss.'

The praise fills me with a warm glow. I'm inspiring the generation of women who are coming up behind me, letting them know that they too can have it all. Look at me kicking at that glass ceiling! Hashtag LadyBoss!

What they don't see is the cool pack I'm sitting on. The one I've had since Nathan was born, that fits into your knickers to bring down after-birth swelling. Turns out, it's great for post-spin crotch pain too. I can hide an awful lot behind a smile and a few grey pubes.

I do feel invigorated though. I've dropped my mid-morning coffee in favour of bottled water. (When I say 'dropped' and 'mid-morning', I do of course simply mean 'moved to' and 'later in the morning'. It's not cheating if I drink the water.) I haven't had one single bit of chocolate since Monday night, and I declared to Paul that wine o'clock is now strictly banned during the working week. It's not been easy, but I want to help my skin regain its youthful glow, help me drop a few pounds and contribute to my reinvention.

In the absence of wine as a distraction in the evenings, I may have gone a bit OTT with online shopping and for once it's not all for the kids. In fact, very little of it is for the kids. I have ordered enough clothes to open my own small but perfectly formed boutique, having analysed my current wardrobe as not fit for purpose. I can no longer justify hanging on to the skinny jeans I loved in 2018 and which are now at least one size, if not two, too small for me. The shapeless but exceptionally comfy T-shirts have been culled from my drawers, leaving only my two favourites.

The local charity shop will soon benefit from a clear-out of my more conservative work clothes. Hours have been spent trawling the internet for advice on how to look good when you're hurtling towards forty, have three children and a muffin top that just won't quit.

I've ordered a few dresses, some skirts, approximately seventy-six T-shirts (only a very slight exaggeration) and a variety of trousers in differing cuts and styles to see what works. And finally some flat shoes, low heels, mid heels and high heels and a pair of knee-high boots which I'm not sure will zip up over my chunky calves. Cleverly, I've arranged for them all to be delivered in-store, so Paul doesn't have a hernia at the number of deliveries rocking up to the house. Not that he would mind. He's a good man. Laid-back. Firm believer in the happy wife equals a happy life method. But he has told me on one too many occasions that I look 'fine as I am', and that word now brings me out in hives whenever I hear it.

I've got a hair appointment for Saturday and my black three-foot roots shall be gone. This will be followed by some bodily waxing, so prepare to say goodbye to all the grey on my body too. That'll show Paul what he can do with 'fine'.

Before work on Thursday, I'm standing in front of my mirror, twisting and turning to see to see how my new black pencil dress fits, ably supported by a pair of sucky-in-knickers. My hair is sadly refusing to behave itself. Whereas I should look a Fifties bombshell, my hair makes me look more like a Nineties bomb scare. Pulling it into a ponytail doesn't work: it's much too severe, the black roots too obvious and the dodgy faux facelift look is not a good one. I try a loose bun. But that's definitely too casual for work. It does not scream glass-ceiling smasher or Hashtag LadyBoss.

After trying to pin it into a French roll (too Eighties yuppy), going casual with some loose beach waves (too Seventies hippy), it's clear that hairstyling is not one of my natural God-given talents. Thankfully, I have a YouTube-tutorial-addicted daughter to hand.

'Gemmmmaaaaaa!'

I am immediately rewarded by her arrival in my room with a grunt that can be roughly translated as 'Wha'?'

'Wha'?' I say, one eyebrow raised. I am pretty sure I raised my children better than this.

'Aye. Wha'? Wha' de ye want?' Her eyes don't leave her phone.

'Darling child of my heart. My firstborn. My reason for living. Let's not go with "wha'?" Let's go with "Yes, Mother who was in labour with me for twenty-six hours and who I love and admire in equal measure. How can I be of assistance to you?"'

She looks up. 'Aye. That's what I meant, bestie.' She is eyeing me suspiciously, taking in my new dress with its figure-clinging cut and my freshly applied make-up, which today includes mascara *and* blusher.

'I need your help,' I say. 'I can't get my hair to sit and you are the only other female in this house and . . . please, Gemma.'

She blinks. Clearly I have confused the child with both my request for her help and my new look. 'You want *me* to do *your* hair?' she asks, and actually slips her phone into the pocket of her school blazer. This is unheard of. Completely unheard of.

'Could you? I've seen you watching those tutorials on YouTube and I saw how you did Mia's hair the night of your party – I know you can do something' – I gesture towards the rats' nest atop my head – 'with this.'

'I can try,' she says, with less than her usual disdain. Dare I say it, is that a flicker of pride? Of love for me, perhaps?

'Thanks, love. You're a life-saver.'

I sit down on my dressing-table stool and she stands behind me, pulling my hair this way and that – examining it as if she is Vidal Sassoon himself. 'You know you need your roots doing?' she says, and I nod.

'I have an appointment on Saturday,' I say.

'By the look of these roots you should've had an appointment last month,' she says, but she's smiling; I won't get on her bad side by telling her she's a cheeky wee madam.

When I was thirteen, the best I could manage for hair care was singeing mine to within an inch of its life by ironing it. Yes, I got more burns to the neck than I care to recall, but my mammy didn't have the money for straighteners – an iron was the next best thing, and lordy me, was that an exercise in danger. One wrong slip and you risked a facial burn you'd struggle to live down at school the next day. Knock the setting too high and the smell of burning and singeing would follow you around like a particularly pungent fart for days. But parted down the middle, with a couple of butterfly clips to hold most of it back from my face, while letting two rather pathetic strands fall forward, I absolutely rocked *Sabrina the Teenage Witch* chic (Nineties version, not cool Netflix Sabrina reboot version).

While Gemma normally wears her long brown hair au natural around her shoulders – her scrunchie remaining steadfastly on her wrist – it seems she can work wonders. She tilts my head this way and that, weaves strands in and out of other strands and slips bobby pins in with ease until she stands back and I see the finished article. She has teased my unkempt, brassy blonde locks into a twisty plait which transforms into a very funky and definitely not dootsy work-appropriate up-do.

Grinning at myself in the mirror, I take her hand and give it a squeeze. 'You're a dote!' I tell her. 'I'm so impressed! This looks great!'

She beams with pride and God, it's so good to see that she hasn't completely lost her ability to smile.

'You look lovely, Mammy,' she says as I hear Paul call her to leave for school.

Kissing me on the top of my head, she runs off in the direction of the stairs, grunting, 'Oh my God, would you calm down?' at her father. I don't care. I'm going to allow this glow to wash over me for a moment or two. Ever since Monday, Gemma has been on her very, very, VERY best behaviour. She's moaned the odd time, rolled her eyes about fifty times, and told Paul and me we are 'so embarrassing' at least three times, so I know she hasn't been replaced by an alien. Maybe she *is* maturing. Maybe twelve was as bad as the 'teen' years were going to get and now that she is thirteen she's settling down?

And look what she has done with my hair! I stand up and take in the reflection before me. I look not bad. Not bad at all. OK, I don't look like I've just walked out of art school, and I'm not exactly 'high fashion', but I look nice. (Fuck! That word!)

No. Not nice. I look good. And professional. And presentable and maybe just maybe I am a Hashtag LadyBoss after all.

I close my eyes and think of positive affirmations. What does Beyoncé say in 'Run the World'? Something about being strong enough to have children, and then get back to business. Yeah, I like that. This is the new me. No, not a new me but a better version of the me I always was. This is the me who can combine parenting with working with being a great wife. This is the me who can be an angel in the kitchen and a sex goddess in the bedroom. I almost feel sorry for Paul. I can feel my libido waking up from its long post-Jax hibernation. This MILF is ready to spend some time with her DILF.

But first, work. I'm going to walk in there and show them how good I am. The interview isn't far away now. Every second at work from this point on counts.

Spraying my new fancy up-do with a liberal amount of hairspray, I grab my work bag from the floor and slip my feet into a pair of black court shoes. (Dear Jesus, I used to wear heels all the time. I used to dance for four hours in a nightclub in them! I loved them. Why do these make me feel as if I'm walking on stilts?)

I'm ready to show off the new me. As soon as I stop walking like Bambi on ice.

13

It's fine, I'm fine but my God he is FINNNNNNE

'Oooooh, look at you!' Molly trills as I arrive at work. 'All dolled up. Are you going somewhere nice after work?'

'Only to Tesco on the way home,' I tell her. 'Then back to the fam.' Fam is a cool word, right? But I'm pretty sure she tuned out at 'Tesco' and hasn't tuned back in. It's OK. I don't need her validation. I know I look good.

I fire up my computer and sit at my desk, slurping from my water bottle (we won't mention the empty grande latte cup in my car) and set to work. It isn't long before I hear the quiet buzz of whispers around me. Now, I know I am looking particularly hot today, but surely it's not that much of a trans-formation?

Smiling to myself, I log into my emails, make a mental to-do list and double-check my Amazon account to make sure the padded cycling shorts that will save my life and my coochie tomorrow morning will definitely be delivered to work today.

Relieved to see they are 'out for delivery', I allow myself a moment to relax and tune into the buzz around me.

To my surprise, it's not me they're talking about. It seems we have a new recruit starting this morning. 'Fresh meat', as Amy describes him, which makes me feel a combination of vaguely nauseous, a wee bit horny and definitely hungry. What I wouldn't give for a dirty big sausage-roll bap for breakfast! I should've taken time this morning to eat something sensible like porridge or natural yoghurt and fruit to fend off the bad carb cravings, but I didn't and now I'll have to go to the shop, ignoring the smell of flaky pastry and sausage meat while I buy a fucking banana. This is some bleak-ass shit.

I throw a dirty look at my water bottle before reminding myself that no pain equals no gain and fewer sausage rolls equals fewer belly rolls.

Is it bad that I'm more interested in a sausage roll bap than I am in the talk of the new starter? Perhaps I shouldn't be. After all, the only spare desk in the office is in front of mine, which means he will be directly in my line of fire. The younger girls will be raging that I've bagged such a prime location even though I've been here longest.

'Oooh, is that why you've dressed up?' Lucy trills in my direction. 'Are you planning on going full cougar?'

'Wise up,' I scoff. 'I've enough younger men in my life to be coping with. I just fancied a bit of a change clothes-wise.'

'Are you sure?' she asks in a very sing-song voice that makes me want to punch her in the face.

'Oh I'm sure,' I say. 'And what age is he anyway?' I bite my tongue before I ask if he is a foetus like all the rest of them.

'Twenty-four,' she says, sighing the deep sigh that only young people who have never dealt with the reality of a relationship that lasts more than three months can.

Twenty-four, I think as I do some quick mental maths. He is closer in age to my daughter than he is to me. The very thought gives me some very short-lived icks, but then the office quietens, and a dark-haired Adonis in a slick charcoal-grey suit with a crisp white shirt glides into the office beside an even more weaselly than normal Mr Handley – holy mama! I can smell the very pheromones off this man and he smells like he'd impregnate you just by brushing past you in the break room.

He has a chiselled jaw, wide shoulders, and hard, tense, toned abs (well, I can't see his abs, but I know, in the way you *know*). I can't quite put my finger on who he reminds me of . . .

'Right, everyone,' Mr Handley says. 'I'd like you to meet our latest graduate recruit. This is Luke. Luke hasn't long finished his post-graduate study in business management, so he is stepping in ahead of the game here. He knows his way around a project.'

I bet he does. I bet he's the kind of big confident, ride of a man who could turn his hand to anything. I blush, as a hot flush rises through my body. C'mon, Tara, get a grip! This man is but a child! I am a woman! A married woman with a husband I love very much indeed and who I also happen to fancy! A married woman with three children, a mortgage, an anxiety

SERENA TERRY

disorder and a pair of sucky-in knickers so tight that I fear the circulation to my lower extremities could be cut off at any moment! Oh, and I've got a grey pube. I need to calm the jets.

Mr Handley walks Luke across the room to his new desk. I offer him a quick smile. 'This is Tara,' Mr Handley says. 'She one of our oldest employees.'

Why the fuck did he have to say 'oldest'? Eugh. Why couldn't he say 'most senior' instead of oldest, although both would be true. I nod at Luke, momentarily struck mute by the sheer rideyness of him.

'It's nice to meet you, Tara,' he says, his dark eyes boring through mine as if he can see my very soul.

'Yes. It is,' I mumble; what a completely shite and embarrassing answer. 'I mean, it's nice to meet you too, Luke. Welcome to ToteTech.'

'I see we'll be neighbours,' he says, his gravelly voice setting me aquiver. He is the wolf and I am Little Red Riding Hood.

'We will,' I squeak and that's it. I'm done. I have lost the ability to speak. My legs, I fear, have turned to jelly again and this time there's no spin bike involved in the process.

'I . . . am . . . I've a wee bitta work here . . .' I stutter, and when he smiles . . . oh baby Jesus! I feel something in the very pit of my stomach tighten and curl, and I can't quite believe I am getting the absolute horn in work from the mere CHILD in front of me. But he's not a child. He's a man. All man. And he's looking at me as if he is hungover and I am a sausage-roll bap. I see it then, I see who he reminds me of.

117

Yer man from that film. The Northern Irish fellah. Aye, Jamie Dornan, when he was Christian Grey.

And I am lost to little a fantasy where Mr Grey will most certainly see me now.

By lunchtime I have a full-on, and completely inappropriate, crush on Luke. I've been trying to fight it, but he is so lovely and he laughed at three of my jokes and asked me for help. He even brought me a cup of coffee and gave me two fingers of his four-finger KitKat to have with it.

I'm about to take myself out for a walk to cool off when Mr Handley appears, vampire like, at my desk. 'Ah, Tara. You don't have lunch plans, do you?'

I shake my head, still in the throes of the horn for the new guy, despite him being much too young and me being much too married.

'Ah great. Well as our oldest employee, I hoped you'd step into the breach for me today. I was to take young Luke here for lunch – you know the drill, welcome him to the company, show him he's made the right decision by joining ToteTech.'

I nod, but I can't lie: I'm nervous about where this is headed.

'Well, it seems we've hit a little bump on the Morrison project and I need to iron it out. And you know the Morrisons – it can't wait.'

'I can do that for you,' I jump in. As it happens, I get on very well with the Morrisons – a husband-and-wife team who launched their own multimedia platform for businesses two years ago and have seen it grow at an exponential rate. I like them. They are no-nonsense people and they seem to like me too and my similarly no-nonsense but no-bullshit approach. 'I'm sure I can calm the waters,' I tell him.

'Maybe you can, but I think this really is a job for someone more qualified, and that as you know, means me.' There he is, waving his qualifications around again like they're his dick. All the qualifications in the world wouldn't make Mr Handley a people person. 'No, I was thinking you could take young Luke here out instead. The reservation is at Browns in Town for one o'clock, under ToteTech. Use your company credit card to pay. And you know the rules: no excessive drinking or ordering double desserts!'

He wags his finger at me as if I'm a child, or at least a lush known for my excessive drinking and double dessert eating. I am neither – not in work anyway.

'I . . . I have a few things I really need to get on with,' I mutter, knowing that it's unlikely a lunch à deux with Luke will calm my raging hormones.

'They can be done tomorrow,' Mr Handley says. 'I know you can do it, Tara. You always get back on track after your unexpected trips out to deal with those delightful children of yours. You can manage this as well.'

I allow myself a moment to imagine what it would feel like to slap him right across the top of his excessively Brylcreemed head.

'Right,' I say, plastering a smile on my face instead. 'Of course I will. That's no problem. I'll take care of that.'

As he walks away I hold my breath for fear that if I let out an exhalation, a very loud and long list of expletives will 'accidentally' escape in his direction. Once I'm sure he's out of the room I allow myself a moment to decompress.

'Yer man's a dick, isn't he?' Luke says with a wry smile, and I nod.

'Well look, I promise I'll behave at lunch and not give you too much trouble. And if you want three desserts, I'll spring for them and the company need never know!' He smiles and I laugh. No, I giggle. Like a schoolgirl. I'm embarrassed for me. But if he had me by just looking like a sexy big ride of a man, he absolutely has me by calling Handsy a dick. And the triple dessert promise is a delightful bonus. As indeed is the look on the face of my youthful colleagues as we leave for lunch together, joking about ordering the most expensive bottle of wine on the menu.

'So,' Luke says, stifling a smile 'You're the oldest member of staff?'

I sip from my glass of wine (I allow myself one glass as it would be rude not to) and grimace. 'Most senior,' I say. 'Although maybe that sounds worse? Senior does have a feel of walking frames and comfy slippers about it.'

'Nothing wrong with a pair of comfy slippers,' Luke says with a laugh. 'You women think you have it all sewn up. Getting home, slipping off your bras and into your jammies. I've seen the Instagram posts.' He's smiling, but my brain is off behaving like a fourteen-year-old thinking 'he said *bra*', causing my face to flush bright red.

'Well, I'll tell you this. I get into the house, out of my suit and into my joggers as quickly as I can. If it's not a five-a-side night or cycling night, I put on my slippers too, and I apologize to no one for owning a pair.'

'Cycling?' I ask. 'Are you a member of a club, or do you go it alone?'

'A club,' he nods. 'Every Wednesday night and most Saturday mornings. I love it. Nothing like getting the miles behind you. Have you ever tried it?'

I think of the spin class I've done and the one I've signed up for and think that, technically, I won't be lying if I say yes. 'Sort of,' I tell him. 'It's a bit different, but I can see the attraction. It's a great workout.'

'One of the best,' he says. 'Although I can think of a better one.' He looks up at me from under his dark lashes and if this were that Christian Grey film this would be the exact moment he would haul me across the table and do unspeakable things to me. If he could get past the sucky-in knickers which make chastity belts redundant, that is.

'Really?' I ask, my heart a-flutter.

'Absolutely,' he says. 'Have you ever tried Twister?'

Before I know what's good for me, I say, 'I'm more of a Buckaroo type girl myself.' As the words leave my mouth, it crosses my mind that as the senior/oldest staff member, my answer could be setting me up as a bit of a 'Handsy' type character. Again I blush, but thankfully Luke is roaring with laughter.

'You're good craic,' he says. 'I mean, I wanted this job – I really did – but when I met Mr Handley I wondered if I'd done the right thing. What kind of a knobber gets his work-mates to call him "mister" anyway?'

I laugh, relieved that Luke has a sense of humour and isn't a Handsy part two – albeit better looking than the original.

'We're all here to work and do our jobs well, but it's good to be able to have a laugh too, isn't it? I was kind of worried you would be a pack of dry shites.'

'What can I say?' I smile. 'We are definitely not dry shites. I'd say we're the opposite, but that doesn't sound terribly appealing either. Look, the thing is, Handley aside, we're all trying to do a good job. Yes, some of the staff – yourself included, if I'm honest – are very young, and some are clearly still learning. I've been with ToteTech for a long time and I know our clients and our business. They'll always be our priority, but I think I'd be for the funny farm if I couldn't have at least some craic during working hours.'

'I'm always up for a bit of the craic,' he says, his eyes twink-ling. 'I mean, obviously, my priority is to get the job done as well as possible, but I agree with you. We spend a lot of time at work, it needs to have appeal outside of the pay cheque. So, fill me in on the other staff members. Is there anyone else, apart from Mr Handley, who I need to give a wide berth to?'

So I fill him in, trying not to let my feelings about the Gen Zs and their immaturity too clear. He does after all tick the same box as them on forms asking his age. I don't want him to think I'm an old, bitter, and – did I say old again? – crone.

Luke is surprisingly easy to talk to and he gets my sense of humour. More than that, he is a great listener. Very attentive. Asks all the right questions. Knows exactly how to flatter me.

'I can't believe you're old enough to have a thirteen-year-old daughter,' he says. 'You must've been very young when you had her. You can't be more than, what, twenty-nine or thirty now?'

I snort. 'You're very kind, but I'm nearer forty than I am thirty. I had Gemma when I was twenty-three. A happy accident.' I say, wondering why I'm confiding in him about something so personal. It's true that Gemma wasn't planned for, but Paul and I were very much a couple when I peed on that stick and we knew instantly that we'd get through this together. A little flash of guilt nips at me as I think of Paul, but it quickly evaporates when Luke smiles. 'No way,' he says. 'You look incredible.'

He looks at me with such an intensity I look away: has the temperature just shot up in the restaurant or is it his gaze that has me all hot and bothered?

By the time we return to the office two hours later I have established that he is a great asset to ToteTech, and a great possible second husband if Paul ever leaves me. Or at least a great possible lover.

I find myself the object of death stares for what remains of the afternoon. Lucy seems particularly aggrieved that I got to spend time up and close and personal with the new guy.

'Mr Handley should've asked me,' she pouts when I bump

into her outside the ladies' loos. 'I mean, I'm more likely to be more on his level, don't you think? Being the same age and all? It must've been a struggle for you, given that you're more used to being around older people.'

'I'm thirty-six, Lucy,' I tell her. 'In many cultures that is still considered young, and I am able to have conversations with people of all ages.'

She blinks, her eyelash extensions fluttering like butterflies. 'I didn't mean . . . I'm not saying you're old. Or that you can't talk to people . . . I'm only saying, y'know, there's a new, handsome single on the loose here and you've no idea how hard it is to meet decent men these days. You've been married for, like, forever. You don't have to impress anyone any more. We do.'

There's a lot to unpack in what Lucy has just said. She's right that I have no idea what it's like to try and meet someone new these days. Paul and I have been together for fifteen years and married for ten of them. I was so young when we got together that I didn't have much experience of the Hunger Games that modern dating has become. But, I do still have to make an effort. And I may be married and I may be a mother of three, but that doesn't mean I've given up on wanting to be desired or that I can't enjoy the flutter in the pit of my stomach that comes with connecting with someone. Even if nothing will come of it.

As the saying goes, I may be on a diet but that doesn't mean I can't look at the menu.

*

On the drive home I have at least twenty-seven conversations with Luke in my head, where I run through a variety of scenarios, from me very calmly telling him I'm very sorry but I'm married, to me snogging the face off him in the stationery cupboard – our very own red room of pain. I indulge that particular fantasy the least because, as Lucy reminded me in her own slightly patronizing way, I *am* happily married to a man who loves me and who says he'd like to have more sexy time with me if I can manage to stay awake long enough.

And I want to have sexy time with him as well. Why am I calling it sexy time? I may as well say fornicate; what am I, seventy-three?

I want to have hot, sweaty, passionate sex with my husband. We rub along nicely together, if you get my meaning. There's something so nice about knowing what makes each other tick, and what the other likes or doesn't like. There's also something comforting and convenient about knowing that sometimes you just have to get the job done and the person helping you knows the quickest, easiest methods. Not to mention the comfort that comes from knowing the person you're sharing your bed with has seen you at your very worst. (There was the three-day hangover that followed my first night on the drink after Jax was born, not to mention the night of being on the drink which ended with us needing to replace the hall carpet.) Not having to worry about belly rolls (of which I have gained an extra one with every baby), stubbly legs and post-breastfeeding saggy boobs is a joy. But maybe this is the issue, the reason Paul thinks I look 'fine'. Have I gotten too comfortable? Is comfort a problem?

I wonder what Luke would make of my 'fine' body. Immediately I'm horrified, not only because I'm sure at his tender age he is only used to seeing nice, pert, firm and bouncy boobs and non-stretchmarked tummies, but also because I have to refer to him as being a 'tender age' and it feels icky. At the time he was Nathan's age, I was already legally allowed into bars. I shudder and push the thought away.

It's all wrong. I need to wise up.

14

All the gear, still no idea

My bravado about the Friday morning spin class ends as soon as I arrive at the Friday morning spin class.

I have come better prepared than last time. I managed to nip into town during the week and bought some actual active wear to go with the shorts from Amazon. I've not gone as far as one of those skinny crop-top efforts because I don't think anyone in the spin class is ready for that particular brand of jelly. But I am wearing the famous padded bicycle shorts and a loose T-shirt which promises to 'wick away' my sweat so that I don't actively drip on the floor mid class. I even bought a sports bra which, from what I have experienced so far, is clearly based on some sort of medieval torture device. My girls will not move during this class as they are bound so tightly to my chest in heavy fabric (which allegedly also has a wicking quality) that nothing is shifting them.

I stopped short of buying a headband to soak up the

inevitable hairline sweat, but already I'm regretting that decision. I dislike being sweaty unless it's somewhere on a sun-lounger, by a pool and with access to all-inclusive cheap non-branded alcohol. I have a pair of trainers on my feet which cost more than a week's grocery shopping for a family of five and which I will have to wear every day for the next five years to cure my spending guilt.

No part of my new look makes me feel any less nervous. Cat, however, has no nerves at all. She bounces into the gym reception announcing that it's her day off so she ran here instead of bringing the car. 'No rush to get to the office today, so thought I'd add a few miles onto my morning.'

She points at the fancy watch on her arm, one of those activity trackers. Paul bought me one once, at my request, but it shit itself after spending three months monitoring my woefully low step count and listening to me spiral that I'm going to die every time my heart rate went up. It seems that Fitbits are not necessarily a good idea for people with chronic anxiety which occasionally tips over into hypochondria.

'Good for you!' I say, and my teeth are only slightly gritted.

'You look great,' she tells me as she stretches her legs and arms. I copy her, wondering if a good stretch first will help me when it comes to being able to walk after the class.

'I bought some new things,' I say. 'Thought I might as well dress for the life I want.'

'Good woman yourself!' she says again. 'I have to say I was half expecting you to call me this morning to cry off.'

Whoa there! She was expecting me to cry off? Just because

I have become notoriously unreliable since Jax was born, and just because I had sent her a series of text messages on Tuesday outlining every ache and pain, including my struggle to first of all bend my legs to sit on the toilet and second of all, straighten my legs again to stand up. Part of me wanted to do an Elvis and expire, right there, mid wee rather than feel the burn as I stood up.

'I signed the fuck-it list, didn't I?' I say. 'I'm all in. This is the new me and all these bitches better all be scared.' I say the last line with perhaps a little too much sass, and definitely with too much volume. Heads turn and look me up and down, and immediately I'm compelled to tell my fellow spinners that I don't think they are bitches, I'm sure they are very lovely ladies.

Cat, for all her supportive friend-itis, is practically wetting herself with mirth. (Except she probably doesn't wet herself when she laughs too much, or sneezes, or jumps up and down. Her vagina, as she often reminds me, has never been brutalized by the birthing process.)

'Tara, you do make me laugh,' she says. 'And I'm all in with you being all in. Not that I don't think you're amazing as you are, but if toning up and making some changes makes you happier then you go get it, girl.'

I smile. Is that what all this is about? Me being happier? I mean, I am happy enough with my life. I don't have any huge tragedy to deal with. I've a roof over my head, three kids, one husband and there's always food on the table. No, it's not happiness I'm after. It's just a sense of who I really am.

I'm about to launch into telling her this when there is a

whistle and a cheer and I hear Connor shouting that it's time to start the 'effing weekend' before a dance track I vaguely recognize as being much too modern for my taste (where are my Nineties bangers?) kicks in and I climb onto my bike and very gingerly sit down. OK, I think. It's not great, but the padded shorts do help. I might be OK.

I do not throw up after spin class. Great success! I do cry, but only a couple of tears. The sweat absorption qualities of my medieval torture device sports bra have been greatly oversold, however, and at one stage I just shouted 'Oh fuck off!' out loud when Connor decided it was time to do some rapid uphill climbs. I'd been sure I only said it under my breath.

My legs are like jelly when I get off my bike but I am smiling a little when the woman who had so gamely held my sweaty hair back as I puked on Monday smiles at me and says: 'I told you the first class was the toughest,' with a wink.

'That was great,' I say to Cat, even though I'm partially sure the euphoria I am feeling at this exact moment is down to the fact the class is over and not that I actually enjoyed it.

'Will we do it again on Monday?' she asks.

The very mention of Monday makes me feel even more weak at the knees than I already do. That's the day of the interviews. Still, maybe it will do me good to go to a class before them – get my blood pumping in a way that doesn't involve any inappropriate thoughts about Luke. I blush instantly, thinking of him, and in particular of him in tight cycling shorts, his muscular thighs bulging, among other things.

'Yes,' I tell her, dragging myself back to the reality of my distinctly non-muscular thighs. 'Why not?'

'Attagirl,' she says. 'Although I'm out on Sunday night – a Tinder date, for God's sake – so I might be a little worse for wear. You don't know how lucky you have it, Tara. Not having to be in the dating pool. It's a jungle out there and one that only seems to have really shitty baggage-laden animals. Like hippos or poisonous snakes.'

She looks sad. I think of what Lucy said to me the day before. Surely it's not *that* horrible for modern daters?

'It can't be all bad,' I say. 'Must be nice to meet new people, and try new things? It's a long time since I've felt the rush of falling in lust or love, surely that's worth the risk?'

'Oh my sweet summer child,' she says. 'Most men these days are not looking to fall in love. Dating apps are modern-day meat markets. I count myself lucky if he pays for half of the bill, doesn't have a seriously weird kink and doesn't try to murder me on the way home. The lure of something new isn't all it's cracked up to be.'

I think immediately of Luke and how we'd laughed and flirted over lunch yesterday and I blush furiously. That's only a silly fantasy, though, isn't it? The reality, according to my friends, would be very different. 'I suppose,' I say. 'I am lucky to have Paul.'

'You've no idea, pet. He's a good man. He loves you. He loves the family you have together and I'm pretty sure he doesn't have seriously weird kinks.'

I smile. Paul's weirdest kink involves him getting absolutely steam-boated, asking me for a cuddle and telling me that he loves me and cuddles are better than sex anyway. Well, that and he often gets the hang-horn when he is hungover – which isn't necessarily a pleasant experience for either of us.

'Ah you're right,' I tell her as I towel the back of my neck. 'I think sometimes it's very easy not to appreciate what we have by thinking about what other people may be up to.'

'You said it,' she says, before pausing. Damn it. Cat has always been able to read me like a cheesy romance novel. 'Is there something you want to tell me?' she asks.

I make an immediate and deadly mistake. I say 'no' before she has even finished her sentence and shake my head vigorously. It's a move I learned from Nathan, and while Cat may not be a mother and used to the complex truth-manipulation of five-year-olds, she's on me straight away.

'Tara Gallagher. There is something! The fuck-it list? The new you? What's going on? Is everything OK with you and Paul?' She looks utterly shaken at the very thought there may be trouble in my own version of not-quite paradise.

'Everything's fine,' I tell her and that's true. 'It's not Paul. It's me. And Gemma turning thirteen and me hurtling towards forty. I don't think I know who I am any more. Didn't I used to be better craic? Didn't I used to be cool and fun to be around?'

'Darling,' she says, 'you're still belter craic and you are definitely still cool. You've just lost your way a little, and you're letting your anxiety get the better of you. We've been here before. We know anxiety lies.'

'Like a bastard,' I say, quoting her own previous take on the matter back at her. She nods.

'Have you been looking after yourself properly?' she asks, and I know she's onto something. My anxiety likes to rise up and look for attention at times when I'm really busy and/or really stressed. Gemma's birthday, and the upscaling of her total embarrassment at being related to me, certainly counts as stress. I feel I'm losing my wee girl, and it's no wonder I'm anxious. I've been a mammy almost as long as I've been a grown-up. I don't know how to adult without a rake of children hanging off me and I fear I'll end up alone after the children grow up and leave home, and Paul realizes he's finally had enough of my not being the sexy siren he wishes I was.

But that is much too heavy a conversation to get into at half seven in the morning on a workday.

'It's probably a midlife crisis,' I sniff, giving her a watery smile.

'Shut your face. Midlife isn't until mid forties or so these days. Not to downplay it, but I'd bet this is a mammy crisis. I've seen it in a lot of my mammy friends. You just have to ride the storm. Explore what will make you feel more like yourself again and don't do anything fucking stupid in the meantime. No rash purchases of roller-boots and/or hot-pants. No getting snookered and crying to a stranger in nightclub loos about your episiotomy scars, and absolutely no, and I mean no, drunken fumbles in the name of finding a bit of adventure.'

I nod and tell her I promise.

Forgetting again that I am but a cheesy romance novel and she is a very adept reader.

15

Cheeses duck!

It's Saturday morning and I am sitting, gowned up and ready for action, in the hairdresser's chair. Sitting down was a struggle – my thighs are screaming after spin yesterday – but now I'm here I am determined to relax and enjoy some me time. The boys had me awake at 5 a.m. There is little as terrifying as having your eyelids prised open and the first sight of the day being a too-close-for-comfort face of a toddler in your personal space.

'Jesus, fuck!' I exclaimed, which was a bad idea as Jax immediately parroted me.

'Cheeses fuck! Cheeses fuck!'

'That's two bad words, Mammy,' I heard Nathan's voice from behind Jax's very up close and very slabbery head. 'I'm going to tell Miss Rose.'

To my eternal pride, I managed not to reply that he and Miss Rose could fuck right off. Instead, I did what all good parents do and I lied. 'I did not say any bad words. I said

134

"cheeses duck". I was having a silly dream about a duck that eats cheese.' I heard a snort of laughter from Paul beside me and I resisted the urge to elbow him in the ribs.

'I don't fink so, Mammy,' Nathan sing-songed. 'And Miss Rose says we should always tell if someone says a bad word.'

'Someone needs to tell Miss Rose that snitches get stitches,' I whispered under my breath. 'I don't think Miss Rose is talking about what your mammy and daddy say at home. But anyway, I did not swear.'

'Cheeses fuck!' Jax proclaimed again, sitting the full weight of himself – overnight nappy filled to near saturation level with pee – much too close to my face.

'Boys,' I said, 'it's still dark. Time to go back to bed.'

'But we are awake,' Nathan moaned. I tilted my head to see him grab his tummy tightly and do a rather impressive impression of a starving child.

'I hungwee,' Jax mumbled, his dummy bobbing up and down in his mouth. I really must train him off that thing, but it works and it's cute and I don't have the energy.

'My tummy is sore,' Nathan said. 'I think it wants Coco Pops.'

'Pops!' Jax parroted, nodding his head enthusiastically. These two are quite the double act. I'll give them that much.

'I was trying to sleep but my tummy was too hungry,' Nathan said. The wee shite was laying it on thick and fast at this stage.

Paul said he'd get up with them if I wanted, but I knew he deserved a lie-in more than I did. He has been so hands-on with the kids this week while I've been flailing around in my not-quite-midlife-probably-mammy-life crisis. And he has done it all without comment or complaint.

So, not long after five in the morning I found myself watching *Peppa Pig* while my children – both having eaten perhaps two spoonfuls of their Coco Pops at most – declared that they were full up and asked if they could go outside to jump on the trampoline.

The neighbours would just love that.

The hours between five and eight became a long attempt at distracting them from their desire to bounce outside. I drank three coffees for sustenance, which might explain why I'm feeling a wee bit hyper and on edge now.

This is a cool hairdresser's. A great salon. I watch as clients arrive and stylists with impossibly cool hair get to work. People are so brave with their hair these days – dying it all the colours of the rainbow and going for undercuts and asymmetric styles and generally pulling it off.

Me, on the other hand? The hairstylist's chair is a cruel mistress. There I sit, my tired face make-up free, looking at my haircut in the same style I have been wearing since I grew it out of the famous 'Rachel from *Friends*' cut in the late Nineties. Blonde, highlighted, shoulder-length. Dark roots, with that grey patch that seems to be growing every day.

It's all so very, very boring. I glance around the salon. There is a woman in her twenties with silver-grey hair, cut into a very sleek, very short bob. She looks amazing. I fear I would just look old, and the bob would look like Lego hair on me.

That's when I see a new client walk in. She's maybe about

my age and she oozes confidence and style as she hands over her leather jacket, brushes down her midi summer dress and follows a stylist to a chair. Her hair is pink. Not bright pink. A lovely, mermaidy pastel tone; and it is cut into a cropped, effortlessly cool style. She looks like she is ready to walk onto the set of a music video and give the performance of her life.

When Rita, my stylist, returns to me and asks if we're doing the same as usual, I shake my head, pushing down Cat's warnings about not doing anything too rash while this crisis is upon me. She never mentioned not dying my hair pink, after all.

'Actually,' I say to Rita. 'I'd like to try something different today . . .'

Three and a bit hours later I am staring at a whole new me in the mirror. Gone are my greys, and my dark roots. Gone is my shapeless, boring cut. Gone is most of my hair, if the truth be told. The blonde that was is now a soft ombre pink, deepening towards the ends of my hair. The back of my neck feels cold and naked as I admire my new look. Rita has done an incredible job.

OK, so I'm not going to be giving the effortlessly cool music-video-ready lady a run for her money any time soon. I should have considered my cheekbone structure a bit more and the fact that my face is a little rounder than I would like. But I feel good. If this is what passes for cool these days, then I am ice cold, bishes! I snap a quick picture and send it to both Cat and Amanda.

Cat replies with six thumbs up emojis in a row, and three explosion emojis. I love it. Total MILF vibes.

Amanda is a bit more restrained in her response. Is that a filter? Or a wig? Tara, is this for real? There is no indication of whether she likes or doesn't like the look and I'm almost afraid to respond and tell her it is 100 per cent for real, but I figure if I don't have confidence in my new look then no one else will.

It's real, I text back. And I love it!

You're very brave. I don't think I'd have the nerve for something so out there, she responds. She hasn't even said if she likes it or not. I don't reply any further. I do not want her to kill my buzz. I paint a happy smile on my face, tip Rita very generously, and walk as fast as my aching, tight leg muscles will allow me into the Foyleside Shopping Centre to check out both leather jackets and biker boots. I have never felt more rock chick in my life. Well, apart from the time I accidentally found myself in a mosh pit at a Kings of Leon concert and lost both a welly boot and got a black eye, but that's another story from my glory days.

In little under three hours from the arrival of the new, cool, pink-haired me, I am fighting the urge to bitch-slap a beautician.

It's not that she deserves to be bitch-slapped. She's lovely, if a wee bit scary. At just over five foot, you'd be forgiven for thinking Tori would be a gentle wee pixie when it comes to waxing. She is not. She is a demon. A master of the dark arts of creating a perfectly arched eyebrow, or a smooth top lip. A killer of bikini lines. A destroyer of rogue grey pubes. She has much better upper body strength than I gave her credit for.

The waxing of both my eyebrows and my increasingly more obvious moustache is relatively painless. I've had it done before, of course, although I'm not as fastidious about it these days as I was in my twenties.

The waxing of my undercarriage is a whole other story. I know it's almost impossible to believe, but at thirty-six years of age I have never had more than a quick tidy up down there. Just enough to make sure no rogue hairs escape from the sides of my swimming suit while on holiday or when taking the kids to the pool. I'm not emotionally able for having Nathan ask (no doubt loudly) why I have a hairy front bum. I have not yet recovered from his asking (again, loudly) to see my willy in the public loos in Foyleside. I don't think he's recovered either from learning that not all people are bestowed with the joy of owning a penis.

Today, a quick tidy isn't going to cut it. I need the grey gone and I figure that's what women do now. We wax ourselves bald to be cool, and sexy and desirable. I have my doubts that any amount of wax can compensate for the slight belly overhang that will not go away post-kids, the stretchmarks and the dimpling thighs, but here we are.

Tori is perfectly lovely. She does not baulk at the sight of my wobbly tummy, nor does she recoil at the sight of my ungroomed foof area, nor the grey hairs.

'And you want it all gone?' she says, looking at me.

I blush, aware that I am lying in an exceptionally undignified position. They say once you have a baby you no longer have any qualms about getting your bits out for inspection. Let me tell you, that is the biggest pile of bullshit known to man, or woman. It's a myth!

'Well, yeah I mean I think so. There's no way to hide the grey, is there?' I ask, only a slight wobble in my voice.

She smiles. 'Sadly not. But we don't have to take it all.'

I wonder if she's secretly calculating how much wax and how much effort she will have to use to get the job done and panicking that she will end up broke and exhausted with two dead arms.

'I know,' I say, pushing that little anxiety demon that lives in my head down. 'But in for a penny, in for a pound. It's on my fuck-it list, you see. My daughter thinks I'm the most embarrassing mother to ever walk the planet and I think my husband and I are in a rut. And did you know that teachers these days seem to qualify when they are about twelve years old, and my friend Cat says she couldn't not get waxed any more. She'd feel like a yeti . . .' This rambling is a nervous reaction to what is to come. Tori doesn't so much as blink. I imagine she has seen and heard it all before.

With an 'OK, lovey,' she steps up on a stool so she can reach my nethers and gets to work. The warm wax feels nice. Along with the soft plinky-plonky music and the gentle whirr of the aromatherapy oil diffuser, it feels almost relaxing.

Until that first strip is torn from my body and I'm pretty sure I feel my soul leaving along with my discarded pubes.

'CHEESES DUCK!' I scream. Tori does not flinch at my outburst. She simply presses down another strip and whips it back with absolutely no hesitation.

'You're doing really well,' she soothes as I cram my fist into my mouth to stop myself from screaming again. This is worse than childbirth, but I can't stop her now. I can't live my life with a half-waxed coochie. It's not like you can do a combover down there to hide it. Paul would be calling me Bobby Charlton for weeks.

I must be brave. This is my Waterloo. If this and spin and pink hair are what it takes to be cool, then this is the price I am willing to pay.

'Now this bit might feel a little more tender,' she says, as my eyes water.

16

Pink hair, don't care

I don't know what hurts more. My crotch or my legs. Either way, climbing in behind the steering wheel of the car is zero craic.

When I pull down the sun-visor, I smile as I get a glimpse of my cool new pink hair, but soon grimace to see the equally pink skin that now glows around my eyebrows and across my upper lip. It will fade, of course, but for now it's not my best look. I dread to think what down there looks like – a freshly plucked chicken, perhaps? It feels like it might be bruised. Jesus, you can bruise your fanny just by waxing it?

At least, I think, the grey is gone. From my head and every-where else. And Tori assured me that Paul will love the new waxed look. I didn't tell her that I have to manage to stay awake long enough to allow him access to that particular area, and that sex in our house can often be a lights out, under the duvet, don't make a sound affair. None of us wants a repeat of the night Paul felt a tiny clammy hand on his back and turned to see Nathan asking if he could play wrestling too.

I can only imagine the wee grass would be running to tell Miss Rose all about it if he caught us at it again. Then she'd not only have us reported to social services for swearing like heathens but for going at it in front of the wains.

I can't believe there are women who do this, willingly, every few weeks. I'm not saying I'm a slattern when it comes to looking after myself, but God, it's fucking painful. And it's so high maintenance. When my eyes had stopped watering after the waxing, I had lifted one of Tori's brochures to see the list of services she has on offer. Lip-fillers, Botox, HD Brows, Micro-blading, Chemical peels – the works. There's not a one of those that is pain-free – and I always thought the salon was about pampering yourself. There is nothing pampering about tattooing your eyebrows on, even if it does look good afterwards.

But still, it is done and cannot be undone. Not immediately anyway. And my hair does look amazing. At least, I'm pretty sure it looks amazing. In this light, and having sweated like a glassblower's arse, it has a bit more of a flump look about it than a sleek, styled cut.

I run my fingers through it. It's nothing that some of the exceptionally expensive 'product' that Rita sold to me as a 'must have' won't fix. Assuming I work out how I'm supposed to use it.

*

143

I would be lying my still-a-bit-too-pink-for-comfort head off if I said I wasn't nervous about how my doting family will react to my new look. The best way to tackle this is head on (pardon the pun). If being a mammy has taught me anything it is that you show no weakness. Let no chink in your armour shine. If I lead with how much I love it, then they aren't really going to kill my buzz by telling me they hate it. Are they? They're not the kind of people who would piss on your chips, if you get my meaning.

With one last tousle and having sung along to Christina's Aguilera's 'Beautiful' to psych myself up (because I *am* beautiful, no matter what they say), I brace myself for whatever will come.

Opening the door with a loud 'Ta-daa! Honey, I'm home!' I'm greeted with an empty hall and family sounds emanating from every room. Long gone are the days when my children would practically fall over themselves to hug me on my arrival back to the homestead. *Paw Patrol* on the TV is more appealing than Mammy doing the same thing she does every day and walking in through the door.

'I'm in the kitchen, love,' Paul shouts and launches into telling me how Nathan got on at his swimming lesson this morning. (He did not pee in the pool like last time, which is considered incredible progress even if he still isn't brave enough to put his face under water yet. To be fair, knowing that he's peed in that same water is probably putting him off; he's smart enough to know that if he peed in it, many others have likely done the same.)

Paul is chatting, his back to me as he puts the kettle on and starts making tea. 'That's great,' I reply, and it is. The peeing incident had left me worried he was going to be the only five-year-old in Derry to be barred from the local pool. The wee monkey hadn't even had the sense to do it discreetly. He had stood at the side of the pool, like a little cherub statue in an Italian fountain, dropped his trunks and peed while calling for me to watch him as he did it. I have never denied my own children before but that day I came dangerously close to saying I'd never seen that boy in my life.

'Did you have a nice day?' Paul asks, as he pours milk into the cups.

'I did,' I tell him. 'It's nice to take some time to look after me for a bit, you know. I don't often get the chance these days.'

He's reaching into the cupboard to grab some biscuits when I hear the thunderous stomping on the stairs which heralds the arrival of our beloved firstborn. I wonder which version of her we will get today – the moody teen, or the new, strangely disarming pleasant teen.

'Mammy, Mia wants to know if I can meet her in Starbucks for a Frappe tomorrow,' she says, her voice travelling down the hall with her. 'Some of the other girls from school are going too and then we're going to Primark and—'

She has reached the kitchen and clearly the sight of my new hair has struck her dumb. I don't react to her silence. 'As long as your homework is done before you go out, you can go. That's fine.'

I make direct eye contact with her and in that moment, I know what it must have been like for all those poor ancient Greeks when they came face to face with Medusa. Gemma may not have snakes for hair, or the ability to turn me to stone with a single glance, but she has a face on her that would curdle milk.

'What is that?' she asks.

'What is what?' I ask, keeping my tone breezy. Showing not a single ounce of weakness.

'Is that a wig?' she asks, which prompts Paul to turn around and see me for the first time. His expression is one of utter confusion.

'No. It is not a wig. It is my hair, because I wanted to do something different and funky,' I say. 'I love it.'

For a moment Gemma looks at me and does not speak. Is it possible that I have broken her? Paul too is eerily silent.

'I thought I was getting a bit boring and wanted to try something new. It's all the style now,' I say, and I realize that even referring to fashion as 'the style' dates me outside of the cool mum era. I used to cringe when my own mammy came out with stuff like that. 'That's the style for all you young ones now,' she'd say, as if she were an expert on teen fashion and didn't buy most of her clothes in Dunnes Stores.

'It might be *all the style* for young people,' Gemma says, and her voice is a mixture of anger and upset. 'But it's not for people like you. Oh my God. Don't be coming to pick me up from school or anything. People will laugh. Are you trying to embarrass me on purpose?'

Part of me wants to do some sort of ninja leg swipe on her and tell her that, as a grown-up, I get to do whatever I want with my hair and she's lucky I didn't do a 2007 Christina Aguilera with dreadlocks. The other part of me feels hurt – both by her words and by her obvious distress. I'd hoped she would like it.

'Wise up, Gemma,' I snap. 'Do you really think I would spend £100 just to embarrass you when clearly I can do it for free merely by breathing in your direction? And what are "people like me" anyway? Mammies? Old people? Because, my dear, I am thirty-six years old and believe me that is not old and it will come around for you too in the blink of an eye. If you think just because I'm a mammy, and just because I'm in my thirties, I should stay in the house wearing leggings and sweaters and hiding from your friends then think on. We "oldies" have as much right to self-expression as you young ones.'

Her lip trembles and I watch as her eyes fill with tears. A couple of years ago, feck it, even a couple of weeks ago, this show of emotion and upset would have me running to comfort her and make it all better, but no, not this time. I get that it is written in the great big teenage manifesto that you must be mortified by your parents at all times regardless of whether or not they are actually performing any mortifying actions, but she has to learn that you can't get away with sneering at people, or making them feel small in order to make yourself feel big.

Gemma, to her credit, is a master of manipulation and on seeing my angry face (and believe me, there is nothing in this universe scarier than an angry Derry woman), she lets a single tear roll down her cheek before barrelling towards her daddy crying loudly. Paul pulls her into a hug but keeps his gaze on me. He's now torn between the devil and the deep blue sea and I'm wondering which he will choose.

'Pet,' he says, and I think he is talking to me, 'maybe we should go easy on Gemma here.' As he says the words, she squeezes him tighter. 'And Gemma, you have to be careful how you speak to people.' His words are soft and she does her very best to drown them out with a new flurry of sobs. I feel a bit like sobbing myself.

'It *is* a big change,' he says. 'And . . . erm . . . very dramatic at that. And I'm sure we'll get used to it. I suppose it does suit you.'

I. Suppose. It. Does. Suit. You.

We will file that along with 'you look fine as you are'.

'You *suppose?*' I ask, and it's time now for my own bottom lip to tremble. I wanted him to like it. I wanted him to look at me differently. With desire.

I can see the panicked expression on Paul's face. I know that right now, inside his head a hundred warning bells are ringing, begging him to abort this current course of action. A fatal husband error has been made.

'It's nice,' he says with a weak smile.

The word does not mollify me. I'm fighting the urge to turn on my heel and walk back out the door – slamming it as I go for extra effect. I'm desperate to phone Cat and tell her I'm gate-crashing on whatever distinctly non-boring Saturday-night adventure she might be having. All I want is to feel good about myself. To feel young, and cool and attractive. My mind can't help but wander to how Luke eyed me up over lunch on Thursday, as if he wanted to spread me on toast and devour me.

It's a stark difference from Paul, who looks as if he's not quite sure who I am any more. When, I wonder, did he last look at me with that same longing? When did I last drive him wild with desire? I mentally work out what date it was nine months before Jax was born because I'm pretty sure that was the last night we completely lost the run of ourselves, and as a result had taken a risk with contraception. OK, so things haven't exactly been wild since Jax arrived – his birth being something we're still processing more than two years later.

Having had two relatively normal, uneventful births I was sure third time would be like shelling peas. I was an old hand at it, after all. Except, it didn't work out quite like that. Jax was eager to arrive and I'd barely cleared eight months when he came out through the sunroof after the doctors spotted my pre-eclampsia. Labour was rushed, scary and messy. Kinda like how Jax is now, ironically.

The experience left both Paul and me traumatized. And trauma isn't terribly sexy. One of my deepest fears, I realize, is that having seen me in such a bloody, weakened state – puking into one of those cardboard bowls, my eyes rolling in my head as my blood pressure soared, Paul no longer saw me as his sexy partner. He just saw me as 'fine'.

My silence must unnerve him, although I wonder how he

can even be aware of it over the din of Gemma's sobbing and hiccupping.

'Tara, honestly. It's lovely,' he says with about as much sincerity as the lifeguard in the pool displayed when he told me 'Not to worry' about Nathan's pee incident.

'Mammeeee, why is Gemma cryin'?' I hear a voice from behind me and turn to see Nathan and Jax, holding hands, both looking ridiculously cute as they gaze up at me. Before I get the chance to answer, Nathan's eyes widen. 'Mammy, your hair is pink!' He breaks into a broad smile and drags his brother towards me. I crouch down enough to pull them both into a big hug. Nathan can't keep his eyes off my new hair. 'Looks like candyfloss,' he says as he raises one suspiciously sticky hand and plonks it right in the centre of my head. Jax leans in too, and he's so close to me that with each suck of his dummy I feel it press against my cheek.

'Teddy hair!' Jax says, and I feel a second hand on top of my head. A hand that will absolutely be stickier than Nathan's as Jax seems to be permanently sticky, no matter how often he is cleaned or how fastidious I am about hiding all the sticky items out of his reach. The boy is made of glue, I'm sure of it.

'Mammy, you are so cool! Like Skye,' Nathan says, and I assume he's talking about the cartoon dog in *Paw Patrol* who wears a pink hat. He immediately confirms this suspicion by adding, 'Can I have pink hair? Or . . . Or . . . blue hair??? I want blue, like Chase!'

'Chase!!!' Jax says, directly into my ear, so close that I can feel the dampness of his warm breath.

I know getting such a compliment from a five-year-old and a two-year-old, comparing my hair colour to a cartoon dog, is a bit of a hollow victory, but as God is my witness I am going to hang on to it tightly. I look up at traitors' corner (this is what the part of the kitchen in which Paul and Gemma now stand will be known as from this day forward) and I smile before pulling my boys even closer and telling them they can have ice cream with chocolate sauce after their dinner.

I don't yelp as the two sticky hands are removed from my hair, leaving behind some sickly sweet residue, I just stand up and brush myself off. 'Let's order pizza for tea,' I declare, and this garners the teeniest bit of attention from Gemma. She sniffs. 'I'm sorry, Mammy,' she says. 'Can I have pizza too?'

There's no point, I realize, in challenging her apology as insincere and pizza-motivated, so I simply tell her that she can. Paul offers to order it and I tell him I'm going for a shower, I want to freshen up after my waxing session and also check for bruises or swelling.

As I'm leaving the room, Nathan grabs my hand and I crouch down again, ready to be enveloped in his adoration one more time.

'Mammy, why is bits of your face pink like your hair?' He presses a small, pudgy finger against my top lip as he examines me.

'Because God is a man and he has cursed all women for all time,' I tell him and he looks at me as if I'm speaking a different language, which I might as well be. It won't stop him from parroting it to Miss Rose on Monday morning though, word perfectly.

17

It's not the menopause, FFS!

'You can do this. You are absolutely the best person for this job and all you have to do now is go and kick this interview square in the dick.'

Cat has me by the shoulders in the changing rooms after spin. Her rallying war cry garners a few odd looks from the other women changing, until Cat loudly informs them I'm up for promotion and any and all encouragement is welcome.

The very friendly holder-back-of-my hair smiles broadly. 'You've got this,' she says with such conviction that, even though she doesn't really know anything about me, I'm inclined to believe her. I need more people like this in my life, I think, women who have my back.

Amanda, as always, has been a little more reserved with her language. She sent out a group WhatsApp a message last night. All the very best, she typed. And remember: what's for you, won't pass you. I admire you looking to take on a new challenge when

Jax is still so young. I hope it doesn't become overwhelming. Let us know how you get on.

I thanked her while secretly seething at her passive-aggressive comments, before immediately telling myself not to be paranoid and she's not necessarily being passive-aggressive at all.

The first thing Cat said to me when I met her outside the gym for our 6 a.m. class was: 'Ignore Amanda. The passive-aggressive witch!'

I'd smiled but it hadn't completely silenced the tiny voice in my head which tells me the only reason Amanda's comment has hit home is that there may be some truth in it. What if I can't manage? What if I become even more tired than I already am? What if I'm asleep by 9.30 instead of 10.30 every night and my sex life has to be consigned to the bin forever?

But no, I remind myself. I won't be overwhelmed because I can do the accounts manager job in my sleep. I've taken the lead with a few clients before and loved it. It was exhilarating, and rather than coming home too tired to chat, I came home buzzing with excitement about my day.

Besides, I've been there for twelve years. I have watched so many graduates come in and work their way up the career ladder before being poached by a bigger company – one based in Dublin or London – and all the while I have been fermenting in my dark corner of the office like a modern-day Miss Havisham.

I love my children dearly – even Gemma, who is still giving me the silent treatment on account of my shaming her for eternity. But I need something more – something that is a part of me, and that sees me as Tara Gallagher, not just somebody's mammy.

Smiling, I nod my thanks at my fellow spinners and allow Cat to pull me into a squishy hug. 'You're amazing,' she tells me. 'And keep me posted on what everyone thinks of your new locks too. I love ya. You got this.'

I feel a little wobbly but draw myself up to maximum Tara-who-is-an-adult height and head home to transform myself into the ultimate boss bish.

I am applying my make-up when Paul pops his head through the door. 'The boys have been quarantined in the living room. Gemma has gone to get her bus. So, there's no risk of any of our gorgeous wains causing a last-minute upset by messing up your outfit. The boys and I will be leaving in five minutes.'

I nod. 'Thank you,' I say. I don't usually wear a lot of make-up to work – a quick dab of concealer and maybe a slick of lip gloss if I have a meeting where I want to look less zombie-like. Today, I've taken the time to do a full face. I've even managed to put on eyeliner without poking myself in the eye, which is a win.

'You look good,' Paul says, looking me up and down. 'Really professional.'

I nod. Good is a great step up from 'fine' or 'nice' in my books, and I'm sure he doesn't mean that I don't usually look professional.

He still isn't keen on my new hair colour, which is making me start to have doubts about it myself. Part of me definitely feels a bit wobbly that his opinion of my appearance matters so much, but hasn't a big part of this whole fuck-it plan been to rekindle that desire between us?

I give him a small smile, my stomach gurgling with nerves. Damn it, my body's reaction to stress is to liquefy the contents of my stomach for quick evacuation. I do not need a dose of the shits right now.

'Thank you,' I tell Paul, resting one hand on my tummy to try and quiet the rumble. 'And thanks for taking the boys this morning. It's a big help.'

He nods. 'I love you, Tara. I really do, and whatever happens today I'm proud of you and I know how class you are.'

'I love you too,' I tell him, and I realize that I really, totally, 100 per cent mean it. I'm not just sticking to a well-worn script. I love this man in front of me. I am *in love* with this man in front of me. 'I'll let you know how I get on.'

'You have it in the bag,' he says, 'They'd be mad not to give it to you.'

'I hope you're right,' I say, and watch as he leaves. A few minutes later I hear the boys shout 'Bye, Mammy!! Good luck!' as they are shepherded out the door.

Amy and Lucy and Molly freak out about my new hair. To the average viewer watching them fawn over me, it would seem like a lovely chat between co-workers, perhaps a bit of girly bonding.

I've seen *Mean Girls* enough times to know that what they say isn't always what they mean. I want to believe them when they tell me it's cool and really suits me. Of course I do. But my confidence has been shaken to its core by both Gemma and Paul's reaction. That and the fact I've had three super-strong coffees already and am basically off my tits on caffeine right now. My body is in full-on fight or flight mode, only it can't decide which direction to go in. Caffeine overload and anxiety are not always the best of pals.

'I properly love it,' Amy coos. 'You look amaze-balls.'

'Totes,' Lucy chimes in. 'It's a total glow-up.'

'A what?' I ask.

'A glow-up,' Lucy replies, eyeing me as if I'm a creature from another planet. And while I'm not actually from another planet, I am from another decade and these days that might as well be the same thing.

'Can't say I've heard that one before,' I say. 'What does it mean?' They look at each other and laugh and there is definitely a little *Mean Girls* carry-on there. I resolve not to let it annoy me. They may be channelling their inner Regina George, but I know how that movie ends and it's not with the bitchy girls coming out on top.

'Oh honey,' Amy cuts in. 'It means you've gone from being an ugly duckling to a beautiful swan.' She beams at me, but hang on one darn tooting minute. An ugly duckling? What the actual fu—

'Not that we're saying you were ugly,' Molly jumps in. 'But maybe a bit basic, you know. A wee bit cheugy.'

I wonder if I might be having a stroke right now. They are talking, but these words are not making sense. Not at all. Glow-ups and ducklings (ugly ones at that!) and basic and cheugy. I think I've heard Gemma use basic, but I'm not sure I really tuned in to what she was talking about. Isn't basic a good thing? Solid. Reliable. Sturdy?

They must be able to see the confusion all over my face.

'What we're trying to say is that you have had a positive makeover and it's given you a bit of your own style. It's nice to see you out of the boomer clothes,' Lucy says.

Now, this one I know. And this one gets my back up. I may indeed be basic (especially the sturdy part), but I am not a fecking boomer. I was born in the year of Our Lord 1985, and that makes me a millennial.

'I'm not a boomer,' I tell her, trying not to use the same scary mammy voice I use when I tell Gemma that I am not a boomer and that I'm from a cool generation.

'Ah, we know that. But you dressed like one – no offence,' Molly laughs, and the others join in. I fake what turns out to be the most insincere laugh of all time. I don't have the energy to try and work out how these young women operate. I've enough to be worrying about with Gemma and this bloody promotion.

At that moment the door to the office opens and sun streams in from outside. With it, as if carried on angel wings, is Luke. Who I must not fantasize about. Who is a mere child in the grand scheme of things. Who is neither a boomer nor a millennial and as such not for the likes of me – even if I wasn't married and in love with my husband.

He does a double-take when he sees me, his eyes widen and a broad smile breaks across his perfectly chiselled face.

Bright white teeth gleam at me and there is a definite twinkle in his eyes.

'Tara!' he says. 'I almost didn't recognize you. Wow! You look amazing! I am loving the new hair. It really suits you.' He's talking about my hair but I don't miss the way he runs his eyes up and down my body. I feel a little ping in the pit of my stomach that, for once, isn't hunger but something altogether more delicious and dangerous. 'Doesn't Tara look incredible?' he asks the others, who I know won't be at all happy that he is directing his attention my way. They mutter their agreement and he winks at me. He knows he is winding them up and it's glorious. Already we have our own way of communicating, our in-jokes, our unmistakable chemistry. That sexy wee shite!

'Thank you,' I smile. 'You're very kind to say. I decided to treat myself at the weekend.'

'I'm glad you did.' Luke says. 'This new look of yours works. Wow.'

It's the second wow that turns my legs to jelly (or again, that could be the caffeine overload), so I sit down at my desk and pretend to start to work. I say 'pretend' because, knowing my interview is at 10 a.m., I also know there isn't a hope in hell of me being able to concentrate on anything but the interview before then. I may be class at my job, but I am not superwoman.

Thankfully the rest of them get the hint and scurry their non-basic, non-cheugy (what the eff does that even mean?) selves back to their desks. Luke turns to look at me. 'I think that's ruffled a few feathers,' he says with a smile. 'But I wasn't saying it just to wind them up. It does suit you. You look incredible.'

I need to focus. I don't need to turn into a simpering idiot when I'm due to sit before an interview panel. And I definitely don't need to be distracted by lustful thoughts. I mean, wouldn't that make me as creepy as Handsy himself?

'I don't think they're too impressed,' I say. 'But they're young and naive.'

'Not all young people are naive,' he says, and he is giving me the full Jamie Dornan in need of a sausage-roll bap look again. As if he'd love to smother me in Heinz tomato ketchup and eat me in one bite. I blush as pink as my hair.

I need to get this conversation on the right track, even if flirting with Luke all day would be much more fun than fighting with a spreadsheet.

'Shall we have a wee look at the Cassidy project?' I ask him. 'I'll get you up to speed to where we're at with it and when we meet them later this week you can sit in and see how we get things done?'

He smiles. 'That would be great, T, thanks.'

He calls me T. He has a little nickname for me. My heart flutters before I drag myself into the Cassidy file to find my bearings.

Ten minutes have passed when there's a creak of the door and a blast of light as it opens and I look up. It's Mr Handley and his eyes widen as he spots me. I know immediately it's not through wanting.

'Whoa, what've we got here?' he almost shouts, with all the subtlety of a brick thrown through a plate-glass window. 'Is this pop songstress Pink before us? Are you going to give us a wee song?' His pallid, bloated face is more animated than I have seen it in a long time. Even more animated than when we got the contract to do PR for a new brand of biscuit, with his 'hilarious' tagline, 'Oh, crumbs, mums.'

'No. No. That's not it,' he says, so loudly that the rest of the office can hear him. 'It's not Pink you remind me of. God, it will come to me,' he says.

'Sure, it doesn't really matter,' I tell him. 'I've some work to be getting on with here before my interview and Luke and I were going to run over some background info on the Cassidy file.' I turn back to my computer but that is not enough to put Handsy Handley off his mission. 'Ah, that's it!' he almost squeals in delight before launching into the first verse of 'Beauty School Dropout' from *Grease*. I want to die.

The Ys are looking on with a mixture of amusement and bemusement. Luke is clearly confused but Mr Handley is giving it his all – and you may be grateful, dear reader, that this book does not come with an audio track of his caterwauling, for you would never be able to watch that Seventies classic again for fear it would trigger your PTSD.

Not having the wit to know when to stop singing, Mr Handley continues long after it has become awkward for everyone. 'Frenchie!' he declares at the end. 'Doesn't Tara look like Frenchie?' He looks around the office for someone, anyone to agree with him.

Well, I'm damned if I'm going to, so I stay quiet.

'Who's Frenchie?' Amy asks.

'Ah come on,' Mr Handley says. 'Frenchie from *Grease*!'

'So is she French or is she Greek?' Amy asks.

'Neither,' he says in exasperation. 'Frenchie is a character in the movie *Grease*. You know, with John Travolta and Olivia Newton-John.'

'Who's Olivia Newton-John?' Lucy asks.

'Oh you absolute philistines,' Mr Handley says, and for once I have to agree with him. '"Summer Nights", "Greased Lightning", "Sandy"? How do you not know about these songs and this movie? It's a classic.'

If it was anyone else other than Handsy Handley making this statement I'd have chimed in with my very best Sandy in leather trousers 'Tell me about it, stud' impression. But there isn't a hope in hell I'm risking that. Besides, I'm fuming. Frenchie? The dropout? With the big, bouffant, dootsy Fifties hair? I have coloured beyond the mildly embarrassed pink to match my clearly outdated hairstyle and on to pillar-box red.

'Are you OK, Tara?' Molly asks. 'You've gone very red? Is it a hot flush? I've been reading about the menopause . . .'

What happens next will go down in the history book of my life in the chapter headed 'Not the Finest Moments in Her Life'.

'It's not the menopause,' I say, and I'm not shouting. I'm saying this in my very best, scariest, Liam Neeson voice. Not quite the American twang he has in *Taken*, but full-on Northern Irish threat, because believe me there is nothing scarier than someone speaking slowly and purposefully to you in a Northern

Irish accent. What we say doesn't even really matter, it's the voice and the implied threat. 'I am thirty-six years old. That is not old. It is certainly not old enough to be anywhere near the menopause. Let me tell you something, I am not some oul' doll drying up and getting ready for the grave. I am young, and vibrant and fertile. I could have another ten children if I was feeling absolutely insane enough. And girls, let me tell you, thirty-six comes around pretty fast. Blink and you'll be here where I am, and some hallion will be telling you that you look like a character from a movie that is forty-odd years old. And someone else will assume you're for the scrapheap. But I can assure you that I am neither. So if you don't mind, I've an interview to prepare for . . .'

I stop short of telling them to eff off, but I don't need to. They get the message and the surreal scene that started with Mr Handley's woeful performance of 'Beauty School Dropout' and ended up with me doing my very best IRA man phoning in a bomb-scare threatening voice is over.

And I think I need another coffee.

18

The slippery wee shite

The interview goes well. Or at least, as well as it could go, given my semi-breakdown half an hour earlier. To his credit, Mr Handley doesn't dare make a joke about it, and there are no further references to musical or hormonal fluctuations.

I answer everything with such ease and confidence that even I'm impressed with how knowledgeable I sound.

The second half of the interview involves me talking Mr Handley and Ms Simpson from HR through a spoof presentation they had asked me to prepare, drafting a dummy launch marketing strategy for a new fashion start-up. Not to be boastful, but I can do this kind of thing in my sleep and, to my delight, it goes down well.

When we're all done, I'm given the chance to ask any questions I may have. I smile beatifically and say I think I've been with the company long enough to know our ethos, goals and structure. But I do ask how many other interviews are being held. Everyone has played their cards really close to their chest about whether or not they were applying for the post, and it has been opened to outside candidates too.

'Just a few,' Mr Handley says. 'But on that note, when you go back to your desk, can you tell Luke we're ready for him now.'

That's when I have my second not finest moment of the day. 'Luke?' I ask quizzically. 'The new guy?' Somehow I stop myself from saying 'My Luke?'

'He's the only Luke in the building, as far as I know,' Mr Handley says and Ms Simpson titters coquettishly at his response.

'But, he's only just in the door? Isn't he not long graduated?' I ask.

'Well, yes, but he was top of his class and . . .' If Mr Handley says much more I don't hear it. Here am I, trying to fight for a job against a twenty-four-year-old. Someone who was born in the same year that B*Witched were leaping around, Irish dancing to 'C'est La Vie'. I knew that dance routine off by fucking heart, I think dumbly.

'OK,' I eventually say. 'Well, I hope you appreciate my commitment and dedication to this company and how much I have brought to the table over the course of the last twelve years.'

'We do, of course,' Ms Simpson replies as I get up to leave the room.

As I walk back to my desk, I see Luke glance up at me. Funnily, in the last few minutes everything has changed. He is no longer the sexy, dominant Christian Grey version of Jamie Dornan, but the creepy, manipulative serial killer in *The Fall* version of Jamie Dornan. He is going for this job. My job. He had chatted over my presentation with me, mined me for information about the company and kept me sweet with tea and KitKats, and all the while he was plotting to take this promotion – my promotion – out from under me.

Well, good luck to him. He's about to learn that experience has some pull over his fancy degree and his well-cut suit and his creepy, serial-killer handsomeness.

'How did it go?' he asks.

I don't reply immediately. I want to unnerve him a little, so I look at my phone, raise my hand in a 'one minute' gesture as I pretend to check it for important emails or messages. There are no important emails or messages, of course, unless you count the picture Paul has sent me of a large spot on his left arse cheek which he wonders if he should see the doctor about. Ah, married life – romance all the way.

When I've clicked out of Paul's message, I plaster on a wide smile. 'Yeah, I think it went really well. They're ready for you now, by the way.'

It's his turn to turn pink as he gathers his laptop and starts to walk across the room. I can't help it, but I give him the sneaky middle finger as he walks away. I don't *think* anyone sees me.

The atmosphere in the office does not improve for the rest of the day. By which I mean, I am pure ragin' that a whippersnapper such as Luke has only just walked in the door to the company and has been granted an interview for a job I've worked years to be in the running for.

I'm more ragin' that he spent his first two days playing Mr Nice and getting a 'how to get a promotion' lesson from me, without me even knowing it. I thought we had genuinely bonded. I thought he had genuinely found me to be a sexy delight. He knew I had an interview scheduled for today. I told him as much on Thursday, which gave him the perfect opportunity to tell me that he was going for the job too. But he kept his perfectly proportioned pouty lips firmly shut – the slippery wee shite.

I should've known he was too good to be true. The pretty boys always are. Men who spend more time than their girl-friends preening in front of a mirror sometimes have a self-serving streak in them. Those ones are the kind of lads who would use the last of your good shampoo, steal one of your face masks, or use you to get background info for a job promotion and – and this is very important – they're the kind of lads who are only concerned with their own pleasure in the sack. Get in bed with a pretty boy and you may as well start watching *When Harry Met Sally* right now to hone your faking-it skills to Meg Ryan levels.

No, give me my reliable, caring, sometimes a complete pain in the hole but still lovely Paul. I never have to fake it with him. He's the real deal.

I'm so relieved that home time has rocked around that I don't even stop to say my goodbyes to anyone before dashing out the door. I've kept quiet most of the day, apart from humming occasional lines of songs from *Grease*, thanks to Mr Handley's ear-worm-inducing singing earlier. Not trusting myself to engage in conversation beyond the bare essentials, I'd kept my head down and got on with what I needed to do. And yes, I jumped every time the phone rang at my desk, or my email notifications pinged, in case there was word of who scored the promotion, but I should've known Handley would draw out the tension for as long as possible. At a minute to five, a message from him declared that a decision would be made in 'the next few days' and the successful candidate would be notified.

'Ah well,' Luke sighed. 'It's out of our hands now.' He'd given me a cheeky wink – one I'm sure that even twenty-four hours ago would have given me a tingle in my padded cycling shorts area, but now? Now it only made me want to, as Cat would say, kick him in the dick.

In my car, I do what any respectable thirty-something mother of three would do: I blast Destiny's Child as loudly as I can while reminding myself 'I'm a Survivor' and giving it the full air-grabbing, pretending-to-hold-a-mic attitude. I don't care if people in other cars can see me. In this moment I am not Kelly Rowland. I am not Michelle whatever her name is. I am Beyoncé – Queen Bey. I am still feeling utterly kick-ass and am power-punching my way through the chorus when I arrive at the boys' childminder's to pick them up.

Jo has been watching my children since I went back to work – although Gemma persuaded me last year as she began secondary school that she is too old for a childminder. I some-what nervously agreed, and she now gets herself home and, it is alleged, gets on with her homework. Jo is the kind of woman who you could totally see living in a shoe, with loads of children running around her all times. But unlike the old woman who does in fact live in a shoe, Jo is a seemingly tireless enthusiast for having the craic with wains. She is a natural – and I have never heard even a rumour of her losing her shit with any child, not even her own. I'd love to know what the secret is to her brand of witchcraft, but also worry that, if I did, I would be expected to be the same jolly, hands-on, let's do some messy play type mother that I am never, ever going to be. So I don't ask her, I just remain grateful that for five days a week she is willing to take on the baby destruction machine that is Jax, and provide wrap-around care for Nathan, who can be a crabbit wee shite after school. She has a way of calming him. Perhaps she puts marijuana in his after-school cookie or something.

Needless to say, my boys are not always excited about leaving her and coming home to boring old Mammy and Daddy and having to do boring things like eat their dinner, or get a bath, or put on their pyjamas. I try not to take their cries of 'But I want to stay' too personally. There are times I want to stay with Jo too and do finger-painting with her while she feeds me marijuana cookies.

'Well, would you look at you!' she enthuses when she opens the door. 'I love the hair, Tara. It's amazing. Wee Nathan was telling me his mammy had hair like candyfloss and I couldn't think what he might have meant, but I love it.'

I blush. A compliment from Jo feels like sunshine breaking through the clouds on a rainy day. She is joy and warmth personified. A compliment from Jo is almost as good as your head teacher in primary school standing up in front of the whole school and telling them you're a very good girl indeed.

'I fancied a wee change,' I smile, deciding not to go into the details of why I was spiralling into acts of ever-increasing desperation to try and still feel relevant.

'Well it has done you the absolute power of good. I love it. Good for you!'

I become aware of a small child peeking out from behind Jo's skirt. Quickly working out that he is not a fruit of my own loins, I give him a smile. He's an unfortunate-looking wee soul – one of those children who has a permanent snotty nose that no amount of wiping or encouragement to blow seems to make a difference to. As he looks up at me, he draws one sleeve of his jumper across his face, spreading his snot along the full width of his right cheek. I try not to throw up. I can deal with my own kids' snotters, but other people's kids, no thank you.

'Fintan,' Jo says, producing a tissue out of nowhere and giving him a very quick clean. 'Be a good boy for me and go and tell Nathan and Jax it's time to go.'

Fintan sniffs, exceptionally loudly for a very small child, and turns his head. 'Nathan! Your granny is here!'

I now officially hate wee snotty-faced Fintan. The little shite! I was willing to see past him using his sweater as a hankie. But calling me Nathan's granny? That was a step too far.

As I seethe, I see Jo crouch down to his height. 'Now, Fintan, what do we not do in Jo's house?'

'Say shit,' he says, with the tiniest look of delight on his face that he has, indeed, said shit, and had a legitimate reason to do so.

'Well, that is one of the rules,' Jo says without a hint of frustration. 'But what do we also not do?'

I can almost see the cogs whirring in his tiny snot-filled mind as he desperately tries to think of something else bold to do or say and get away with. His hesitation sinks him, though, as Jo steps in. 'We don't shout, do we, Fintan?'

Fintan shakes his head.

'If I had wanted to shout, I would've done it myself. Now be a good boy and go and tell Nathan and Jax that their mammy is here for them.'

Fintan eyes me with suspicion then looks to Jo before looking back at me.

'That lady is a granny not a mammy,' he says with a degree of scorn which is quite impressive for a child of his age. I'd say he's five or six at a push, and he can already throw some serious shade. Ouch!

Jo smiles. 'Now, Fintan, why do you think this lovely lady is a granny and not a mammy?'

'She has hair like my granny,' he says. ''Cept my granny's hair is blue.'

Jesus, Mary and the wee donkey, is snot-features saying I look like a little old lady with a blue rinse? Is this how the world sees me? Should I give in now, buy some slippers and a cardigan and a family bag of Werther's Originals? (I do actually love a good cardigan, if I'm being honest.) I'm wondering if it is ethically questionable to fashion a voodoo doll in the image of a child, when Jo gives a little laugh and smiles. 'Lots of people have different coloured hair,' she says, 'And they're not all grannies! Anyone can dye their hair a new colour.'

There's something about the way she talks to him that reminds me of the Jedi mind trick from *Star Wars* – I can almost see the words seep into him.

'Can I dye my hair a new colour?' he asks.

'Green might be a good idea,' I chirp before I can stop myself. I do, however, manage to stop myself from tagging on the 'to match the colour of the snot all over your dirty wee face' to the end of that sentence. Again, I like my own kids, that's it. Jo is a fucking saint!

19

Fuckssake patriarchy

Mr Handley is a sadist. There's no other explanation for it. He is silent throughout Tuesday, and through Wednesday, except for sending the briefest of emails about new projects, forthcoming pitches and some godawful training on social media curation – no doubt to be delivered by some sixteen-year-old hipster who is 'down with the kids' and makes the symbol for hashtag with his fingers every three seconds.

As the last wee while has taught me, so brutally, I am not down with the kids and if I wanted a teenager to lecture me on what is so great about social media, all I'd have to do is spend an hour in Gemma's company as she shows me at least ten of the latest dance crazes from TikTok and tells me about a video she saw where this teenage girl 'like saw an actual ghost and no one believed her and then she died'.

As for any mention of the promotion? Handley remains tight-lipped but has taken to walking through the office and giving us little smiles, winks and on one particularly cringe-worthy occasion making that finger-gun gesture, for fuck's sake. It is not good for my anxiety levels.

I have been trying to channel my inner Jo and remain zen at all times, which is not easy. What I really want to do is grab Handley by the lapels and shake him vigorously until he tells us who got the promotion – with the preferable answer being me.

'No news is good news,' Paul says as I stab a turkey dinosaur with renewed viciousness. 'It's a bit like the cat in the box.'

'The cat in the box?' I ask him, fork freezing midway to my mouth, nervous as to where this is going.

'Aye, there's some scientist or something who has some theory about a cat in a box. I can't think of his name – but until the box is open you don't know if it actually contains a cat, so there is both simultaneously a cat *in* the box and not.'

'Eh, that's a load of shite,' I say, which immediately earns me an extreme eyebrow-raise from Nathan, but I'm tired and frankly not in the mood. 'Yes, Nathan. I said shite. Mammies are allowed to say shite because we are grown-ups and those are the rules of the world. When you are a grown-up you too can say shite whenever you want.'

'But . . . But . . . Miss Rose says . . .' he starts.

I point my fork, the back end of the dinosaur dripping in ketchup now skewered to it, to stop him. 'Nathan, my darling, at this exact moment in time I don't give a flying shite what

Miss Rose says or thinks or does. At this precise moment, Miss Rose can kiss my cellulite-covered ass.'

I'm sure I hear Paul choke on an oven-baked smiley face. I'm not stupid, I know I've gone too far.

'Schrödinger,' Gemma pipes up, which stops us all in our tracks.

'What?' I ask her.

'The cat in the box. It's Schrödinger's cat – and it's a hypothetical cat and not a real cat,' she says with an air of authority that freaks me out a little. 'I saw a TikTok about it.'

'That's the very boy I was thinking of,' Paul says, triumphant now the smiley face is dislodged from his throat.

'But if it's not a real cat to begin with, then surely the cat is never in the box because it never existed. That aside, I'm failing to see what this has to do with my job interview.'

Gemma shrugs and goes back to looking at the phone she is absolutely not supposed to have at the dinner table. I don't bother arguing with her. Sometimes, you have to choose your battles.

'What it has to do with your interview is that, at this moment in time, while the pretend cat is still in the box, then you both have the job and don't have the job. Or something. I've kind of lost my train of thought here, but what I'm trying to say is: keep the faith.'

I look at him and a wave of fondness washes over me. He tries so hard to keep me content and to build me up. He never burns the turkey dinosaurs and I never have to remind him to leave the bins out.

'I love you,' I tell him with genuine warmth, because in that moment there's no hypothetical metaphorical question about it. I do love him. 'I mean, you do talk a load of shite sometimes, Paul, but I really do love you.'

Out of the corner of my eye, Nathan is shaking his head, resigned to my use of the word shite, like a very tiny, disappointed male version of Miss Rose.

There's a buzz in the office as soon as I walk through the door. Or at least there was a buzz in the office when I walked through the door. It seems as soon as people spot the muppet with the pink hair, they shut up. I find myself wondering if I've left the towel on top of my head that morning, or forgotten to do my make-up, or have my skirt tucked up into my knickers (all things that have happened to me in the past). But as soon as they go quiet and look at me, they all suddenly seem to find something very interesting indeed to look at on their computer screens, or their desk, or in their handbags. Not even Molly, who normally greets me with a rundown of her previous night's antics, looks up. Instead, she lifts the phone on her desk and starts typing random numbers in.

I have a bad feeling about this. I'm tempted to scream at them all to ask if the cat has been let out of the box (or the bag? Or am I mixing my hypothetical cats here?) and a decision has been made about the big promotion. But I don't scream, because I think I already know. If it was good news they would be fawning all over me. They'd be doing their very best to stay on my good side, knowing that some of them would be working under me. My heart sinks.

OK, I tell myself. Front it out. Don't cry. Beyoncé Giselle Knowles would not cry. She would take this moment and turn it into an absolute banger of a song like 'Irreplaceable' or 'Best Thing You Never Had' or . . . or . . . It's no good, I feel tears prick at my eyes and I've not even heard any official news yet. Taking a deep breath, I walk to my desk. This doesn't have to be a bad thing. I mean, it's tough combining this working carry-on with being a mum and . . . and . . . Nope. I've got nothing. It is a bad thing. All I can do is hope that it is not the worst thing in the world. Because the absolute worst thing would be if Luke steals the job out from under my nose. I can lose a fight gracefully if I can see that the winning candidate deserves it more than I do. I'm not a big child, or a sore loser. I can take my oil. But my oil will not be taken if Luke, who probably still only shaves twice a week, becomes my superior. I mean, I shave my damn legs more than that. (Or I do when I'm on holiday. The rest of the time, as Tori the wax lady will attest, it's pretty much fur in the leg department.)

Luke is not at his desk. The others are huddled at the water cooler (and they had the nerve to call me basic!). They glance at me quickly before resuming their whispering. This must be what walking the green mile feels like. But I have to do it. I can't turn and run out of there. I am a 'growed up' as Nathan would say. I have responsibilities.

'Ah Tara,' I hear Mr Handley's dulcet tones from behind me. 'If you could just step into my office a moment?'

'Of course,' I say, in a voice that is a little too bright, as I turn on my heels and follow him. I'm surprised to see Luke already there, sitting in front of Mr Handley's desk. He stands and gives me a silly shrug in a kind of 'no harm done' gesture and I want to punch him in the face. (I'm feeling quite violent these days, I think briefly, between wanting to yeet Fintan, Prince of Snotsville, out a window, wanting to kick Miss Rose up the arse, and now wanting to punch Luke square in his perfectly chiselled jaw. I do a very quick sum in my head. Fucking great. My period is also due. Could this day get any worse?)

'Please sit down,' Mr Handley says. 'Look, I'm going to cut to the chase here because there's no point in beating around the bush. Sometimes it's better to view these things as a sort of sticking plaster – better to pull them off quickly than prolong the agony, if you get what I mean?'

I nod.

'I know it is perhaps a little unusual to invite you in here with Luke, but I think it's important that in all this we remember one key thing: team work makes the dream work. I've always seen ToteTech as a real family environment and as one of the elders—'

'I thought you were going to cut to the chase?' I interrupt through gritted teeth. I cannot take one more metaphor.

'I was. I am. Right, well . . .' Mr Handley takes a deep breath and if I didn't know better I'd say the man looks scared. No, not scared. Terrified. It gives my pre-menstrual self a sense of satisfaction. 'On this occasion, I regret to tell you that you have not been successful. We've decided to go a different direction with the promotion.'

He glances to Luke, who at least has the decency to shift uncomfortably in his seat.

'So you've gone in a Luke direction?' I ask.

'We have,' Mr Handley says. 'But Tara, I want you to know – or rather, both Luke and I want you to know – that you are a very, very valued member of the team and we believe you have a lot to offer the company.'

'We really do,' Luke says sincerely. Luke, who started here a week ago. With his fancy degrees and his fancy suit that his mammy probably bought for him. 'You're really great, Tara. A real fount of knowledge.'

I bite my tongue because if I do not bite my tongue I will absolutely lose my shit on a level the likes of which has never been seen before and which will become a thing of legend retold in story and song for generations to come.

'I asked Mr Handley if I could be here at the start of this meeting because I wanted to stress that to you. That I think you're a strong asset for the company. I was kind of hoping maybe you would come on board my team. Be my deputy?'

I nod. My first thought is to ask if there would be a pay rise, but fuck that, money isn't important here. I remain silent. This should worry them both. Paul has long said the only thing scarier than a screaming angry woman is a silent angry woman.

'I will leave Mr Handley to answer any questions you may have,' Luke says, standing up and reaching across the desk to shake Handley's soft, clammy, treacherous hand. 'Thanks for believing in me,' he says before leaving the room.

I do not speak.

'Tara, I know this must be a disappointment to you. You were so close, but you see, Luke is fresh. He is brimming with new ideas. The kind that will shake this place up a bit. He thinks outside of the box, and that's what we need to stay relevant. He was top of his class . . .'

I may not have a haemorrhaging turkey dinosaur on a fork to wave as a signal for him to shut the actual fuck up, but I do have a twitchy raging right eye and my Medusa stare, which I give him.

'It doesn't mean you will never get a promotion. You are welcome to try the next time a similar role comes around. As I said, it was very close. Sometimes we just have to make tough business decisions and this was one of them. Things have been tight recently and if we don't move with the times, we will lose out. And as Luke said, he would love you to deputize for him.'

'Is that a promotion for me?' I ask, because I didn't come up the Foyle in a bubble and I can see where this particular boat is sailing.

'Well, I mean, it is in a way. We'd be utilizing your experience, and it would give you more face-to-face time with some of the key clients. I do know you love that side of things and you're very good at it—'

'Yes, I am very good at it. And yes, I do enjoy it. But if you could rewind a wee second. It *sort of* is a promotion? So that means it also *sort of* isn't?'

It's Mr Handley's turn to shift uncomfortably in his chair. I hear the squeak of his polyester trousers against the faux leather seat cushion. He clears his throat. 'As I have said, things are tight at the moment and this is a time for re-strategizing and streamlining. So, at this stage, we're not in a position to offer a salary increase, but if all goes well, that's something we could certainly look at in the future.'

I nod. 'So you want me to help Luke do the job I'm more than capable of doing myself, but for no extra money and just a vague possibility that I might get a raise at some undefined stage in the future?'

'Well, it's not quite like that. I mean, you would be working more with key clients. That's a bonus in itself, and the job would come with a title, and industry kudos. I mean, there's a reward to that in and of itself, don't you think?'

There is anger building up inside of me. I can feel it bubbling away, like I'm a kettle about to boil. I will myself not to tell Mr Handley to fuck off because, even though I very much want him to fuck off, I'm not in a position where I can walk out of a job without an immediate backup plan. Not with three children to feed. I bet the wee bastard was relying on that, as so many do. They know working mammies are over a barrel of needing to feed their wains and can't afford to take chances with their careers.

'If you want to take five or ten minutes to compose yourself before you start work, then please feel free,' he says, in a tone that implies he means 'get the feckity feck out of my office right now'.

'I am perfectly composed,' I tell him in a voice so menacing that I even sorta scare myself. Inside, I want to run away because, hot on the heels of my raging anger, the tears are coming. Hot, angry, it-should-have-been-me tears. I want to run out the door and drive to Jo's house and cry on her lap for a bit before driving to Cat's house and getting her to break out the vodka. I want to get so utterly shit-faced drunk that I perform both the rap from 'Gangsta's Paradise', and the entirety of Kelis's 'I Hate You So Much Right Now'. I want to cry into a curry chip, throw up in a basin at the side of my bed and sweat the badness out of me. I want to savour the hangover knowing it was one born out of a mad night as opposed to born out of three glasses of rosé wine in front of *Gogglebox*.

I want to do all that, but I don't.

Because I am an asset to this company. And I am fucking good – no *great* – at my job and I'm going to make Mr Handley desperately sorry. He has bet on the wrong horse.

My head held high, I stand up and walk towards the door. Before I leave, I turn and with a voice as cold as ice despite the internal storm raging within, I say, 'I hope this doesn't all blow up in your face. Luke's a great kid, but I'm a great project manager.'

Mr Handley blinks and I see his Adam's apple bob up and down as he swallows his nerves. I have rattled him. I'm a Derry mammy. I know when I put the fear of God into people. It's satisfying to see that moment of doubt on his face before I turn towards the door again and leave the room.

I walk back to my desk and start to work as if my whole professional life has not just crashed around my ears. I'll be damned if the bastards are going to get me down.

FUCKSSAKE PATRIARCHY, ARGH!

20

In my defence, it was my jeans that got me stuck

By lunchtime I have rage-raced through my to-do list and decided the only way to make it through to the end of the day without killing someone is for me to cash in some of my flexitime.

The rest of my colleagues have given me a wide berth all morning and I totally get that I've been sending off huge fuck-off vibes since I sat down. I've not gone to the breakroom and joined in the officer banter. I've not listened to their chatter about whatever reality show they're currently obsessed with. I have put on my headphones as a clear and undeniable sign that I, like Greta Garbo once famously said, 'want to be alone'.

Molly set a cup of coffee on my desk at eleven, with a Penguin biscuit. She didn't look at me or speak, which was perfect because I didn't want to see pity in her eyes and I certainly didn't want to talk about all the feelings whirring inside of me right then.

No, that's not true. I couldn't speak, because if I did, I would break and all my crazy would come out. I'd no idea if it would spill out as anger, or tears, or a mixture of both, but I couldn't let myself lose my cool like that. Anxiety curled its fingers around my stomach and squeezed tight.

When Luke turned around in his chair, a look of faux concern on his face, I glared at him with such ferocity that he immediately turned back to his own computer and started working. He knows he has joined the ranks of supreme office dicks.

I'm immensely relieved when lunchtime arrives. I just want to get to my car, drive to a quiet spot and have a good, long, sweary cry at the unfairness of it all. Then I'll do what every working mammy in the world does: I'll pull myself together and go and pick my child up from school. Maybe we can even collect Jax early and go to the park.

Perhaps spending some quality time with my children will remind me that it's OK that I didn't get the promotion – even if it absolutely isn't OK that I didn't get the promotion.

I've already sent a text message to Paul, Cat and Amanda about the decision. Paul replied with a sad face emoji and a promise we'd talk about it later. Cat sent a suitably Cat-like string of expletives and Amanda sent a wishy-washy, Oh I am sorry. Maybe it's for the best? I haven't replied to any of them because I don't know what to say. Maybe Handley is right and I'm just not fresh and vibrant enough to grow the business. Maybe Amanda is right and it might be for the best – extra responsibility comes with extra hours, and I don't want to be the kind of parent who never sees her own children. Although there are times when they drive me so mad I want to run away and join the circus, deep-down I always have mom-guilt about not spending enough time with them. Yes, I'm career-driven too, but they're only wee once, as my mammy says, so why not enjoy them now, before they get to Gemma's age and want nothing to do with me?

Maybe I have been flogging a dead horse trying to prove that my best days are still to come and I should give in to early old age with grace. It would be less stressful, I suppose. I could wear my cardigans and get heavily invested in the *Antiques Roadshow*. I could let my hair go grey, and my body continue to spread like jelly tipped out of a bowl. I could embrace being the permanently embarrassing parent and I could embrace being the slightly irrelevant office elder who people are nice to only because they've heard she's perimenopausal and really quite scary.

On my way to the school to pick up Nathan, I stop at the corner shop and do the biggest FML shop of all time. Do I buy vegetables? Fruit? Low-fat dairy produce? Lean proteins?

No. No. I do not.

I buy several multipacks of Twixes, Mars and Chocolate Buttons. I buy two bags of Wispa Bites (one to inhale in the car during the remaining five minutes of my commute to the school, and one for later). I buy full-fat Coke and a big bag of Drumstick Squashies. I add in a share-size bag of Doritos (extra cheesy, of course), several dips, two bottles of wine and twenty cigarettes. I feel a little rebellious, out of work early, with my pink hair, scowling as the cashier tots up my bill. Look at me, I am hard. I am a bad bish. I can buy my own alcohol and cigarettes and I can eat chocolate until I throw up and there is nothing any of you can do about it.

'Wee party in the house tonight?' the cashier asks with a broad smile – which is remarkably brave of her, given the look on my face right now.

'Something like that,' I say, stony-faced.

'Well have fun and don't go too mad. It is a school night, after all,' she says in a super happy sing-songy voice.

I take a breath, glance at her name tag and start to speak. 'Jessica, let me tell you a wee secret. I don't care if it's a school night. I intend to go totally mad. In fact, I think I might already be halfway there. If you had the day – no, the week and possibly even the month – that I have had, then you would absolutely do the same.'

She smiles back at me but I can see fear in her eyes. She's probably wondering who this crazy pink-haired lady is. Part of me wants to tell her that she's young. She might not understand where I'm coming from yet, but she will. One day. When the world starts seeing her as invisible and irrelevant and the high-lights of her weekend include finding a dried poo in the toy box and going head to head with a teenager who wants the world handed to her on a plate.

I lift my bag of feelings and leave. I don't want to be late for Nathan. I've already told Jo that I'm going to pick him up today and I don't want him traumatized because no one is there to collect him. Also, the school does not like it when parents are late. Actually, I'm not overly sure that's true. The school secretary doesn't seem to mind one bit, if I'm being honest. It gives her the perfect opportunity to be legitimately judgey and passive-aggressive about it. 'Oh Mrs Gallagher, was there something really important happening at work today? Poor Nathan here has been beside himself thinking his mammy loves her work more than him.' I am not in the mood for her self-righteous bullshit today.

Standing in the playground with all the other mammies, daddies, grannies and childminders, it strikes me that I'm one of the oldest 'mammies' from Nathan's class. I am not one of these young and lithe twenty-something mammies, in their Lycra sports gear, fake tan and full make-up with a designer buggy in front of them containing their newest offspring. I hear them talk about their weekend plans – both admiring and failing to understand how they can possibly have the energy to get dressed up to leave the house after eight in the evening. I watch as one of them holds a conversation, scrolls through her phone and takes a banana from her bag to hand to her beautifully behaved toddler in his pristine, high-end pram. I think of Jax. How there'd be a reasonable chance he would yeet (I'm starting to love the word 'yeet', which means it will only be cool for another fifteen seconds) it across the playground. I think of his buggy – neither pristine nor high end. It has been through the wars, having served Nathan admirably in his day. It has a slightly wonky wheel from being thrown around like a sack of spuds on a budget airline flight to Spain, and no matter how often I clean it, it always retains a faint whiff of cheesy Wotsits.

Thankfully I'm distracted from this particular chapter of 'How to Feel Inadequate in 100 Different Ways at the School Pickup' by the opening of a door and the sight of two hundred children being vomited out of the building into the playground. The noise level rises, hands are flung in the air to indicate that mammies have been found, coats and school bags are thrown to the ground as children explode with energy after being forced to behave all day.

My mood immediately lifts the moment I see Nathan, and he breaks into a huge smile at the sight of me. He comes running towards me at the speed of light, barrelling into me and almost knocking me over, but I don't care. This is a big, deeply lovely hug and it is exactly what I need. Even more than Wispas and wine. I gulp down the tears I didn't know were so close to the surface and lean into this wee bundle of love. It's like exhaling after holding my breath all day and I squeeze him tight, as if doing so will transfer some of his inherent goodness and innocence into me. This is what matters, I remind myself. I've not failed him. I can do this mammy thing and my child adores me. I need that feeling of being adored.

'Mammy, I didn't know you were coming to get me today,' he says, as if my showing up is the most incredibly exciting thing that has ever happened to him.

'I thought it would be a nice surprise,' I tell him. 'And I

missed you so much that I needed a big squishy cuddle from my best boy.'

'Am I your best boy and not Jax?' he asks, his eyes wide.

'You are my best boy and Jax is my best baby,' I tell him.

'And Gemma is your bestest girl?' he asks.

I nod. 'She is. I love you all very much. To the moon and back a million times. So, I was thinking me and you could go for a wee sneaky visit to the park? I'll push you on the swings.'

'And watch me on the slide?' he asks, excitement writ large across his face.

'Yup. And help you on the big climbing frame.'

He punches his small, five-year-old fist in the air and says, 'Yes! Best day ever!' before hugging me again. 'I love you, Mammy.'

It's shaping up to be quite a touching scene, even if I do say so myself, but then of course, because this is my life and nothing ever goes quite to plan, I hear my son whisper in my ear: 'Miss Rose says she wants to talk to you about kissing her ass.'

The conversation from the previous night flashes into my mind. Well, not today, Miss Rose. Today I do not have to be the sensible parent. Today I am not going to be the sensible parent. I'm not going to show my son a good example by apologizing to Miss Rose. No. Not a chance.

'Well,' I say, still crouching close to him (and hopefully out of Miss Rose's eyeline), 'how about we get out of here as fast as we can before we have to talk to her?'

Nathan looks at me as if I have lost the run of myself, which in fairness I have. 'Really, really, Mammy? Will we run from Teacher?'

'Really, really,' I nod, and grabbing his hand I start to lead him out of the playground, walking at first and then we are both running and giggling like eejits, past the yummy mummies and their perfect little banana-eating designer toddlers. If that's Miss Rose I can hear calling me in the background, I take no notice. Today, this mama is going rogue.

Nathan is still giggling when we reach the park. Probably because I have let him eat a Twix and given him a Fruit Shoot to wash it down with. He is now running on giddiness and sugar. I know how he feels, the hit of the chocolate is in full effect, as is the release of the tension that had been pinning me down all morning. We walk together hand in hand, laughing and joking, into the playpark and I imagine that I'm some sort of uber mummy, who does fun things with her children all the time and is always up for the craic.

I launch into swing-pushing with great enthusiasm before helping Nathan shimmy up the climbing frame with slightly less enthusiasm, but still, you know, being an uber mummy. I cheer as he climbs up, almost but doesn't fall off, climbs again and pretends he is Spiderman. I play along admirably in a faux American accent, saying things like, 'Hang on one minute, dude! You can't get away from me!' And he shouts back, 'Yes I can, 'cos I'm a Spiderman and you is a big, smelly, poo-bum doofus.'

I have to be honest, I don't remember either of those lines

from any of the successful movies in the Spiderman franchise, but they'll do.

By the time we get to the slides, Nathan has positively and without question lost any semblance of sense and begs me to have a go on the slide too. I'm watching him take his turn and I realize that it really does look like great fun, and I used to love going on slides when I was wee, so I agree.

'You go first, Mammy, and I go after,' he says as we climb the steps to the top. 'You have to sit on your bum and not go down with your head first,' he says solemnly, and I nod. But now I'm up here, at the top, the slide itself looks much thinner than I remember. Still, I'll be grand. I tell myself. Anyway, it's not like I can chicken out now, with Nathan looking at me as if I'm a total legend. I like how that makes me feel.

So I sit down and grin. And I try, I really do, I try to slide my ass over the edge and down the slide, but it doesn't want to move. 'Do you want me to push you, Mammy?' Nathan asks, his impatience and that of the four or five children queuing behind him starting to show.

'No, no, pet. Mammy is fine. I'm going to go now.' I shuffle forward, and slide perhaps two inches at most before my hips and ass decide they are now at one with the metal slide and they will be staying that way for the foreseeable future.

'Mammmeeee,' Nathan says, 'you're 'posed to keep going till the very bottom!'

'Aye, pet,' I tell him, trying to wriggle my way free. 'I know. I think someone might have put glue on the slide or something!' I laugh, externally at least. Internally, I am dying a thousand deaths. Dear Jesus, what if I don't start sliding again and soon? Will they have to call the fire service? Will my fat ass have to be cut out of this contraption?

'I don't fink it's glue,' a child who looks like he could actually mug someone shouts from the queue. 'I fink it's 'cos your bum is too big!' The other children waiting fall about laughing. Nathan is giving me the strangest of looks, as if he is willing his humiliation to transform into a force strong enough to propel me to the bottom of the slide without further delay.

I pull my knees up so that my feet are sitting flat on the slide and try to use them to lever myself down, inch by inch. Naturally, the sight of a grown-up with pink hair fighting her way down a slide is one which attracts the attention of some passing teenagers who waste no time in taking their phones out and starting to record.

They do not stop even when I tell them to pack it in. If anything, that renews their determination to capture the moment for posterity. Sweet Jesus, I'm gonna end up as a viral internet meme.

I momentarily consider faking my own death to see if that might evoke some empathy from them but realize that I've probably traumatized Nathan enough already, and having him think that I may have just croaked it might be a step too far.

With humiliatingly slow progress I make it to the bottom of the slide. The teenagers, to their credit, give me a round of applause before running away as fast as they can. Nathan slides down after me and runs to take my hand.

'I fink we should go get Jax now, Mammy,' he says. 'You're a very brave girl coming down the slide,' he adds solemnly.

Not half as brave as I'm going to have to be if those wee bastards post that video online. Gemma will disown me entirely.

21

Well, Oprah, it's like this . . .

Of course, those wee teenage shites posted the video online. It has put the tin-hat on what will go down as the shittest day in history. As if it's not bad enough that I have been overlooked for a job I would smash out of the park in favour of an inexperienced new recruit, I have now been humiliated by a bunch of obnoxious teenagers.

Why do younger generations have to be such completely entitled shit stains?

As expected, Gemma announces her intention to disown me while I'm sitting on the sofa in my Lion King fluffy pyjamas, wondering if it's worth opening the second bottle of wine and more importantly how I can persuade Paul to do it for me so that I don't have to get up off my slide-filling fat arse.

'I am never going to school again,' my daughter declares in a pitch so high I'm surprised that anyone other than dogs can hear her. She is seething with rage. This is worse than the

'Tragedy' of her birthday party (see what I did there?). This is worse than me dyeing my hair pink. This is the ultimate mammy betrayal. I have made a dick of myself, and I have done it online for the world to see.

Clearly, the fact that I did not intend to do it online and I didn't want anyone to see isn't important here.

'All my friends will be laughing at me. Mammy, are you actually trying to make sure I have no friends and end up never leaving my room ever again?' (It would seem my daughter has the same touch for the dramatics that I have.)

'Here, Gemma, calm yourself. And don't speak to your mum like that. You know she's had a tough enough day.'

'*She's* had a tough day? Have you SEEN the state of the video?' Gemma is practically hyperventilating with rage at this stage.

'Video?' Paul asks, completely confused, because I've not told him about the great slide humiliation. I was all out of humiliating myself after telling him about Luke scoring the promotion over me. I'd cried, then cried some more, then said a lot of words that Miss Rose definitely would not approve of, cried again, and then Paul had hugged me tightly before opening a bottle of wine.

Gemma thrusts her phone in his face and I watch as he takes in the sights and sounds of me scooting down a slide like a dog with an itchy arse while a queue of children tell me to hurry up. He looks at me then back at the phone, and then he looks at Gemma.

'Well,' he says, and I know that he is doing his absolute best to try and work out what to say next and also not to laugh. 'That is quite an interesting video.'

'An interesting video?' Gemma shouts, her face puce with teenage indignation. 'Can she not do anything without making a show of herself?'

'Whoa!' I jump in. 'She? She? Do you mean me, your mother? The woman who gave you life?'

'Yes! You! You big embarrassment!' She storms off, in another hail of teenage tears and rage, and because she has been extraordinarily rude, and because I too am exceptionally pre-menstrual, and because it has been a complete and utter fucker of a day, I promptly burst into tears myself.

Paul, God love him, looks on in horror. 'Jesus Christ,' he mutters.

In my wine and sugar-infused sleep, I dream that the video of me stuck on the slide, goes viral. It becomes a meme that is shared for generations. My daughter properly disowns me until she writes a bestselling memoir *Oh. My. God. My Mother, the Embarrassment* and we are invited onto *Oprah* to be interviewed about our 'difficult relationship'.

'Well, it's like this, Oprah,' I tell her. 'Teenagers are absolute assholes.'

In a second dream, Paul is having an affair with Miss Rose, and Nathan has already taken to calling her 'Mammy'. Paul is absolutely besotted with her and tells me it's not personal, it's just I was getting on a bit and he fancied a trade-in. He speaks with all the emotion of a man upgrading from a 2008 Ford

Fiesta to a brand spanking new Ferrari. In case you are in any doubt here, I am the 2008 Ford Fiesta.

When my phone rings at 5.30 a.m., I am grateful to have been pulled from my sleep. It's Cat.

'Yoohoo! Good-morning sunshine!' she coos. 'Are we all set for spin? I've heard a rumour there's a new playlist being dropped this morning.'

Christ on a bike. Spin. I'd forgotten all about that. I'm in a sugar crash that would fell even the hardiest of my children, and the bottle of wine I drank has left me feeling as if I'm seasick and there's no land in sight.

'I . . . I think I'll give it a miss,' I say, throwing in a fake cough for good measure. 'I'm not feeling the best.'

'I can imagine,' she says. 'I know yesterday was shit. I know your boss is a wanker. And I've seen the video that's online. Gemma sent me a rather long rant about it all last night.'

Now she has my attention. 'Gemma sent *you* a rant?'

'Aye,' Cat says. 'We chat quite a bit, you know. Perks of being the coolest adult she knows. You've a great kid there.'

'Hmmmmm,' I mumble.

'Seriously,' Cat says. 'Obviously she's a teenager and they can be problematic . . .'

I laugh, snorting so loud that Paul cracks open an eye with a look that screams 'could you ever have that conversation somewhere else, it's too early in the morning for this shit'.

I sneak out of bed and scoot downstairs.

'You need to cut her a bit of slack maybe,' Cat says. 'You must remember being that age? Do you not remember how

197

shamed you were of your mother's big hair and short denim skirt rig-out? She thought she looked like that singer . . .'

'Bonnie Tyler,' I offer.

'That's it. And you thought she looked like Julia Roberts in *Pretty Woman*, before Richard Gere picks her up.'

'Yes,' I concede. 'But it's not like I'm wandering around dressing like a prostitute, Cat. I coloured my hair and got stuck on a slide. I didn't even plan the slide thing. Trust me, it's humiliating for me too. As if yesterday hadn't been humiliating enough before that!'

'Ach pet, look I know you had a shit day. A really shit day. And I'm so angry on your behalf for how that fucker at work has treated you. I really am. But Gemma is going through a lot at the moment. It's a shit age. Everything seems bigger than it is when you're thirteen,' Cat says. I pour a pint of water and down it as if my life depends on it. Which it actually might. 'Anyway,' she says, 'you've twenty minutes to get your arse to spin class or, so help me God, I will come round there and drag you out of the house myself.'

'But I'm sick!' I protest, with another fake cough.

'Do your legs still work?' she asks.

'Well, yes.' Cat can be quite scary when she wants to be.

'Then no excuse!'

'But . . . I had a shit day yesterday and I'm not in the form. I might cry.'

'So cry,' she says. 'Tara, I am serious right now. Get your ass into your gear and get here now, or a viral video will be the very least of your worries.'

She hangs up and I know she has me, because Cat does not make idle threats. With all the grace of huffing teenager, I haul my sports gear from the drier, change and tie my hair into the shortest ponytail in history before leaving the house. This is so not fair.

'Good girl yourself!' Cat applauds when I walk into the studio. I don't even try to hide the two-fingered gesture I give her before climbing onto my bike. To add to my woes even further, my uterus has started on its monthly mission to kill me and I've no goals in mind other than surviving this class without killing myself or anyone else.

I don't think I can feel any more wretched, but then Connor comes in, full of the joys of a very youthful spring, and asks if we are ready to feel the burn. While everyone else cheers and whoops excitedly, I find myself shaking my head – a gesture that Connor pointedly ignores.

'OK!' he shouts, which frankly there's no need for because the music isn't even playing yet. 'It's Friday morning. Almost the freakin' weekend! And we're going to kick this off with a few bangers.' Does he secretly think he's a DJ in some cool Ibizan club and not just a fitness instructor at the local council-run gym?

I don't have time to think about it any more before the 'beat kicks in' as Connor would put it and we are warming up and I am indeed distracted from all my worries because the only thing I can focus on now is not throwing up.

Sadly, about three quarters of the way through the class I

199

lose that battle. Thankfully I'm able to make it to the bathroom in time, so I'm at least saved the humiliation of puking on my shoes while a roomful of perfect people watch.

Like a turkey, I'm done, I think, as I sit on the floor of the bathroom – although perhaps not yet done with this particular purge. I'm tempted to curl up into a tight little ball to help ease my period cramps. It wouldn't be that weird to have a wee sleep right now, would it?

When I hear the door to the bathroom open, I fully expect to see Cat ready to inflict some 'for your own good' type punishment on me, but it isn't her. It's the Lovely Lyrca Lady (as I will forever think of her) – she who recommended the padded cycling shorts. Her face is filled with concern. 'How are you feeling?' she asks.

If you are from Ireland, the polite response to this question is always considered to be, 'I'm grand, thank you very much'. Even if you are clearly not grand, like if there's a limb hanging off, or there's a shark sinking its teeth into your leg. We are supposed to be hardy people. But I am not feeling very hardy.

'I've been better,' I say, which is the Irish equivalent of 'call the undertakers and plan my wake because I'm on my way out'.

She sits down beside me, and hands me a water bottle. 'Take a wee sip,' she says. 'I promise it's only water. Although, there are times when I wish it was something more.'

I smile at her, and gratefully accept the water.

'I saw the video you're in,' she says, and I wonder is it possible to drown myself with half a bottle of Evian. 'I've a teenager in the house – obsessed with Snapchat and TikTok. He showed me the video yesterday evening and, well, I recognized the hair.'

I go beetroot red, which at least makes me look like death warmed up. 'I'm so embarrassed. My own teenager – my daughter – is threatening to disown me. As if I did it on purpose. I was just playing with my son, and he wanted me to go down the slide and I didn't think I'd get stuck. I mean, I know I've put on a bit of weight . . .'

'That slide is designed for children, you know. Small children. With skinny bums. It's also the least slidey slide in the world, according to my eight-year-old. He says everyone gets stuck on it.'

I'm not sure if this very lovely stranger is saying this just to make me feel better, or if it is actually true, but I appreciate the lie. 'Thank you,' I say. 'I'm Tara.'

'I'm Eva,' she says with a smile. 'I'd shake your hand, but I'm a sweaty mess and it would be unpleasant for both of us.' I smile back and it's genuine. I feel honest-to-God warmth towards this Lovely Lyrca Lady with her water, her kind smile and her in-depth knowledge of slidey slides.

'How many children do you have?' she asks me.

'Three,' I tell her, 'Gemma – who wants to disown me – is thirteen. Nathan is five and Jax turned two last month.'

She nods. 'That's a handful,' she says, but there's no judgement in her words. 'I've three as well. Charlie is fifteen. Joe is eight and my baby, Cara, is five.'

'Solidarity!' I say with a smile and an embarrassing burp that manages to slip out.

'Whoever said this motherhood gig was easy was either lying, or a man,' Eva laughs. 'I struggled for a few years after Cara was born. Nothing to do with her, mind. I love the bones of her, but I think I was so busy trying to be a great mammy and a brilliant wife and a kick-ass employee that I sort of, well, I sort of forgot to be—'

'Yourself?' I interrupt, because I know exactly where she is coming from.

'Yep. The one person in the whole equation who was getting ignored was me. I don't know if it was because I didn't feel I deserved attention, or I valued myself less than everyone else, or I was just too bloody tired, but I do know I ended up feeling as if I didn't matter and I never would.'

I nod because I know if I speak, I will cry. And that last burp has taken me way over my embarrassment quota for the month.

'So, I decided to move myself nearer the top of the list. And I decided to trust my own voice too. You know, we are constantly being told what a good mammy should be, or what a good wife should do – well stuff that. It makes us ignore our own instinct and try and become some sort of Stepford Wife. I don't know about you, but my husband did not fall in love with a perfect version of me. And my own mother was not perfection personified, but she was still a brilliant mammy.'

I want to hug Eva. I want to pull her into the giant, squishiest, sweatiest hug I can. 'How did you get round it?' I ask her, throat tight, because this woman in front of me does not look like a woman being pulled in a hundred different directions.

'Ach, it was a few things. Coming here was one of them. If I'm stressed or angry or whatever, I just go at these classes full steam ahead and take all that rage out on them. I completely recommended boxercise. I often imagined my opponent was my boss – and believe me, that was cathartic,' she laughs. I imagine pummelling Mr Handley's face and I smile. I can totally see how that would help.

'And the other thing was that I joined the Rebel Mums group – it sounds much more cringe than it actually is. It's not all yummy mummies talking about buggies and sleep training. I'd have had to shoot myself in the face if it was. The rebel bit is key. We're the anti-yummy-mummy brigade. Real, down-to-earth, warts-and-all mammies who know they're not perfect, never will be, and accept that they don't need to try to be. We've done things like rally car driving, Xbox tournaments, a weekend away to Liverpool to watch a match. We've done a cocktail-making course. Body painting. Dry ski slopes . . . and we have a night out at least once a month which starts at six for dinner, and those who need to go home in time for night feeds can leave early while some of the rest of us party on.'

It sounds bloody brilliant. It sounds cool! Really cool!

'The thing is, all our members get to choose an activity – either something that they loved before they had kids, or something they've always wanted to try – and we all give it a go. I can't believe some of the things I've done that I never ever thought I would. I think you might love it, you know? Is there anything you've always wanted to do, or missed doing since you became a mum?'

I think about what I'd like to do, given the chance. Aside

from having a night of passion with Tom Hardy, one thing springs immediately to mind.

'Have you ever done a dance class? Like hip-hop? To, you know, maybe Nineties music or music from the early Noughties?' I ask.

'That's strangely specific,' Eva laughs. 'But I like it. We've never done it, but I'm thinking it could be right up our street. What kind of songs?'

I'm thrust back to the school talent show. Fourteen-year-old me wearing enough Pan Stik and blush to make a drag queen take the staggers, walking proudly on stage to dance my little heart out to 'Bootylicious'. Beyoncé and the girls had nothing on me. I knew I was good. And the high it gave me was unreal.

'You know, Destiny's Child, Backstreet Boys . . .'

'*Steps*!' Eva chimes in and I smile.

'Definitely Steps,' I say.

'Look, let's get out of here and get our phones from the lockers. We can share numbers and I'll talk to the gang, but I bet they would love it. We'd just need to find a teacher. I'm sure it won't be too hard. A friend of mine went to a hen do and they had a dance teacher in. I'll get the details from her. This could be really exciting!' Eva says, and I feel it too.

The sadness that has been sitting on my chest since yesterday, the feeling that I can't do anything right, begins to fade a little. The thought of hanging out with other mammies who genuinely get it, who like to shake off the mammy shackles every now and again, sounds great. Dancing again, even if we make an unholy mess of it, sounds like exactly what I need. When my tummy tightens now it's not with nerves, or fear, or lust – it's with excitement.

'Here, give me your number,' Eva says. 'I'll ping you a message so you have mine too and we can keep in touch. I think you'll fit right in.' She seems to mean it, too. 'This is going to be brilliant!' she says with a grin.

I have a feeling she's right.

22

I could fake my own death, right?

I am still buzzing when I get back to the house after class. Standing in the shower, singing along to the Spice Girls, I remember how good dancing used to make me feel. The wee kernel of excitement over giving it a go again is enough to distract me from the video trauma, and maybe more importantly from the great disappointment in work yesterday.

As I condition my hair, I vow that I will not let them see my hurt today when I go in. I'll put my best foot forward. I will kick ass and do my job to the best of my ability, embodying girl power while I figure out what I really, really want to do about my future with ToteTech.

I'm still singing as I get dressed for work. Paul looks at me quizzically. 'Erm, Tara, are you OK, love?' he asks.

I turn around and give him a huge thumbs up. 'I am indeed OK, and even better than OK.'

'Last night you cried so much about work you made yourself sick. And a couple of hours ago you were literally begging me to help you fake your death across social media,' he says. 'You asked me if I could put you up for adoption and you'd just leave me and the kids to it.'

'That was then and this is now,' I say.

'And what's changed in the ninety minutes between now and then?' he asks. 'Not that I'm complaining. I mean, obviously I much prefer the version of you that doesn't want to fake her own death or leave us in the lurch.'

'You know what, Paul. I think I've finally realized that I'm a grown-up and if I'm not happy with how things are then I can change them.'

For a moment he looks stricken. 'You're not happy?' he asks. 'With us? With me?'

'Oh God, no! I'm not talking about you or us. I love you. I love us. I will always love you and us. But you know I've not been particularly happy with me and how my confidence seems to have fallen off a cliff lately. And I'm definitely not happy with what has happened in work.'

'Are you sure things are good with us?' he asks, and I see a flicker of fear on his face.

'Paul, we don't have the perfect relationship. No one does. But that doesn't mean things aren't great with us. Through all this, and especially since Jax's birth, which turned me into an anxious wreck, you have been my constant. I don't think you'd know how to make me unhappy.'

He's staring at me, his expression soft and full of love, and I feel tears prick at my eyes.

I reach out and stroke his face while the Spice Girls croon about two becoming one in the background. He probably thinks I'm losing it altogether, but I'm not. Something has shifted this morning. Something in me is different, but not in a bad, scary way. 'I love you,' I tell him and kiss him full on the mouth, without worrying if any of the children, even Gemma, walk in and see our display of affection.

I make myself a little promise: I'm going to book us a night away. In a fancy hotel. And I'll wear my fancy new underwear, and maybe even high heels to boot. If necessary, I'll even get waxed again. I will take this man of mine away and I will seduce every part of him.

There is no way I'm sliding (ha) back into the pit of despair I was in last night. No matter what might surface online, or how much of an asshole my daughter is. Not even if Miss Rose makes me write one hundred lines about not telling my children she can kiss my cellulite-covered ass. Not even if Mr Handley promotes all of the Gen Zs ahead of me. My worth is not dependent on his ability to see it.

Nope. I am gonna find the real me again. Watch me shine, bishes.

When I arrive at work I am determined not to let yesterday's trauma show. Part of me would love to throw a hissy fit and tell Mr Handley to go fug himself. But I won't, because it would achieve precisely nothing except give me something else to cringe about at a later date. And that man would probably love nothing more than to fug his own brains out. The new me will keep my cool. I also resolve not to rise to the bait from the Gen Zs, who flock around me with faux concern for my mental health now that yesterday's storms have somewhat cleared.

'It must be such a disappointment,' Lucy trills. 'I mean, we all totally thought you'd get it. Are you devastated?' She tilts her head to one side, giving me a doe-eyed look that oozes insincerity to the trained eye. I watch as Molly and Amy adopt the same head pose – the three of them standing there looking like dazed pigeons.

'No, I'm not devastated,' I lie. 'I'm sure that Mr Handley knows exactly what he's doing and chose the best person for the job. To be honest, I'm looking forward to taking my foot off the accelerator for a while. No need for me to push myself so hard now, is there?' I smile so brightly, you'd almost think I'm being paid to advertise toothpaste.

Lucy gives me a small sympathetic smile, which Molly and Amy copy. But I see it. I see the faltering look and fear on their faces. These girls are not stupid. They might not have the emotional intelligence that comes with having a certain amount of life experience behind them, but they are smart. They know exactly what will happen if I take my foot off the accelerator. They know that shit is about to go down.

'And the best bit?' I say with a smile. 'Those weekly reports won't be my responsibility any more.'

They look at each other. The weekly reports – collating a snapshot of what we have achieved that week and putting together a document outlining our current state of play and updating any projected budgets – are an essential part of housekeeping which really should be done by a senior account manager. They aren't for the faint-hearted and I know Luke will struggle with them while trying to get up to speed with the rest of his new role.

I imagine that's why they wanted me onboard for the in-name-only promotion to Luke's deputy, aka Luke's dogsbody.

'But will Luke know how to do them? I mean, you do them so well,' Lucy trills.

I shrug. 'He has to learn, I suppose. And it is *supposed* to be done by someone on a higher paygrade than I am.'

'But you'll still take the lead on the BumbleTots project, won't you?' Amy asks.

I shrug again. 'You'll have to ask Luke about that.'

I can see each of them clocking that things are about to change and that sweet, malleable, get-the-job-done Tara is about to make a stand. For too long now, I've been keeping this ship afloat: I've done more than I've been paid to do, pushed harder than anyone to make this company a success and been singularly generous with my experience to those newer to the company. I'm not bragging – it's just how it is. It's why that promotion should've been mine. And they know it.

I'm not going to get angry about it all, but I *am* going to get even. Tara the Walkover is gone. Tara the kick-ass dancing queen who gets right back on her spin bike even after she pukes her guts up is taking over and the Gen Zs and Luke, and yes, even Mr Handley, should be very afraid. This mama has had enough of cleaning up other people's shit. From now on, my cleaning skills are reserved entirely and solely for people who entered this world through my vagina. Everyone else can go and take their face for a shite.

I spend the morning doing my job but not stretching myself to any great lengths. I'm not rude to anyone. I remain resolutely professional, but if Luke thinks we can still be besties and bond over shared confectionary, he is wrong. When he tries to hand me a peace offering of half a king-sized Twix, I show him how serious I am about maintaining a professional distance by refusing. Even though in my hungover state it almost kills me, he has to learn my forgiveness cannot be bought – not even with caramel biscuity goodness.

I keep my head down and power my way through my immediate to-do list, and then I allow myself a little Friday office downtime. I don't normally faff about online at work – but this is a whole new me. I take the business card that Eva handed me before I left spin class and do what every self-respecting woman would do in the circumstances. I log into Facebook and Instagram and hunt her down.

I need to find out more about my new BFF and her Rebel Mums club. I want to be sure she is telling me the truth and her story of solidarity between fed-up mums isn't just chat designed to hook me into some multilevel marketing scam. I've heard of it happening – one minute you think you're being invited over to an old school friend's house for wine and nibbles, and the next you find yourself being badgered into signing up to sell organic skin cream made from the discarded toenails of Tibetan nuns.

Thankfully, Eva is easy enough to find and doesn't seem to have any affiliation whatsoever to Tibetan nuns. I locate her Facebook page – should I send her a friend request? I don't want to come across as desperate, even though I am in fact exceptionally needy and craving her approval.

Her Instagram account gives a better idea of her life – not being tied up in privacy settings. It's open for all to see and she has one of those accounts which I both envy and despise. Of course, Eva has a perfectly Instagrammable life by the look of it, and I'm not just talking about the fact she is lithe and gorgeous and has almost unnaturally white teeth.

Her home is tidy *and* clean – which is no mean feat when you have children. Speaking of which, her son looks as if he just fell out of a One Direction poster. I must make sure he and Gemma never meet, as I can only imagine the drama that would accompany her first big real-life crush. Eva's daughter, Cara, could be a child model. Long dark curls, the bluest eyes.

Her husband doesn't appear in many photos but when he does, I can see why she would want to keep him away from the gaze of other female eyes. He looks like he should be wandering around the halls of Grey Sloan Memorial in scrubs, shouting at some poor first year attending to get him the goddamn results he asked for, stat. Yup, he is an absolute ride.

I blush crimson when I realize I'm staring slightly open-mouthed at my computer screen. 'Are you OK?' Lucy asks, clearly worried that my slack facial expression means I'm having some sort of mini-stroke.

'I'm fine,' I tell her, but as I've said, the girl isn't stupid. She knows when there is scandal afoot and she is up and out of her desk in seconds and by my side before I have time to click out of the page.

'Who's the hottie?' she asks. 'And is he single?'

'Erm . . . it's his wife's Insta that I'm looking at,' I say, and scroll through to show her.

'Why are all the good ones taken?' she asks with a sigh. 'Men my age are either trolls or self-obsessed posers.'

'I thought you had your sights set on our new glorious leader,' I say. 'Didn't you say you'd like to eat him on toast?' (Although I'm not sure if Lucy actually did say that, or if those were my own thoughts. I know she fancied him though – she'd made that much clear.)

'Meh,' she says, wrinkling her nose. 'I don't like how he's waltzed in here and bagged a top spot already. Feels a bit sneaky – and sneakiness takes away from rideyness.' Maybe I haven't given Lucy enough credit in the past.

'I suppose,' I say. 'He is arguably very handsome though.'

'If you don't mind me saying so, Tara, he has nothing on your husband. You're a lucky girl. He is a pure ride.'

'My what is what now?' I gasp, and now it's her turn to cringe with embarrassment.

'I'm sorry,' she mutters, her voice quiet, 'that was really inappropriate of me. But he's a very handsome man.'

I examine Lucy to see if she's coming down with something.

213

Maybe she has a fever and doesn't realize what she is saying. A wee dose of the bubonic plague, perhaps? But she looks perfectly normal. No sweat on her brow, or flushed features. She's scrolling through Eva's Instagram feed and making approving noises.

'My husband? Paul? Paul, my husband?' I ask.

'Yes. Your husband. You are married to that mechanic, aren't you?'

'Yes,' I tell her.

'Then yes, I'm talking about your husband. He's a hottie. You know I have friends who go to his garage just because of him.'

OK, so that's a little bit too *Fatal Attraction* for my liking, but there is something quite nice about being told my husband is a ride.

'Who is this woman anyway?' Lucy asks, returning to her scroll through Eva's feed life. 'Is she a new client?'

I don't want to tell her the truth – that Eva is not a new client but in fact a potential new friend, because that would make me sound like Nathan does when he tumbles in the door from school and excitedly tells me he has a new bestest buddy in the world. Nathan can get away with being ridiculously enthusiastic about making new friends because he is five and his social circle is a bit shite, if we're being honest. But I don't think it's the done thing for grown women to start talking about their potential new mum friends in the same way. It would make me look needy, and a wee bit lonely – which of course I totally am, but I don't need Lucy to know that.

'Potentially,' I lie. 'It's very early days. I'm just being nosy.'

'Well, she looks like the kind of woman who knows exactly what she wants out of life and how to get it,' Lucy says, and I have to agree. She looks like exactly the kind of woman I wish I was.

The fuck-it list is now getting a little crumpled and worn, but it's still providing a nice template for the new me. As I tick off some more items, I get a real deep-down thrill at the thought I'm making genuine change in my life.

I've had the 'out there' haircut (with limited success, but look, I was brave and I did it. That counts).

I've now done four whole spin classes and I'm still alive.

I have bought some fancy knickers, though I've not had the energy to use them in an attempted seduction of Paul yet.

Mind you, despite the spin classes, I still have my mummy tummy. It's extra round today, thanks to the arrival of my period, and the shedloads of crap food I ate last night. So losing weight and toning up is still on my list. I want to be able to wear Lycra leggings and a crop top like Eva does and not feel at all body conscious.

Making sure Lucy is distracted with her own work and not likely to try spying on my screen again, I click into the gym's website and read through their list of classes. I'm sure I could make lunchtimes work for me. Has to be better than sitting here, working for free, eating limp sandwiches and talking reality TV. Think how virtuous I could be each day as I nip out to the gym.

Booking myself in for Zumba, Beginners' Yoga, Body Pump and an induction session with a personal trainer, I feel smug enough to get out of my seat, walk to the shop next door and buy my own bloody king-size Twix. (I'm hungover, I have my period. Do not judge me. The diet proper starts tomorrow.)

By late afternoon I'm scanning Facebook pages of nutritionists and slimming clubs, and finding myself sucked down a rabbit hole of YouTube videos and customer testimonies on the power of juicing. The joy of the new online era means that within five minutes I have a top-of-the-range Nutribullet ordered, along with extra cups. Fifteen minutes after that I have done an online grocery shop that would make the man from Del Monte proud. For the first time in my life I have steered clear of the biscuits and the crisps and gone straight for the chia seeds and the goji berries. (For the record, I have absolutely no idea what chia seeds or goji berries are, but I'm told they fall into the 'superfoods' category and that now makes me super.)

I even go super mom and add to my shopping a list of ingredients to make my delightful younger children a healthy 'happy meal' from scratch, all by myself. How do you like them apples, Ronald McDonald?

When I leave work, I'd swear I am already walking taller and feeling less bloated. I feel as if I am finally in control of my own life and promotions be damned.

I'm still grinning as I drive home, a motivational soundtrack of Nineties R&B classics pounding in my ears. I can't wait to get home to my lovely family and to my DILF of a husband.

I can't wait to see his face when I tell him about the sneaky weekend away I've booked for us in a hotel in Inishowen. It might only be an hour from home, but it will be a strictly no kids allowed zone and that's all we need. We'll even be able to have sex with the lights on if we're feeling particularly daring.

Things get even better when, as I pull up at home, my phone pings and I see it is a message from Eva.

> Spoke to the girls. Big thumbs up all around!!! We've messaged a dance teacher already and look good to go. We're actually meeting up for drinks tonight if you want to drop in and introduce yourself? Would be great for them to get to know you!

She sends me details of the city-centre bar where they are meeting in . . . shit . . . just over half an hour. I need to shift my ass if I have half a chance of getting there on time.

Grabbing my bags, I'm in through the front door in seconds and have the two boys hugged, kissed and told that I love them very much within a minute. Paul looks at me, probably thrown by my continued good mood after yesterday's histrionics. He may have seen me wearing my best positive pants this morning, but that was before I spent the day in work having salt metaphorically rubbed into my no-promotion wounds.

When I kiss him and tell him I love him, I suspect that he thinks I've had some sort of mental breakdown but is too scared to ask questions. I'm smiling, that's probably enough for him. He knows I'm a rollercoaster of emotions at the best of times.

'Where's our beautiful princess?' I ask as I swing Jax around without a care as to whether or not he may have consumed something that will make for a truly impressive projectile vomit.

'In her lair,' he says. 'She's not long in. Went up town with Mia for a Starbucks.'

'A Starbucks? Is she a coffee drinker now?'

'That's what I asked her. Her response involved eye-rolling and grunting and stomping upstairs. Hopefully she'll have worked through whatever is annoying her before dinner.'

'Being a teenager is annoying her, Paul. We're hammered for the next five years. At the very least,' I smile.

'In that case, I think I'm going to need to drink more,' he grimaces. 'Will I order pizza for tea? I've been a good husband and made sure there's wine in the fridge if you fancy a glass now? I'm going to grab the first of my medicinal beers.'

'Pizza sounds good. It should put Gemma in a better mood too. But, if you don't mind, can I skip the wine? And the pizza too? There's this new group I'm interested in joining . . .'

He raises an eyebrow. 'What kind of group meets on a Friday evening? I mean, I know we joked about the amount of wine you put away last night, but those were exceptional circumstances, no need for a twelve-step programme.'

'Oh God no. It's nothing like that. They're meeting for drinks and they've invited me along to see if they like the cut of my jib and I suppose to see if I like the cut of their jibs too.'

'Mammy, what's a jib?' Nathan asks.

'Haven't the first notion,' I tell him, which miraculously he accepts as an answer.

Paul is still looking at me. He, however, doesn't seem to be particularly happy with my answer. 'It's a mum thing. There's a woman at spin class, Eva, and I thought she was going to be a total nightmare at first, but she's not. She's lovely and was very kind to me this morning when I puked and cried on the floor.'

'You did a bokey on the floor, Mammy?' Nathan asks. 'It's OK. Was only a wee accident,' he says, parroting something I've said to him many times through gritted teeth in the past.

'I'm OK now, sweetie,' I tell him. I look back to Paul. 'Anyway, she is part of this group of mums, the Rebel Mums club, and they get together to do fun things like playing the Xbox and going drinking.'

'Are you sure these are actual adult women and not teenage boys?' he asks, and his tone is a bit cold. I ignore it. I don't want to come down off this buzz. Not any time soon.

'Well, I'm pretty sure,' I say. 'Eva is definitely not a teenage boy. Anyway, it just so happens they are having drinks tonight and Eva had asked me what kind of class or activity I'd like to do if I joined and I said I'd love to do some dance classes, you know. You know how I loved to dance.'

'Dance classes?' he asks.

'Yes. But songs from the Nineties and the like. Songs that had dance routines. Some Steps or something. It's all for fun, but can you imagine? I'd love it. It's exactly what I need right now, Paul. Something outside of this.' I gesture around me at our very ordinary living room in our very ordinary house.

As soon as I see his face, I realize I have fucked up on a monumental level, again. Only this morning I'd told him he was more than enough, and now I'm saying I need something more than what we have. 'Not that I don't love this. Obviously I love this,' I stutter. 'I love this, and I love you and I . . . I just need something for me.'

'But it's Friday night,' he says, almost mournfully. 'We get pizza. We have a wee drink together. We watch *Gogglebox* in our pyjamas and then play Spotify karaoke until Gemma tells us to shut up.'

'I know, love,' I say. 'But we do that every week. This is just one time and it's really important to me.' I glance at the clock and see I am now definitely fighting a losing battle to be on time. 'They're meeting at six,' I say.

'You better be getting ready then,' he says, standing up and taking Jax, who is now a lovely shade of green, from my arms. As I leave the room, I hear my youngest child empty his stomach contents onto the floor and Nathan immediately tell him, 'Is OK, Jax. Was only a wee accident,' followed by a frustrated moan of 'Jesus, Mary and the wee donkey' from my husband. I pretend not to hear as I rush up the stairs and start pulling clothes out of my wardrobe as if my life depends on it.

23

That's my jam

I am working my way through my wardrobe, discarding top after top after dress after 'good' jeans. My going out-out wardrobe, it seems, has shrunk in recent years at the same rate as my ass has grown.

It doesn't help that my desire for sparkly tops and cleavage-hugging frocks has been replaced by a deep and personal love for brushed cotton pyjamas and fluffy bed socks. I get the same thrill now picking up a pair of cosy PJs as I once did picking up a skirt with a good thigh split.

I do still have a few killer outfits though and currently they are all lying on my bed vying for attention, as if they are all screaming 'pick me, pick me' as I look at their sequinned, glittery beauty. I have to say, I admire their self-confidence. I'm not sure any of them will look as good as they think they might.

It's early evening drinks so I discard anything too body-con and which risks a flash of knickers. I don't want to look as if I'm trying too hard or give off full-on 'hot-mess mammy out for the first time in forever' vibes.

Spotting a gold satin cami top, and a pair of dark denim skinny jeans, I decide that is exactly the kind of cool, wee bit sexy, not too slutty look I can rock. I manage to haul the jeans on with the help of a serious intake of breath and reassure myself they will loosen with wear. Jeans always stretch, don't they? I'll be fine. I'll totally be able to breathe.

The cami hides a muffin top of sins, and I pull my favourite navy velvet blazer from the back of the wardrobe and slip it on. Feet in strappy sandals, a quick slick of lip gloss and a dab of mascara and I look presentable. I'd love to fix my hair, or slap on a bit of fake tan but it's already after six and I'm conscious of making a bad impression by arriving ridiculously late.

Paul offers to drop me in town and Gemma is ordered to keep an eye on her brothers while he is out. When I say ordered, I of course mean bribed. Paul's going to pick up the pizza on the way home and she's been promised ice cream after.

Paul doesn't say much in the car. He seems distracted and if I'm honest I'm distracted too. I'm so nervous I can feel my stomach twist and turn. (Though that could be the jeans cutting off circulation to my large intestines, in fairness.) I'm not usually nervous meeting new people: I get along with most folk I come into contact with. But there is something about this group of women that makes me desperate not only to get along with them but to love them and, maybe more importantly, have them love me. Even though I've not met them and know very little about them, I already know I want them to think I am the soundest person they have ever met, that I'm stacks of craic and that they simply couldn't function as a unit without me as a member.

The last time I felt this nervous was probably my first day of secondary school. Eleven-year-old me, with a coat that I would grow into in about five years and a school bag that weighed more than I did, stumbled into a packed assembly hall, eyes wide with fear at all the new faces in front of me. That worked out, though. I met Cat and Amanda and we formed a pretty solid bond – one based around our absolute adoration of Westlife.

'Well, have fun,' Paul says as he pulls the car over outside Silver Street, where my fate awaits me. I smile at him. 'I'll do my best. Look, pet, I probably won't be long. I just want to meet these people and see if we're a fit. I'll probably make it home in time for Spotify karaoke.'

He shrugs. 'Sure, see how it goes. I'd better get these pizzas picked up before the wains go feral and start eating the cushions or something.' There's a smile there, but it's small. Not terribly sincere. I push it down because I don't have the time or energy for mammy–wife guilt right now. It's not like I'm always out running round the town. I can't remember the last time I was out on a Friday night, between lockdowns, being pregnant and subsequently fighting the anxiety monsters that seem to have been delivered into my life along with Jax and his placenta, it's probably been the guts of three years. *I deserve this*, I tell myself.

Watching Paul drive off, I straighten my cami top, give my hair an extra fluff and take a deep breath. Here goes.

Seeing Eva as soon as I walk in is a huge relief, and she grins when she sees me and ushers me to sit beside her on the edge of the group. 'We just put a drinks order in. I ordered a French Martini for you. Is that cool?'

I nod. 'Thank you.'

'Don't look so nervous,' Eva says, grabbing my hand. 'We're all lovely. Honest.' I look around at a group of smiling, waving women who start throwing their names at me and telling me they love the sound of learning some dance routines. Thankfully, and I mean this from the bottom of my soul, this is not a group of Eva clones. The mums gathered here range in age from, at a guess, mid twenties to mid forties. They are a mixed bag of perfectly imperfect women. A collection of mum tums, eye bags, dark roots, hastily applied make-up, and all giving off a total 'I don't give a shit' attitude. There are no airs and graces. Instead, there is a group of women who immediately welcome me into their fold and who exude honesty about the highs and lows of this motherhood carry-on.

I'm on my second French Martini when the conversation moves on to the unwritten rules of the Rebel Mums club.

'We do permit talk about our kids – the good, the bad and the ugly,' Eva says, taking a long sip of her Pornstar Martini. 'But competitive parenting is strictly forbidden. No "my labour was worse than your labour" nonsense. No preaching on epidurals, breast versus bottle feeding, sleep training or any of that bullshit that people use to make themselves feel smug. We run on the assumption that we're all doing the very best we can, and as long as our children are content, fuck the begrudgers and judgers.'

The other mums whoop a little and shout 'preach it', some even raise their hands.

'Sounds bloody great to me,' I say, clinking glasses with a few of the women who are closest to me.

I can get behind this vibe. I never fare well in the competitive parenting stakes anyway. I've had an epidural – two of them, in fact. One with Gemma, which made me throw my guts up, and one with Nathan, which was so effective I proposed to the anaesthetist. With Jax and my rapidly increasing blood pressure, coupled with a nightmare of an induced labour, I took every form of pain relief on offer. At one stage, when the midwife had left the room, I told Paul I was pretty sure there was a bottle of Calpol in my bag and if he could just get it for me, I'd sink the whole lot too. That was before the shit hit the fan and I found myself being put under general anaesthetic for an emergency C-section while poor Paul was left to wander up and down the corridor outside not knowing if either Jax or I would make it out of the room alive.

I bottle-fed Gemma, breastfed Nathan and combined the two for Jax, even though my poor body was so bruised and battered I struggled with the demands breastfeeding put on it. But I felt as if my body had let him down by almost killing him in utero, and sore boobs were the smallest sacrifice I could make for him. It almost broke me at the time, but I got through it. Just about. When he was three months old and I felt a little of the old me come back, I'd switched to formula full time and the result was a happier baby, and definitely a happier mammy.

I've done what I thought was right for each child, going with the 'Aye, we'll get there' methodology. And we have. I've never felt the need or desire to judge any mother on the decisions they make when it comes to raising their children.

It's so refreshing to be with women who just support each other, and these women seem like my kinda gals.

The conversation is flowing by this time – bouncing from person to person – and I let it all wash over me, like a new puppy desperate to become part of this family of friends.

My head is swimming a little, but in that delicious 'this is really nice' way and not a 'one more drink and I'll puke on my shoes' way. I can feel the tension from the past week seep from my body with every sip of my drink and I soon find myself dancing in my seat while embracing the craic around me. I may not have got the job I wanted, I think, but fuck it. I'm enjoying myself right here in this moment.

I know that I should probably be heading home in time for the aforementioned Spotify karaoke with Paul, but I'm having so much fun that I really don't want to. As I reluctantly slip my blazer back on to leave, I'm met with a chorus of 'Oh no, don't go' and 'Sure the night's only getting started'.

'No, ladies, sorry, I promised Paul I'd be home by nine,' I call, but I'm drowned out as the music in the bar ratchets up a gear in both volume and tempo and the opening beats of 'In Da Club' by 50 Cent kick in.

The mums around me whoop and cheer, and most of them are now on their feet and moving en masse towards the dance floor. I'm swept away not only by them actively linking arms with me and dragging me to the dance floor with them but by my own desire to really let loose. By the time good old 'Fiddy' is telling Shorty that we're going to sip Bacardi, I'm wondering if I can still master the running man.

This is what it feels like to be young and relatively free and just to have the craic. I used to do this shit every Friday night – and I'd still get up in the morning for my Saturday job and then go out again on Saturday night. Those are among the happiest memories of my life.

'Oh my God, you're a class dancer,' shouts one of the mums, who I think was called Jacinta, over the music. 'I bloody love this song!' she cheers as she twirls and punches her hand in the air in time to the beat.

'Me too,' I shout back over the thrum of the base as Jacinta dances up beside me and we start rapping along like two badass bishes. We may both have saggier boobs than we'd like and episiotomy scars, but right now we are gangsta-level cool.

As 50 Cent gives way to Missy Elliott getting her freak on, I know I'm going nowhere fast. I think I might have just found my tribe.

I'm not sure what time it is, but I do know that someone has moved the lock on my front door. I've been fumbling with my keys in the darkness to find it for a good few minutes and now I'm seriously considering lying down to go to sleep right here on the front step.

If I wasn't bursting for a pee, that is exactly what I would do. A pelvic floor that has birthed three children is no match for five French Martinis, half a bottle of Prosecco and some other alcoholic stuff that was put in my hand long after I'd lost my ability to taste anything.

I cannot piss myself. Even in my drunken state, I know that would not be a power move. Missy Elliot would never piss herself. But I am now reaching a level of desperation where I'm sure I can hear my bladder screaming for mercy.

'Feckinstupidbuggerindoor,' I slur, jabbing my keys at my door again, sure that the lock really should be there this time. It evades me once again. I'm starting to think my front door is haunted and the lock is moving around out of sheer badness. I let out a muffled sob, and lean my head against the front door, only to stumble forwards as it opens wide into a very dishevelled and exhausted-looking Paul.

I don't have time to chat, to answer the twenty questions he's asking with his eyes. I barrel past him to the downstairs loo where I just about make it in time before my bladder explodes. I look up and see him standing at the door (which I left open), staring at me.

'Sorry,' I mutter. 'I was desperate.'

'Did you have a good night?' he asks.

'It was absolutely belter!' I grin at him, giving two thumbs up. I haul myself to standing, wrestle my jeans back up and move to hug him. For some reason known only to Paul Gallagher and God, he pulls back from my enthusiastic embrace.

'Pet, you smell like a brewery, mixed with a chip van, mixed with a faint aroma of boke. And is that coleslaw down your top? Please tell me it's coleslaw?'

I look down and sure enough there is a clump of what I too hope is coleslaw clinging to the fabric of my top and, if I'm not mistaken that's a shred of lettuce poking out of my cleavage. Perhaps the kebab I'd gorged on was not the best idea in the world, but I'd not eaten and I was – am – drunk.

'Oops,' I say, with a giggle that I hope is playful and flirtatious. 'I suppose I'd better take it off.' Now, even on an ordinary day my attempting to do any sort of a sexy dance would have Paul slightly panicked – but me, drunk as a lord and coming at him at two in the morning, covered in shredded cabbage and mayonnaise, and smelling of boke (which I swear isn't mine. One of the mums had a moment in the taxi queue) is enough to send him over the edge. And not in a good way.

'Pet, why don't you just go up to bed. I'll bring up a pint of water and a basin.'

'Whaddy-I-need-a-basin-for?' I slur as I lift my top over my head and the full impact of the not-actually-coleslaw-but-mum-boke smell hits my nose. I retch immediately.

'Maybe because your stomach doesn't appear to be the strongest right now, does it?' He takes my top from me and wets the ends of a towel to wipe off whatever suspect substance is smeared on my cleavage. He's such a good man.

'I love you,' I tell him, suddenly feeling more than a little emotional. He turns me towards the stairs, but I turn back and look up into his gorgeous face.

'I really, really love you, and I'm not just saying it because I'm drunk, honest.'

'I know,' he says. 'You love me. And I love you. But I think we could all do with getting some sleep. Go up to bed. I'll follow you up as soon as I have the water.'

He looks cross. Even in my pie-eyed state I can tell that he is cross. 'Are you annoyed with me?' I ask, and I feel tears prick at my eyes.

'No. Tara. I'm just tired. Please, go to bed. We can talk in the morning.'

'No, if you want to talk it means you're annoyed with me and I can't handle it . . .' I sob. And it's not in a dignified way. It's in a make-up having slid down my face, wearing only a bra and jeans that are too tight, and with my hair pasted to my forehead with sweat kind of a way.

'Jesus, Tara!' he says firmly. 'You'll wake the boys. Believe me, you don't want to wake the boys. Bed. Now.'

Suitably chastised, I climb the stairs, crying and hiccupping, my head spinning. And there, like the unwelcome wee bastard she is, anxiety walks in and the horrors hit before I've even had the chance to fall into an alcohol-fuelled coma first.

In our bathroom I attempt to remove my make-up but, let's face it, it's a half-arsed job, if that. Like the damn lock on the front door, my features keep jumping around. What I do see scares me a little – pale face, red eyes, mascara making a run for my chin and hair that wouldn't look out of place on a troll doll. Is it any wonder Paul is cross? Look at me, for fuck's sake. Drunk. Messy. Can't-even-get-a-promotion. Useless. Anxiety pokes at me like an annoying child as I slide out of my jeans, grab one of Paul's old T-shirts from the drawer and pull it on. There's a comfort in the smell of it. The smell of him. I remind myself that anxiety lies. He is my constant. He has seen me worse than this. He loves me. And I really, really love him.

My head is on the pillow and I'm almost asleep when I hear him come in and rest the pint of water by my side of the bed.

'Lucy thinks you're a DILF,' I mutter before I drift off to sleep.

24

I can hear colours

If I'm ever asked to give a TED Talk, my chosen subject will be a stark warning to young mothers everywhere, and I will consider it my duty to get this message across as loudly as I can.

Never, ever go on the lash when the only supplies you have in the house to treat the inevitable hangover are a fucking Nutribullet, chia seeds and enough fruit and veg to open your own market stall.

In my haste to be healthy, I neglected to put in our weekly supermarket order. So, the only food that arrives is my super healthy, super green, super leafy veg collection. This is closely followed by the arrival of my Nutribullet (with extra cups, because I am going to be SO virtuous) by a smiling delivery man.

I can't actually see that he is smiling, for the record. I'm still in bed. But I can hear his cheery banter from where I lie, half dead. I can hear everything. I have woken with the kind of supersonic hearing that only comes with the mother of all hangovers. I can hear our next-door neighbours breathing. I can hear the flap of the wings of the little sparrow flying thirty feet above our house. I can hear the way Mr Delivery Man's facial muscles move and contort themselves into a smile. I can hear colours.

I can hear the beads of alcoholic sweat form in my pores and squeeze their way out of my dehydrated, shrivelled and wrinkled body. With superhuman effort, I unpeel my tongue from the top of the mouth and open my eyes.

I almost shit myself when once again I come face to face with an extreme close-up version of Jax, whose nose is touching mine, his sweet baby breath warm on my face.

'Mammy smell yucky,' he mutters, pulling a face before clambering off the bed, running to his room and returning to throw a clean nappy in my face. 'There go!' he says, climbing up again. Great, so I smell like a dirty nappy.

'Are you sick, Mammy?' I hear Nathan's voice and push through the pain of moving my head to see him standing at the door, his eyes wide with concern.

I try to speak, but little more than a whisper comes out. I remember, vaguely, scream-singing to Gwen Stefani's 'Hollaback Girl' last night, among other things. I have broken my voice. BANANAS indeed.

'Naw,' I hear a sullen-voiced Gemma. 'She's not sick. She's hungover.'

'What's that?' Nathan adds.

'Too much wine,' Gemma says, her voice thick with disgust. 'So we'll have to spend the day checking there are no more videos of her online, shaming us all.'

Nathan looks from Gemma to me while Jax does his best to make me throw up by bouncing up and down on my tummy. 'But it's Saturday, Mammy – 'member you said we could go to the Bounce House on Saturday.'

Dear Jesus, I did. I did promise him that come Saturday we would indeed go to the Bounce House – the black hole of craic for parents on their own. It's actually a soft play centre with trampolines and bouncy castles and children who have lost the ability to speak in any volume other than deafening roar. It's hot. It's sweaty. It always smells of a heady mix of smelly feet, Fruit Shoots and vomit, and the only thing a parent can console themselves with during the hour their child is going buck mental is a lukewarm cup of beige coffee in a polystyrene cup.

I cannot adequately express how much I regret my decision to promise this trip today.

'Where's your dad?' I croak.

'Downstairs, trying to figure out why you ordered twenty-eight carrots and four bags of celery. He says you don't even like celery.'

'For smoothies,' I say.

'Aye, good luck keeping that down,' Gemma says, lifting Jax off me and ushering both him and Nathan downstairs. 'Let's give Mammy peace to get ready for all that bouncing.' She sing-songs at them. I hear the glee in her voice. The joy that comes from knowing she has thrown me to the wolves. That child of mine has a streak in her that scares me sometimes. I only hope she decides to use her powers for good.

I'm going to have to drag myself out of bed and into clothes and into a noisy, sweaty dungeon of a place while I feel so hungover it wouldn't be hard to believe that I'm actually in my last hours on earth.

I have to do that while feeling a deep sense of shame that my children have seen me in this state – again – mixed with a deep state of fear that there might indeed be photographic evidence of my busting some moves from last night. And God . . . did Paul and I fall out? I can't quite remember, but I sense all is not well between us. The fear is a killer and I pull the duvet up over my head to try and block it, and all the noise around me, out. As it turns out this is a huge mistake as under the duvet smells even less fragrant than the rest of the room.

Gasping for fresh air, I emerge from my duvet cocoon and try my best to fight the urge to sleep. My head is sore, and my stomach is sick and I feel that special kind of hyper emotion that only comes with a hangover. Yup, there's the hangxiety. It seems last night was only the pre-game. She's here for the party now. I drink the tepid water from the pint glass by the bed, sit up, and lift my phone. Parts of last night are worryingly hazy. I believe there was twerking. Possibly an attempt or two at a slutdrop, which for the record I can still do like a boss. I'm just not so good at the slut-get-back-up these days. There may have also been swearing, and rapping.

Images of disembodied heads float in and out of my mind. People laughing and chatting and singing and maybe a tearful conversation in the loos. I can't remember if I was the tearful one or if it was some other poor unfortunate soul. I have a very vague recollection of a rap battle with Jacinta.

I figure if I'd done anything truly awful – like the kind of awful that would have Gemma pack my bags for me and yeet me out the front door – my phone would be buzzing with notifications. As it happens, and much to my relief, there is only one. And it's from Eva.

> Morning Tara. Quick note to apologize for last night. We're not usually quite that loud, or drunk. Swear! Hope we didn't put you off.

So far, so good, I think. It definitely sounds as if I have nothing to be wanting to fake my own death over. Phew! I read on.

> Please apologize to those lovely girls from your work for us gatecrashing their night out. I think we might have mentally scarred them!

Shit.

Eva has added three rolling-about-laughing emojis and one embarrassed emoji and I don't know whether to laugh or cry. The girls from my work? I have no memory of meeting them – or maybe I do. Something niggles at the back of my mind. It's just a whisper of a conversation and I can't remember the details, but I think I'm starting to remember seeing Molly. Or maybe it was Amy. I can't trust my brain right now. I need caffeine and carbs and paracetamol too. A bacon bap would be the absolute dream, but then I remember I've not ordered bacon, or baps. Superfood super mum ordered fucking kale and spinach. I want to cry.

I weigh up which would be worse, messaging Eva back to ask her what exactly happened with the girls from work, or messaging one of them and pre-emptively apologizing in a general enough fashion that it covers a multitude of sins.

I opt for the first scenario, trying my very best to word it in such a way that hides my absolute panic from Eva.

> Had a great night. Feeling it this morning. LOL. Some details are a bit hazy – can you remind me what we talked to the girls from work about?

She messages back almost immediately: Things are a bit hazy here too. I think you showed them the slide video, a couple of times as it happens. And then we started on the birth stories . . .

Oh Christ.

> Just make sure to tell them it's all worth it in the end when you get your baby handed to you. You know, the usual bullshit. You forget about the pain blah blah blah . . .

All I wish in this moment is that I could forget about the pain in my head right now. It feels as if my brain is actively trying to burrow its way out of my eye sockets.

I send Eva a smiley face and a heart to pretend I'm not living slap bang in the centre of the horrors. Why is it that I can't seem to take two steps forward these days without promptly taking four steps back straight after?

I must atone for my sins, so I haul myself out of bed and into the shower before dressing in my most comfortable, and definitely not fashionable, joggers and a T-shirt. If I could get away with wearing my jammies and fluffy dressing gown, I would, but there's been enough embarrassment for my family recently.

I plaster a smile on my face as I walk downstairs to find my three children watching TV.

'Can we go now, Mammy?' Nathan asks, and I note he already has his socks, trainers and jacket on. Jax is similarly attired.

'I packed the baby bag,' Gemma says. 'Nappies and juice and snacks.'

'Can we have fizzy juice at the Bounce House?' Nathan asks, his eyes already wide at the very thought of a sugar hit.

'Not sure, wee man,' I tell him. 'Will we wait and see?'

'I want fizzy juice and chicken nuggets,' he says defiantly, and I get the impression he has been prepped for this moment by Gemma. Well, two can play that particular game.

'Are you coming too?' I ask her. 'I'm sure your brothers would love for you to play with them.'

'Ah Mammy, I would, but I've an extra homework project on this weekend and you always tell me schoolwork has to come first,' she says with a shrug. There are times, I think, when I see my own dastardly ways playing out in front of me and I want to phone my own mammy and apologize to her. Well played, karma.

'That's a shame,' I say.

'I know,' she says, 'maybe next time.'

'Can we go now, Mammy?' Nathan asks, pulling at my leg and trying to push me in the direction of the door.

'In a wee minute,' I tell him. 'Mammy needs a coffee.'

'Ah, Mammy. I made you a smoothie,' Gemma trills. 'I hope you don't mind me using the blender thingy, but I looked up the best smoothie to detox a hangover and we had all the ingredients so I thought that might be better for you.' She darts from the room and returns looking proud as punch with a large cup filled with a greenish, brownish sludge not dissimilar to the kind of poo emergency level-ten Jax had been known to produce as a lactose-intolerant infant.

'Hmmm,' I say. 'Looks yummy.' Every cell in my body is telling me to get as far away from this sludge as possible, but Gemma is looking at me with a combination of anticipation and excitement. She can't wait to see my reaction to this. I cannot show her weakness. Not now. Flipping the lid open I very gingerly put it to my lips, only wishing I'd been as reserved as this with the Prosecco last night, and I take a long, slightly lumpy, definitely foul swig.

'It has antioxidant qualities, and is good for cleansing your liver. It's also supposed to be good for hormones, you know, in older ladies,' she says, and I realize she is actually trying to be nice, in her own twisted teenage way. She *is* trying to help, even if I do want to smack her up the side of the head for referring to me as an older lady.

I give her a thumbs up because I don't feel brave enough

to open my mouth to speak in case I do an *Exorcist* and spew everywhere.

'Let's go, let's go, let's go!' Nathan is now shouting, much too loudly, while hopping up and down, and Jax has decided to join in with the noise. If I'm hoping Paul will swoop in from the kitchen to rescue me, I'm in for a rude awakening.

'Where's your dad?' I ask.

'Gone to the supermarket to get some proper food,' Gemma says. 'I'd better go and start my homework.' And she leaves me there with two very hyper children, a very serious hangover and a bucket of bile to drink.

25

Shove your organic parenting up your hole, Janice

In Dante's epic, *Inferno*, he describes the nine circles of hell. I have no doubt in my mind whatsoever that if Dante was alive in the year 2021 there would be a tenth circle of hell and it would be the Bounce House on the Derry ring road on a Saturday morning. Even without a hangover it's a feat of endurance. With a hangover, it's like the Hunger Games with ball pits.

I'd like to go find a table in the darkest, least populated corner of the play centre, but generally it's frowned upon these days to allow your two-year-old and five-year-old to run about without any supervision whatsoever. So, I am confined to the least comfortable bench in the world in the 'tiny tots' area of the Bounce House. I have to watch as Nathan and Jax fling themselves down slides and throw balls at each other screaming 'Look at me, Mammy!' every seven seconds. They're not happy simply to have me look at them though. They want reassurance they are the best boys, and so clever, and I've never seen anyone throw a ball as well as they have – and they want that reassurance constantly. It's hard to keep up that level of enthusiasm on the seventy-fifth toss of a ball. I watch as other mammies sip from those fancy coffee carry cups they've picked up in fancy coffee shops on their way here and fight the urge to beg them for one wee sip.

I have to be strong. I have to continue with my penance and my detox, so I sip from my cup of bile as frequently as I can without being sick.

'Oh, are you doing one of those cleanses?' a super-smiley mammy who is bouncing a very cute, very compliant baby girl on her knee, says to me.

I nod. 'Yeah, trying to look after myself, you know.'

'You're brave,' she says. 'I've been meaning to try one of those, you know, to shift the baby weight.'

Super Smiley Mammy is a size eight at most. I nod.

'I've a friend who did one and lost like a full stone in a week,' she says. 'Says she never felt better and she wasn't even hungry while doing it. Said she spent a lot of time on the loo, mind. It really does cleanse everything, if you get my meaning.'

I nod, vaguely aware of a slight rumble in my stomach which I'm sure can't possibly be related to what I've had of the smoothie so far. Surely it can't work that fast?

'Do you find it hard, doing the prep?' she asks. 'My friend said she felt like she never stopped chopping veg, but I spend so much time preparing food for Flora here that I'm always in the kitchen anyway. Doesn't take much to do a few more than usual. Did yours take long?'

'Erm, actually, my daughter made it for me.'

'Oooh, aren't you lucky? Hopefully, one day little Flora here will be as kind to me. I'm really hoping she develops my love for healthy eating and living as organically as possible. Did you do baby-led weaning with yours? That's what we're doing with Flora. It's so important to give them a real sense of self and independence. I want her to have a really varied diet, you know. It's so important to open her up to as many different tastes and textures as possible. Apart from flesh, of course.'

She smiles really brightly at the word *flesh*, which makes me suspect she may be a serial killer in disguise who harvests scummy-mummy kidneys in her bathroom.

'Flesh?' I ask, the word making the bile rise to my throat.

'We don't eat anything with a face,' she says. 'Meat is murder, don't you think? I mean, what kind of a planet are we leaving for our children if we're teaching them it's OK to eat other mammals? We're all equal in the eyes of God, you know. And my goodness, the impact of factory farming on global warming . . .'

I nod because I don't have the energy to do anything but nod. Jesus, this woman is a grade-A dick; I cannot cope.

'As soon as we started trying to get pregnant, I cut out all non-organic, processed food. I stopped putting all poisons in my body. You know, alcohol, caffeine, anything that isn't plant-based.'

'Plant-based?' I ask.

'Yeah. Vegan. But I'm not one of those really annoying vegans. I mean, I'm not being preachy, but we're determined it should be only the best for Flora.'

I look at my children, throwing themselves down the slide without fear of injury while screaming 'I'm gonna get you, sucka!' at the top of their lungs in a fake American accent.

'It's fascinating really. Have you heard of attachment parenting? Our children are so intuitive, we really should listen to their wants and needs more. I mean, so many people have children today and don't put in the proper effort with them. So many are raised by iPads and YouTube. Can you imagine?'

Clearly, Smiley Mammy does not read people very well. One look at me, or indeed my children, would tell anyone watching that I'm a firm fan of the old iPad. I'd give anything to be handing them out to the kids now, at home, while I die properly on the sofa. The gurgle in my stomach is now definitely more a rumble and it is moving downwards. Fast.

'It's the very least we can do, don't you think?' Smiley Mammy witters on. 'You can't be selfish when you have children. I've no time for mammies who take the lazy approach. You understand?'

I nod and smile. Cramps are now kicking in and I know, instinctively, it's not worth trying to take a chance on it being just a quiet fart that needs releasing. OK, karma, I get your point. Have a night on the lash and make me pay for it by leaving me to fear shitting myself in front of the ultimate sancta-mummy.

She's launched into a monologue on gender identity in toddlers when my stomach rumbles so loudly that it wakes a baby in a car seat by the next table. It stares at me, big startled blue eyes, and I want to say, 'Baby, you shit yourself every day. You're not one to judge.'

I need to make an emergency exit.

''Scuse me,' I say, with a saccharine (agave?) smile. 'BOYS. Do you want a drink?' They jump and run to me, their faces red and hair damp with sweat. Nathan digs into my bag and pulls out two Fruit Shoots and hands them to me to open for him and Jax.

Smiley Mammy is no longer smiling. She is looking at me as if I'm drawing up a couple of syringes to inject heroin directly into their veins. Well, I may be hungover, I may be feeling emotionally vulnerable and I may be about a minute away from losing control of my bowels, but that isn't going to stop me from striking a blow for the good, doing our very best imperfect mammies of the world.

'Right, boys,' I say. 'Let's get our shoes on, and then how about we go and get some chicken nuggets on the way home?'

They whoop and cheer. 'Mammy, can I have my tablet in the car?' Nathan asks, while I hand a now tired Jax his dummy. (I'm fully expecting Smiley Mammy to have a stroke at this stage.)

'Course you can, sweetheart,' I tell him, and he cheers, then downs his Fruit Shoot as if his very life depended on it, handing me the empty bottle and letting out a very loud but contented burp. ''Scuse me,' he laughs. 'My mouth did a fart.'

Smiley Mammy is edging away from me on her seat, as if she is worried she might catch 'normal' from my two. I ignore her while I get the boys into their shoes, then I lift Jax, who snuggles against my shoulder, and take Nathan's hand. My bum cheeks clenched as tight as I have ever clenched them, I turn to Smiley Mammy. 'I love my children as much as any mammy loves their children. And here they are, content, happy and healthy. Raise your children how you see fit, but don't tell other mammies they're doing it wrong.'

With my head held high, I waddle as fast as I can to the loos and all hell breaks loose. Thankfully my boys both seem to be at a stage where they find diarrhoea, and the associated noises coming from my body, hilarious.

Twenty minutes later, we arrive at McDonald's, where I buy them both Happy Meals and finally give in to my need for caffeine and allow myself a huge coffee. It is probably the nicest coffee I have ever tasted in my entire life and I swear I can feel my bruised and battered body start to come back to life with each sip. The rumbles are back to being gurgles. The worst is over. I hope.

Now I just have to repair the rest of the damage done last night. First up, I text the girls from work:

I hope youse had a great night, feels so good to let your hair down doesn't it? Those other mums I was with are sooo much fun, and honestly, you should pay no heed to what we were saying. You'll understand in time (or not!), if you become mums yourselves.

One by one they text me back with variations of 'You go, mama! We were lashed too, can't remember a blessed thing this morning – but go you for living your best life and enjoying yourself!'

I get a warm fuzzy feeling from it: maybe I should try cutting them some slack. After all, it's hardly their fault that they are young, gorgeous, single and talented. And it's possible I was equally as cocky and entitled when I was in my twenties (although, given that I was a mother at twenty-three, I don't think I ever had the time to be cocky and entitled about anything). I accept it's possible I've been judging them harshly – too harshly – all along. I've been judging them in the same way Smiley Mammy was judging me and people like me.

I'm feeling as if a weight is lifting from my shoulders when Nathan, his face clattered in ketchup as if he has forgotten where his mouth is, tugs at my sleeve. 'Mammy, Mammy, them boys and girls are looking at you and laughing.'

I follow Nathan's gaze to where a group of four vaguely familiar-looking teenagers are sitting slurping milkshakes, looking at their phones, then at me, and they are indeed laughing.

Well, they've picked the wrong day to mess with me. This mama is taking no shite.

'Excuse me, but is there something you want to say to me? Maybe you might want to tell me what's so funny?' I call to them, getting up and walking across to their table.

I sort of expect them to shut up, look embarrassed and leave me alone. That's what I'd have done as a teenager. I might even have burst into tears at the thought I might be in trouble with a grown-up.

But this particular lot have grown up in a very different time. They don't automatically defer to their elders (not that I like to think of myself as an elder). They look at me, open-mouthed for a moment and then one of them points his phone at me and I don't know if he is taking a picture or recording a video.

The girl opposite him, with tumbling red hair that honestly has no place on a teenager and would look much better on me, snorts. I swear I know that snort from somewhere, but I can't quite place it. Meanwhile the second lad in their group straightens himself up and, with a face you wouldn't get tired of slapping, says to me, 'We're just enjoying our drinks . . . Karen!'

That's enough for all of them to descend into laughter. Well, if they are expecting that pointing a phone in my direction, and calling me the worst name a woman can be called at the moment is going to shut me up, they have another think coming. My ass stuck to a slide has already been all over the internet and I've already faced down a Smug Mum today. Asking some teenagers to have manners is nothing in comparison.

'My son, over there, has noticed you pointing and laughing, and I've always taught him it's not very nice to point and laugh at people. He understands it, and he's five years old.

Clearly you lot don't. So if something is funny, why not share it with the group?'

'Chill your boots, Karen,' the same lad who spoke before says again. Curly Red Hair is laughing and the fella with the camera is still pointing at me. The fourth member of their group at least has the sense to look embarrassed by the actions of her friends. She has her hood pulled up round her face and seems to only be interested in whatever is happening on her phone.

'First of all, my name is not Karen,' I tell him. 'Second of all, my boots are perfectly chilled. Now if you have nothing to say outside of calling me names, then I'd ask you to mind your own business and leave me and my children alone.'

'But it is you, isn't it?' the smart-arse with the camera asks. 'You're Slidey Arse.' Curly Red Hair is now in fits of laughter and I'm wondering if I'd have the strength to take out both her and the smug article who called me Karen.

'Slidey arse?' I ask.

'Yeah, from the meme. You're famous.' Curly Red Hair turns her phone towards me and shows me a full page of memes featuring stills of me, stuck halfway down a slide, with various facial expressions of mortification captured at different moments of my humiliation. It dawns on me that this is exactly where I know these youngsters from.

'And you'd know exactly why that was, wouldn't you?' I ask.

'No need to get your knickers in a twist,' the smug one grins. 'It's only a bit of a laugh.'

'Yeah, boomer! Are you not able to take a joke?' the smart-arse with the camera chimes in. 'You've gone viral. Everyone is talking about it.'

Curly Red Hair is still laughing, verging on hysterical now. The hooded one still has her eyes locked on her phone. I glance down and spot something familiar on her screen. It's a picture of Gemma, and her friends, taken on the night of her sleepover.

'Erm, why do you have a picture of my daughter on your phone?' I ask. Smug, Smart-Arse and Curly Red Hair stop laughing. The girl in the hoodie tilts her head up towards me, and I know I probably shouldn't but I do anyway. I pull the hoodie back from her face and I realize the reason Curly Red Hair was laughing so much was probably down to sheer nerves. Because I recognize Hoodie Girl immediately.

'Mia?' I say, staring at my daughter's best friend. 'You've been involved in this? Posting my video online?'

'It was only a joke, Mrs Gallagher,' she mumbles, her face blazing red.

'But you knew that Gemma was getting a hard time in school about it. Does Gemma know you were there?'

She looks at me but doesn't speak. I see tears well in her eyes and I don't know what's making me feel worse – that I've made this wee girl, who has been in and out of my house since she was five years old, cry – or that this same wee girl who my daughter loves has been involved in her humiliation by posting the video of me online for everyone to see.

'I'm really disappointed in you,' is all I can come up with.

I turn on my heel and go back to where Jax has now smeared tomato ketchup all over his high chair. With as much dignity as I can muster, I give the boys and their surrounds a quick clean and we head for home.

As we walk out of McDonalds, I can't help but notice the teenagers have stopped laughing. Well, good enough for the wee bastards. Now, what do I tell Gemma?

26

They messed with the wrong mammy

'Is Gemma in?' I ask as I carry Jax, now fast asleep, through the front door, with Nathan following behind, his head buried in his tablet. I can hear some very loud, very excited American children screaming in whatever YouTube video he is watching.

Paul takes Jax from me and lays him down on the sofa, while I remind Nathan we got him headphones for a reason. It's a conversation we have many times a day, but that's what life is like in this house. Routine and repetition; no fuss, just a nice familiarity. I feel a wave of emotion and realize I have moved on from 'The Fear' to 'The Great Sorrow' stage of my hangover.

Because, while this is a well-rehearsed routine, I know there is a tension bubbling underneath it. Paul has told me where Gemma is (in her room, allegedly doing her homework) but he has made no joke about her. There has been no 'will miracles never cease' banter from him. His voice is flat. Not rude, but just, you know, not like him. He has not asked me if I need a drink after the Bounce House or if, on a scale of bit rubbish to total shitshow, where the experience fell on the horrible things about parenting chart.

'We need to have a chat with her,' I tell him. 'And I think it's going to be a bit sensitive.'

I have his attention now. 'What kind of sensitive?' he asks. 'She's not smoking or drinking, is she? Jesus, tell me she's not on drugs! Or . . . or . . . Tara, is Gemma pregnant?'

'Keep those words out of your mouth!' I tell him. 'No. Jesus. No. She's not pregnant. She's only thirteen, Paul. She hasn't even kissed a boy yet.'

'Are you sure?'

'Well,' I shrug. 'I can't be one hundred per cent sure, but I think she would tell me. We're not as close as we were but she still talks to me sometimes and the last time we had a heart-to-heart she had a crush on Adam from her old primary school but was too shy to tell him.'

'And when was that? Because she's been out of primary school a wee while now.'

'About three weeks ago,' I tell him. 'So I very much doubt in the intervening time she has had the chance to woo him, seduce him *and have sex with him.*' I whisper the last few words because the very thought of my baby even thinking about having sex any time in like, maybe the next seventeen years, is too much to take.

'So, what do we have to talk to her about?' Paul asks.

I usher him into the kitchen – which is now stocked with

an assortment of fine carbs and the kind of processed food that would send Smiley Mammy from the Bounce House into a full-on Facebook rant. I open a bag of Wotsits and stuff a handful in my mouth.

'I thought you were doing a juice cleanse?' he asks, one eyebrow raised.

'I am,' I spit through orange, sticky lips, and I pour the rest of the bag of Wotsits into the Nutribullet. After all, they can't make the smoothies taste any worse. They might even be an improvement.

'Look,' I say as I load a banana, chopped pear, strawberries and orange juice into the blender. 'We went to McDonalds after the Bounce House. There's a story behind that, by the way. I'll fill you in later. Anyway, we went to McDonalds, and I was drinking a coffee and the boys were creating modern art with red sauce on everything but their nuggets. Then, get this, Nathan tells me that there are group of teenagers pointing and laughing at us.'

'So, knowing that teenagers are mostly dicks, you ignored them, helped the boys and then came home?' he asks, knowing full well that is absolutely not what I did.

'Almost,' I lie. 'Look, I went to talk to them and they called me Karen and started filming me . . .'

'Oh Jesus, Tara, don't tell me there'll be another video of you doing the rounds? I don't think Gemma will cope.'

I shake my head. 'No, I don't think there will be another video. You see, when I got closer I realized they were the same teenagers who had filmed me at the park.'

'Did you kill them? Is the sensitive issue that the peelers are about to land here and lift you for murder?' he asks.

I shake my head. 'No,' I tell him. 'It's worse than that.'

'How on earth can it be worse than murder?' he asks.

I pause from chopping and peeling and point at him (which is definitely a bad idea as I've still got the knife in my hand). 'Because, sitting with them – as part of their group – was Mia.'

'Mia? Gemma's Mia?'

I nod.

'And had she been at the park when the slide video was made?'

I shrug. 'I can't say for sure. I don't know. She had a hoodie on today, and there was one of them in a big hoodie on Thursday. So, here's the deal, she has been party to this video being posted online – and she'd have known that Gemma would've got stick about it. She didn't stop them, Paul. So she didn't stand up for her best friend.'

'And you think Gemma knows?' he asks.

'Does Gemma know what?'

Between the chopping and the peeling and the noise of the blender I haven't heard Gemma come down the stairs, which is just fan-bloody-tastic.

Paul and I turn to see her looking young, fresh-faced, innocent and very, very confused. I'm so used to her bringing shedloads of attitude for every interaction that seeing her looking vulnerable is like a stab to my heart. She may be a teenager, but she is still a child. She is still only thirteen. She's still finding her way. Can it really be the case that her best friend is making her life more difficult? Has Gemma been extra challenging because of something more than the usual teenager hormones?

'Sweetheart,' I say. ''Mon over and sit down a wee minute.'

She looks between us and her brow furrows further. 'Am I in trouble?'

'God, no,' Paul says. 'It's nothing like that. Here, let me get you a drink or something.'

'Daddy, can you just tell me what it is I might or might not know, please? Youse are freaking me out.'

'Pet,' I say, glancing at the smoothie in the blender and really, really regretting throwing the Wotsits into it. 'Is everything OK between you and Mia these days?'

She bristles a wee bit and my mama bear instincts kick up a gear. 'Aye,' she says, but she doesn't meet my eye. 'For defs.'

'Really?' I ask.

Gemma shrugs. Paul takes a seat at the table too and reaches across to take her hand. To my surprise she doesn't pull away, which is her standard reaction to any physical contact these days. 'You'd tell us, wouldn't you? If something was wrong or anyone was bothering you?' he asks.

She looks down at the table and nods, but I'm getting serious 'things are not OK' vibes. Sure enough I see a single tear plop onto the table and watch as she drags her sleeve across her face to mop up the flurry that follows.

'Pet,' I say gently, 'I know she was involved in posting the video of me on the slide.'

'I had nothing to do with that, swear,' Gemma says, looking

up at me, panic on her face. Does she really think I'd believe she had been in on it all along?

'I know that, dote,' I say. 'But you knew Mia did?'

She nods. 'She sent me the link after it was posted. It wasn't her, but it was one of her new friends that did it. She's got some new pals and I'm not cool enough to be part of that gang.'

I think of the cluster of arrogant wee shites in McDonalds, with their bad attitudes and total lack of respect, and I want to scream.

'I saw her with some new people today,' I say. 'A girl with long, curly hair? Two boys?'

She nods. 'The girl is Sorcha. She's in our class in school. Mr Devine paired her and Mia up in Science and they've become pure besties. Mia never shuts up about her, Mammy. Everything is always about Sorcha and how Sorcha is so cool and isn't afraid of anything. They've been hanging out together after school and at the weekends. I asked to come along but Mia says I would be bored. That Sorcha and her friends are not into the same things I am. And Mia likes one of those boys and Sorcha is kissing the other. So I'd just be a spare part anyway.'

I'm not sure which emotion is stronger in me right now. It could be sadness, seeing that my daughter is clearly upset and going through the agony of outgrowing a friendship, which at thirteen, is worse than any heartbreak could be. But I'm also angry. Like, Incredible Hulk levels of angry. How DARE anyone not like my daughter? Yes, she can be a right royal pain in the hole, and I've wanted to throttle her more times than enough of late, but that's OK: I'm her mammy. I'm allowed to feel that way, because ultimately, I love her.

'You're so much more than a spare part,' I tell her, breaking down and pulling her tight while we both sob. Poor Paul is looking completely traumatized at this stage. Here are the two females in the house bawling and he's not sure what to do about it. But I get it, you see. I get that fear of being pushed aside because it's exactly how I've been feeling with Gemma this last while. That we are the ones growing apart. That I am surplus to requirements. I know how that hits.

'I begged Mia to take the video down,' Gemma sobs. 'I said she knew what school was like and how people would pick on me. I even told her that it was cruel of them and that you didn't deserve to be embarrassed like that. You've been really kind to her, Mammy.'

My heart swells again with love. Seriously, she is killing me right now.

'But she wouldn't. She said she wasn't going to be called a snowflake or have Sorcha and the boys fall out with her over it. She said it was only a joke and I need to lighten up instead of being such a borebag.' Her words are coming out between great, heaving sobs now. 'She said . . . she said . . . it was no wonder no one wanted to hang around with me, 'cos I'm a total gimp. But she knew, Mammy, she knew that everyone would laugh at me. She just didn't care as long as Sorcha didn't fall out with her. You should've seen her after my birthday. She was telling everyone about you trying to teach us that dance routine and—'

'Whoa there one minute,' I say, raising my hand to stop her. 'She was telling people about that? What . . . why?' I've always liked Mia, but right now I'd drop-kick that child into the middle of nowhere.

Gemma shrugs. 'To get a laugh. She tells people all the time that I'm a big baby and not cool. Because I do my homework instead of going to the park after school. And Sorcha saw a picture I'd posted of me and you on my Snapchat, so she said I was a wee mammy's girl. Then Sorcha had her thirteenth birthday and I wasn't invited – which I was OK with because I don't like her. But Mia told me Sorcha's mammy and daddy went out and then Sorcha had a bottle of vodka they were all drinking.'

Vodka! Jeez, teenagers are hardcore these days. I was fifteen when I had my first drink, and the worst me and my friends did was neck a bottle of cider up on Derry's Walls. We eased our way into an unhealthy relationship with alcohol like every good teenager out on the sesh; we wouldn't have touched spirits. We couldn't have afforded spirits! Certainly not at fifteen and absolutely not at thirteen.

'Have you had a drink with them at all?' Paul asks. 'You're not in trouble if you did, but if you're going to drink, I'd rather we were all open about it.'

Gemma shakes her head. 'No. I swear. I don't want to drink. Not yet anyway. I think it's disgusting.' She grimaces. 'Remember when I was eleven and I sneaked a taste of your wine? Why would anyone drink that and say it was nice?'

Feeling personally attacked, I'm about to launch into a

heartfelt defence of wine and why anyone would drink it and why they would say it was nice when I stop myself. This is not the time.

'Anyway, then it was my birthday and I didn't invite Sorcha because she's a . . .' Gemma pauses, and I can tell she is trying to think of an acceptable way to describe Sorcha in front of her parents.

'Bitch, pet,' I finish for her. 'Sorcha is a bitch.'

'Tara,' Paul's voice is soft. 'Language.'

'She is though, Daddy. And I know that's a horrible word and we're all supposed to be mad into the sisterhood, but she's not nice. At all.'

Paul nods. Huh, that battle was easy won.

'So, I didn't invite her and she was really angry about it and started telling everyone it was because it was a child's tea-party and there was only so much ice cream and jelly to go round and it would be rubbish anyway. Mia didn't stand up for me then either. She said she didn't want to get stuck in the middle and Sorcha was still angry with her for going. So I think that's why, after the party, she told her about the dance routine and how there was no vodka, or any drink, at my party, and that you were wearing your pyjamas and had put balloons and streamers up everywhere as if I was five.'

'But you were still speaking to her?' Paul says. 'You went to Starbucks with her yesterday?'

Gemma nods. 'She goes there with Sorcha on Fridays now. So I went to try and talk to them and get them to take the video down. Have you read the comments, Mammy?'

The truth is, after the first hour or so, where the comments were mostly OMG. *I would die* or *Ha ha ha, that's so funny*, I didn't. I didn't see the need to pick at that particular plaster, but maybe I should now.

Paul is already scrolling through his phone and I can see his Hulk-like anger growing. 'Oh Gemma,' he says as he hands me the phone. I'm fully expecting to see a long list of *Look at her fat ass* type comments but instead it's a long line of comments tagging Gemma into 'Yo Mama' jokes, telling her she's a sad case (as am I) and taking the piss.

27

Shit happens

As an adult, I can take my fair share of shite. Yes, I can have the occasional breakdown but I'm only human and hormones are bastards of the highest order. As an adult I can see bullying for what it is: some insecure, horrible person targeting someone else to make themselves feel good.

But I know that as a teenager – especially one who is finding her own way – it feels like the end of the world. It feels real and personal and justified. Well, there isn't a hope in hell I'm going to let this go on. Taking a big gulp of my smoothie, then remembering the manky Wotsits, I gag. No, I need coffee for this. Juice cleanse be gone. It's time for the hard stuff.

I pop a new pod in the coffee machine and down two paracetamol with a glass of water. 'Just give me a minute to try and get my head around this, love,' I say.

And it's times like these I realize again how well the tag

team of Paul and I work as parents. When I need to step out of the ring, he is there to step in.

'Gemma, things can get messy in your teenage years and the sad truth is not all friendships last forever. No matter how much they have meant to us,' Paul says. 'And that's especially true when you're younger and trying to figure out who you are and what you want from life. But here's the deal, love. Friends don't put each other down. Friends stand by each other. It's OK for people to grow apart. It's sad, but it happens. What's not OK is for people to be really shitty to someone just to try and make themselves look big and clever.'

'But I thought we'd be best friends forever,' Gemma sniffs, and I know this is breaking her heart. I wish I could take her pain away and put it on me.

'I know, darlin',' Paul soothes. 'And look, maybe the pair of you will come through it and she will realize she's made a huge mistake and you are absolutely one hundred times cooler than this Sorcha person.'

'You have to say that, you're my daddy,' Gemma says through a watery smile.

'I don't have to say anything,' he says. 'But it's true. You're a good person. You're a pain in the arse some of the time, but we'll cut you some slack because being thirteen is hard.'

'It's the worst,' I chime in. 'There's so much going on in your body, and in your head and sometimes it feels as if everything is shifting under your feet, but it does get easier. Things have a habit of working out.'

Even as I say the words, I have a moment of doubt. Things

don't always work out. You won't always be happy. You won't always get the promotion you deserve. You might find yourself a viral sensation for all the wrong reasons. You might find yourself in your mid thirties with a thirteen-year-old daughter who thinks you are totally cringe too. I wish I could protect her from it. But I've only made it worse. I've left her embarrassed and vulnerable to bullies.

The coffee machine gurgles and splutters and I add some milk and come back to the table. 'Look, your dad is right. I'm sorry if what I've done has added to this. I never meant to be a source of embarrassment, but we all get it wrong from time to time. Or we all get it right, but someone else doesn't vibe with our sense of humour. You know, I'm learning about this all myself too. I've never had a thirteen-year-old daughter before. This is all new to me too, and things are so different for your generation than they were for mine. We didn't have the internet, or Snapchat, or Instagram or whatever to deal with, thank God.'

Gemma looks horrified. Truly horrified. 'How did you cope?' she asks, eyes wide, as if I've told her I grew up during a zombie apocalypse where we had to eat weaker family members in order to survive.

'We just did. We never had it, so we didn't miss it. I know you won't believe this, Gemma, but the sky didn't fall in and the world didn't crash around our ears. It was easier then, in a lot of ways. Things weren't as pressurized,' I say.

'I still don't think I'd like it,' she sniffs. 'Like, youse didn't have Shein or anything for clothes shopping?'

'We went to a clothes shop,' I say slowly. 'There was no such thing as big online retailers. You went up the town and into a shop and you bought something there. Or maybe your mammy would send off for something from the catalogue.'

She shakes her head. 'That sounds awful.'

'It was grand. It wasn't like we were living through the famine or a pandemic. And we still had Primark, only everyone called it Pree-mark back then.'

'Youse are all mad,' she says with a sniff and a smile, and I suppose part of me is glad to see the Gemma I know so well come back into the conversation. The Gemma who thinks I'm ancient, who would actually die without Shein and ASOS, and would have her phone surgically attached to her hand if she thought she could get away with it.

'Sure there's nothing wrong with being a bit mad,' I tell her. 'All the best people are, isn't that right?' I look to Paul, who nods in agreement.

'But look, see what's going on with Mia? I'm willing to bet she's just trying on different personalities to see what fits. She might grow away from you, or she might come back. Hopefully, she will wake up to how nasty Sorcha is and distance herself.'

'I don't know if we could ever be friends again anyway. She's been so mean about you, Mammy,' Gemma says, and her lip is trembling again. 'She didn't have to post that video online.'

'No,' I say, shaking my head. 'She didn't have to post it. And she should've fought to get it taken down when you were upset by it. But if you're thinking Sorcha, or Mia, or any one of their

265

gang are making me feel bad? Not a bit! So what if I got stuck on a slide? I was playing with your wee brother at the time. And see, trying to teach you dance routines? I was only trying to have the craic with you all. If that's what makes someone want to embarrass me or you, then they're the weirdoes, not us. There's a wee saying round here that I wouldn't normally say in front of you, but in this instance I think it's allowed: up her hole, with a big jam roll.'

Paul splutters his coffee over the table while Gemma looks on, not sure whether she's supposed to express shock and horror at my turn of phrase or laugh at it.

'Look, in this life there is always going to be a Sorcha waiting in the wings. Sometimes, ignoring them is enough to make them go away. Sometimes, you have to fight back. But what you always have to do is hold your head high and be proud of who you are!'

I feel as if I've just delivered the equivalent of Bill Pullman's speech as the president in *Independence Day*. If only there was a Will Smith to sidle in here and kick ass with me.

'Thank you, Mammy,' Gemma says. 'And Daddy. I love you.'

'To the moon and back,' I say, squeezing her hand and enjoying this rarest of moments where she hero-worships me again. It's nice to try that feeling on for a while.

As I vow to think about the very best way to tackle Mia, and the awful Sorcha, Gemma excuses herself to go back up to her bedroom. 'I really am doing some homework,' she says. 'It's an art project. I want to get it just right.'

'OK, love,' I tell her. 'Have fun.'

When she is gone there is a silence between Paul and I as we sip the remains of our coffee. I'm tired now, bone-tired. The kind of tired Morgan Freeman says he is in *Shawshank Redemption* – except *he* didn't have a hangover when he said it. I'd love a wee nap, but I'm acutely aware that I have landed Paul with more than his fair share of parenting duties recently. He deserves a rest too. When I glance up, I see he is looking at me but I can't quite read his expression.

'What is it?' I ask him, suddenly worried I've something on my face or that Nathan has used my T-shirt as a hanky again and I've not realized I'm covered in snot trails.

'Do you really believe what you just told Gemma?' he asks.

'Of course I do!' I tell him.

'That you should hold your head high and always be proud of who you are?' he asks.

I nod. 'Absolutely.'

He sighs. 'Then why are you turning yourself inside out and upside down trying to change who you are?'

'I'm not!' I protest.

'Really, Tara? You've joined a gym, changed your clothes, dyed your hair pink and now you've joined some rebel club . . .'

I shake my head. 'We're not out burning our bras. It's only a group of mammies who are trying to live a little away from their families and their commitments.'

'And their husbands,' he says flatly. It's more of an accusation than a question.

'Wise up, Paul. You know it's not like that.'

'Do I?' he says. 'Do I really know what it's like? Because this last fortnight I don't feel as if I know you at all, Tara.'

'You're being a wee bit dramatic there, Paul,' I say, trying to keep my tone light-hearted but really not liking where this is heading.

'Says the woman with the pink hair and the viral TikTok video,' he says. 'Look, I know that Gemma turning thirteen has been a big deal for you. But she's my baby girl too, you know. I have my own feelings about it. And I know you've been disappointed with work. I know that working and looking after three kids, especially our three kids, is tough going at times but, God, it's not that bad. It's bloody good, if you ask me.'

I shake my head. My hangover is ramping up for the afternoon stealth attack.

'I never said it was bad,' I tell him, the pressure behind my eyes mounting. 'I never said it was about you or the kids, or even work. It's about me, Paul. I know we have a good life. And I feel guilty that it doesn't always make me feel fulfilled in the way it used to. Maybe it's my age. Maybe it's Gemma turning thirteen. Maybe it's still the fallout from Jax's birth. All I know is, like Gemma and Mia and that Sorcha one, I don't really know who I am any more and I want to find the real me.'

'You're right there,' Paul says, looking directly at me. He sounds defeated. 'You're right there, Tara.'

I'm trying to think of what to say when the stomach rumbles return, like any good sequel, with a vengeance. Thanks to the frankly traumatic experience in the Bounce House, I know where this is headed.

'I need to go to the bathroom,' I mutter, wasting no time in rushing towards the downstairs loo, praying that it is empty, the door is open, the toilet seat is up. (It would be sod's law that the one time I need to access the loo as quickly as possible would coincide with the one time anyone but me in our family put the seat down after they used it.)

Here we are in the middle of a huge heart-to-heart and my bowels decide to take themselves swiftly out the back door. Great bloody timing! Thankfully I make it to the loo before all hell in unleashed, but this time there is no one laughing at the humiliating noises my body is making.

28

No one's gonna piss on my parade

The equilibrium at chez Gallagher has not yet returned, and it's a week and a half since the poo-cident put an end to our big heart-to-heart (the Nutribullet has been consigned to the cupboard of gadgets that I thought would change my life but which quickly became redundant; I see you, omelette maker; I see you, pressure cooker; I see you, health grill). Between home and work, we've not had the time, or maybe the courage, to get back into it.

Luke has taken a 'new broom sweeps clean' approach to his team without really knowing how to operate the new broom. I've been biting my tongue when he delegates task after task to me and the other girls that really he should be doing himself. I imagine one day – soon, hopefully – someone will call him out on it, but then again men have been getting away with this shit forever. And although I've made an uneasy peace with it, I'm not going to be the one to dig him out of his own hole.

He's still trying to be my friend though. Still trying to get me to reconsider the 'promotion' he is offering me.

'We do make a great team,' he says in the breakroom as I eat both sticks of my own Twix without so much as offering him a bite.

'ToteTech have always prided themselves on a strong team work ethic,' I parrot, sounding as if I swallowed the company handbook for lunch.

'Yes, but I didn't mean the whole company. You and me, Tara. You have to know your experience is invaluable to me.'

He smiles, giving me the full Christian Grey smoulder, but I'm immune to his ways now. I don't think he's all bad. I think he's young and ambitious. He saw an opportunity and ran with it, but that doesn't mean I have to hold his hand as he learns how real life works in a fast-moving firm. If ToteTech want me to do that, then ToteTech better do a Jerry Maguire and show me the damn money.

'Yes, I'm aware my experience is useful to you,' I tell him.

'Especially at the minute, preparing for the Wilson pitch,' he says.

'Yes. They can be tricky, but it helps to know how best to handle them,' I say, taking a sip of my tea and brushing the Twix crumbs off the table. 'I'd better get back to work. I want to be out of here on time tonight.'

He sighs and there is a hint of 'Gemma' about it. A teenage melodrama – sigh loudly enough and I'm bound to ask what's wrong. Except I don't. I just rinse my cup in the sink and set it to drain. Luke, it seems, isn't for giving up though.

'I'd been wondering if you could work a few extra hours this week. You know, build up your flexitime or something. So you can help me out on this.'

I smile and shake my head. 'I'm really sorry, Luke, but things are crazy with Paul's work, and the kids' childminder is so precious about them being picked up on time.' Neither of these things are strictly true, but he doesn't need to know that. 'Besides, I'm still working through the BumbleTots project. That's taking all my energy.'

The expression he gives me this time reminds me not of Gemma but of Nathan when I tell him his last five minutes of Roblox is most definitely up and it is definitely time for bed.

'Have confidence in yourself,' I tell Luke. 'You were top of your class, weren't you? You know how to do this.'

It feels good to walk out of the room. By keeping Luke in his place I feel as if I'm winning on one front at least.

I'm certainly not winning on the home front. Jax seems to have transformed from a destructive but generally well-mannered toddler into the demon child from hell. It's either teething or the terrible twos. Maybe even a combination of both. We've tried teething powders, Calpol, ibuprofen, a teether, ice-lollies, even that special medicine your mammy tells you about that makes them sleepy (it's legal, honest) but to no avail.

Added to this, Gemma has been clinging to us, taking the middle seat on the sofa – the one usually reserved for snacks – to watch TV each night. When I ask her about Mia and the horrible Sorcha, she just shrugs. 'I don't think I want to be her friend if that's how she goes on,' she says, then looks so sad that I find myself guilt-buying her a new top or ordering a pizza or booking us both manicures. I'm enjoying basking in the glow of her admiration again, which I suppose is something, even if I know that underneath it all is an unhappy child who should be having the craic with her friends and not her really boring parents.

I've been intending to carve out a distinct time for Paul and me to talk about everything properly, but with my high levels of exhaustion thanks to lunchtime gym classes, I'm generally asleep by ten at the very latest. And that's only if I haven't fallen asleep while reading the boys their bedtime stories.

As I watch him laugh and joke with the boys, and even get the odd smile from demonic Jax, I tell myself that everything is fine. We've hit a bump in the road, but all couples do. It's not the end of the world by any stretch of the imagination.

But then I catch how he's looking at me sometimes and I feel a little scared of where this could be going and how I can pull it back. The little voice in my head tells me that the time will come when even sweet, loving and ever-supportive Paul will have had enough of my shit and will leave me in the lurch. Or even worse, we'll become one of those couples who stop laughing together and having the craic. I wouldn't only be losing my husband, I'd be losing my best friend.

Maybe a conversation would put my mind at rest but, truth be told, I'm terrified that it won't. It's easier to carry on as if nothing is wrong – or at least it has been easier. Now, it's just getting bigger and my fear is growing.

I've an email on my work computer confirming my reservation for our night away in a hotel on Friday and I wonder whether it would be sensible to cancel. It would definitely be easier to cancel. I'd find an excuse quite easily. I'm already bringing out the big guns to secure a babysitter willing to take on the task of keeping our children alive in our absence. I've warned Cat that it is highly likely that one of the wains will bite her, and may even draw blood – it's only fair to give her a chance to make sure her tetanus shots are up to date.

Cat, thankfully, dismissed my concerns with the confidence of a woman who has not yet had children of her own and has no idea of how evil those little cherubs who usually fawn over her as she hands them sweets and toys can actually be. She has agreed to babysit – and even better to babysit in our house and sleep over with them so I don't have to worry about packing a bag for them or dealing with any emotional breakdowns at having to leave a prized toy behind.

But still, with Gemma being clingy and Jax being a nightmare and Nathan being really good because 'Miss Rose says it's nice to be nice', I'm afraid it could all go horribly wrong. I know Nathan. He may have an infatuation with Miss Rose now, but this 'being nice' all the time isn't going to last. There will be a meltdown and I should probably be the person here to deal with it.

I text Cat. Think I might cancel Friday night. Doesn't feel right. Kids a bit out of sorts.

A message pings back almost immediately: You're not cancelling. I will physically kick you and Paul out of your house and lock the damn door until Saturday lunchtime at the VERY earliest. You need this.

But the boys . . . I text back.

Will be fine, she replies. They have me. Auntie Cat. The coolest auntie in the world. And it's one night, Tara. It's not like you're abandoning them to go on a forty-day trek of the Sahara! You're going down the road to Ballybofey. For ONE NIGHT.

Aye but still . . .

Still NOTHING, she replies and I can almost hear her shouting at me through the screen. Remember the fuck-it list? Remember? You wanted to get jiggy wid it? You wanted time alone with Paul to do special adult-alone things and get the fire back? This was on your damn list, so you'd better go and enjoy yourself. Go get you some of dat DILF ass.

It's really unsettling to see my best friend write this way, even though it's exactly the kind of thing she would say in real life, to my face. And it's exactly the kind of thing I would say to her if our roles were reversed. Still, it doesn't matter that I know she is right. I know it was on my fuck-it list, but that was before the great awkwardness.

No, even though she doesn't know what's going on between Paul and me, Cat is right: we have to force ourselves out of our comfort zone and have this conversation.

I confirm the booking, tell Cat that I will indeed go and get 'dat DILF ass', and switch off my computer.

Before I do any of that I have bigger fish to fry and my stomach is bubbling – thankfully this time with excitement and not as a result of some rotten Wotsit-infused vegetable smoothie.

Tonight is my first dance class with the Rebel Mums. I have a bag packed with my sports gear in the car. I'm sticking with leggings and a loose, sweat-absorbing top. Part of me wanted to go full 'kid from *Fame*' and wear leg warmers, but I decided to dial it down a bit. 'Keep your cool, Tara,' I whisper to myself as I get in the car, switch on the engine and start singing along to 'Hot in Herre' by Nelly.

I'm giving it the full head wobble, shoulder shake when I notice that Molly is in the car parked next to me and she's looking at me as if she can't quite work out what the hell is going on.

Nothing is going to piss on my parade though. With all the stress there is in my life right now, this is the one thing that has me buzzing with excitement. I wave at her, and sing just a little bit louder.

29

Dig for spuds, ladies

'I'm so excited, I've been dancing around my kitchen all evening. I think the kids think I've lost the run of myself, which isn't far from the truth.' Eva greets me with a rush of enthusiasm and excited chatter as I arrive at the community centre where we've commandeered a small room for the class.

'The other girls are inside. And they're hyper as a box of frogs. Jacinta bought herself a pair of sparkly dancing shoes like the ones they wear on *Strictly*, and Erin is threatening to put us in to perform at the fundraiser for the hospice.'

Whoa. Perform? I didn't think that was going to be anywhere on or near our agenda. 'Perform?' I say. 'Like in front of people?' Memories of enthusiastically jumping around like a loon at school shows to eager applause flood my mind. (At least, I think the applause was eager, and not just a 'yay it's over!' reaction.)

I've never thought I would have a chance, or the balls, to try and recreate that high as an adult. I'm not sure I do have

THE SECRET LIFE OF AN UNCOOL MOM

the balls, even now. It's one thing to set about dancing with some like-minded mammies up for the craic, and another thing altogether to consider dancing in front of an audience of strangers.

Eva must see the fear on my face. 'It's only an idea,' she says. 'God, we might be absolutely shocking. In my head I thought I could be a backing dancer for Madonna. In the real world, I was booted out of Irish dancing classes when I was six because I kept tripping over my own feet. I don't think my skills have improved much since then.' She laughs and I admire that about her – how she can shamelessly rip the absolute piss out of herself and still laugh. I aspire to such levels of not-give-a-fuckness.

In fact, I'm going to add that to the fuck-it list. A simple 'Give no fucks' should sort it. As Eva grabs my hand and we walk through to the hall, I steel myself and push down the unexpected level of emotion that is clawing at me. This will be fun. We will laugh. We won't care too much if we get it wrong. The goal is to relax and have the craic, and if we manage to feel a little like sultry, sexy bishes while we're doing it, then that's a bonus.

Eva scans the room. 'Erm, has Linda not arrived yet?'

I rack my brain for memories of a Linda but come up blank. Jacinta looks up from her phone. 'I'm trying to get through to her now,' she says. 'She definitely should've been here by now.'

'Who's Linda?' I ask, although the penny is starting to drop as I glance around me and see only confused and slightly disappointed faces.

'The teacher,' Jacinta says, and she looks like she might cry. She puts the phone to her ear before shaking her head. 'It's going straight to voicemail,' she says, and that's when I think I might cry. I need this. Like, really need this.

'What should we do?' Jacinta asks, and all eyes automatically go to Eva, who looks as bereft as I feel.

'I suppose we give her another ten minutes and keep trying to get in touch? Maybe she's stuck in traffic or something?' she says.

There's a low mumble of agreement, but the mood in the room has already changed from charged with excitement to a bit fed-up. Does Linda not know how much us mammies need this release?

I excuse myself to go and change in the ladies. Stay positive, I tell myself. What would Gemma do? She would manifest that dance teacher right into the room.

'Do you hear me, universe?' I say out loud as I pull on my trainers. 'Can you get that dance teacher into the hall now please so we can throw some shapes?'

The universe, however, is a dick and by the time I'm finished changing, Eva comes in looking flustered. 'No need to hurry,' she says. 'It seems tonight is a no-go. Linda has double-booked – a mix-up with the dates or something. Long story short, she's currently teaching the foxtrot to a bunch of pensioners at a tea-dance in Eglinton and not here teaching slutdrops to a group of mums.'

My heart sinks. 'Can she reschedule?' I ask hopefully. 'Next week maybe?'

Eva sighs. 'That's the thing: she thought the booking was for next month and she's committed to the pensioners for the next three weeks. I mean, we can try and find someone else . . . but we'll be out some money in the meantime. The only way to get this hall was to block-book it for four months.'

'Well, that's a bit shit,' I say, but I'm downplaying the disappointment I'm feeling. 'Bit shit' comes nowhere near.

'I know,' she says. 'You're not the only one disappointed. Everyone was really excited about this one. I've two left feet and even I was looking forward to it.' She looks genuinely disappointed. I hate it when people look disappointed. Maybe . . .

'Eva,' I say, my voice shaky. I can't quite believe I'm about to say this, but at the same time, I know that I have to. 'Look, this might be completely mad – and feel free to tell me no – but since the hall is ours, and we have an hour to kill . . . Look, I'm no expert, but I used to dance all the time when I was a teenager. I can still remember some of those moves.'

Her eyes widen a little and I see the glimmer of a smile on her face. 'You can. You're a great dancer. I saw you shaking your thang on our night out.'

'It'll give us time to find a new teacher, but I'm sure I could throw something together for tonight. Do they have a sound system I could hook my phone up to?'

'I think so, yes,' Eva says, and the glimmer of a smile is now a grin. 'And I think that would be absolutely perfect. You're a bloody life-saver!'

I feel a shiver of nerves. 'Oh, don't say that – I might be awful. But it's worth trying, isn't it?'

Eva links her arm in mine. 'It's always worth trying.'

All eyes are on us as we walk back into the hall. 'OK,' Eva says, 'Tara here is going to come to our rescue tonight and lead the class.'

'It will be rough and ready,' I say, a slight tremor in my voice. 'I've not done this before and most of my dancing these days is done around the kitchen – and my issues, ha.'

'You were brilliant on our night out!' Jacinta chimes in, and I want to hug her.

'I was also pissed as a fart,' I laugh. 'My powers might not work without alcohol.' I'm joking, but part of me worries it might be true. I'm not used to being as loud, gregarious and confident these days as I once was.

'You'll be great,' Eva says. 'And if nothing else we'll have a bit of fun.'

'What are we going to be dancing to?' a small, short-haired lady who I think is called Oonagh asks.

'Well, we want to have a bit of fun with it,' I say, mentally scanning through my Spotify playlists until it strikes me there's one song that almost everyone knows at least some of the signature moves to and I definitely have it downloaded. 'How about we try "Single Ladies"?'

There is a collective whooping and cheering and an immediate raising of hands and turning them in time à la Beyoncé's iconic dance routine. OK, so it's not a Nineties banger but, look, it takes a while to build up to the classics. You need to work up to dancing with the passion needed for Gina G's 'Just a Little Bit' or to remember that 5ive will make 'Everybody Get Up'.

I'm elated by their reaction and start to lead them in a warm-up and practising some of those familiar moves. We point our toes, pump our fabulous bingo-winged arms and sway our hips.

'Ladies, you know the moves,' I say, punching my hands downwards towards the ground. I'm sure there's proper dance terminology for it, but given that we're in Ireland I christen that move 'digging for spuds'. The wiggle of our butts to the rhythm of the verses is 'baby on your hip', and that iconic hand twist I name 'buy me diamonds'.

I know I sound like a madwoman running through a series of instructions. Anyone walking past will no doubt think we're completely mad. 'Dig for spuds,' I shout. 'Dig deeper, Jacinta. Put your back into it, girl – c'mon, get them spudddddds!'

I let the music wash over me and I feel as if I could be Beyoncé. If I close my eyes, I can imagine I'm wearing the black leotard and stiletto heels that she wears in the video. I might be breaking out in a sweat, but I'm also filled with joy to see these new friends of mine having fun, looking sexy and embracing how bloody great we all are.

We may be a rag-tag bunch of mummy tummies, eye bags, comfy knickers and greying bras, all feeling a little less mumsy and lot more feisty. It doesn't matter that we don't always get the steps right. It absolutely doesn't matter that we end up laughing at ourselves so hard we miss our intro and have to start the song all over again. All that seems to matter is that we are having fun and being silly and doing something completely different to our normal, humdrum mum lives.

Because that's not all we are. I'm not only Gemma's mum, or Nathan's mum, or Jax's mum. I'm not just Mrs Gallagher. I'm not just Luke's second in command. I'm me: Tara. In my activewear teaching some new friends some new moves, and it feels bloody class.

More than that, it looks class. We look class. I'm watching these women and marvelling at how fucking amazing our bodies are. The things we can do. The moves we can make.

'Eva,' I say, between takes, 'can I borrow your phone a minute?'

She looks at me quizzically. Sure my own phone is sitting right there, propped on the edge of a stage by a speaker. 'I want to record this,' I say. 'You all need to see how good it looks.'

'Oh, right, OK,' Eva says, and I see a little seed of doubt on her face. Eva – gorgeous, lovely, inspirational Eva is having a wobble. 'I might stand it out though. I'm not very good, and I hate seeing myself on camera.'

'Eva,' I say, 'you look amazing. I'm not just saying that. Don't think about the camera – throw yourself into it like we've all been doing this last forty-five minutes. None of us is perfect but, believe me, you have to see this.'

I can see the reluctance on her face as she agrees and sets her phone up on the edge of the stage, facing out to where we stand in the hall.

'Ignore the phone!' I shout as the music starts to play. 'Now! Dig some spuds, ladies!'

Five minutes later we are huddled around Eva's phone and the laughing and whooping has stopped. We are watching in silence, transfixed by the images of us on the screen. I'm not gonna lie. I am feeling totes emosh.

By the moment of quiet when the video ends, I get the feeling I'm not the only one.

'Jesus, we're actually not bad,' Oonagh says.

'I didn't realize my body could move that way,' Jacinta says. 'Or that I'd enjoy it so much. I mean, I wanted to give it a go, but that was brilliant.'

Eva is smiling and I give her a quick 'are you OK?' tilt of my head. She replies with a broad grin and a thumbs up before the rest of the mammies chime in with how much they enjoyed it.

They leave five minutes later, singing and laughing, and I stand with Eva in the now quiet hall and allow myself a moment to feel all the good feelings.

'Thank you,' I say to Eva.

'What the hell for?' she asks. 'You pulled us out of a hole here.'

I can hardly speak because what I want to say is that it's been her, and these mums, who have pulled me out of a hole.

Dancing my way in through my own front door shortly after nine, I walk into the living room to find Paul fast asleep on the sofa. The low hum of music from upstairs tells me Gemma is in her room. The lack of shouting, screaming or pealing laughter tells me the boys are, thankfully, asleep.

It's just Paul and me in a dimly lit room. I'm on such a high – so sure that I have turned a corner – that I want to wake Paul up. I want to tell him I'm sorry for how insane I've been. I want to kiss him hard on the lips and show him how much I love him and how much I fancy him. And right now, believe me, I fancy this man of mine. He's lying on his back, his T-shirt pulled up, exposing a little band of skin, and I have an almost uncontrollable urge to lick it. His hair is messy, but in a sexy way. It's no exaggeration to say this man of mine is an absolute ride. I could mount him like a bucking bronco right now.

But with the perfect timing of children who know their mama might be about to get some, I hear a whimper and a cry from upstairs. Jax and his mouth of doom have struck again. Quick as a rocket, I bolt to get to him and extract him from his room before he wakes Nathan and there is all hell to pay. The only thing worse than a crying Jax is a crying Jax and Nathan. God love my eldest son, but he is not good at waking up. I want a shower, a cup of tea and a quick cuddle with Gemma, but if I'm to have even half a chance of that I need to get this situation under control and fast.

On my bedside table sits a virtual arsenal of teething aids. Calpol is first. Jax slurps at the pink liquid like an alcoholic getting his first sip of the day. Then I bring out the Bonjela and risk my fingers by trying to reach into his mouth and find the offending swollen gum. He gags and my heart stops. Please, I beg, please let him not boke. Not now. Thankfully he gives a little cough and then resumes his sleepy half-crying. It's utterly pitiful. When I look up, I see Gemma at the door, holding his favourite sippy cup, filled with warm milk.

'This might help,' she whispers, and she sits down beside me, holding the cup to her baby brother's mouth as he drinks, his cries already subsiding and his eyelids growing heavy. We both sit there and very quietly sing 'You Are My Sunshine' and Gemma rests her head on my shoulder.

In a day of good moments, this is the best. I wait for it to implode in the way things so often do for me these days. I wait for Jax to shit out of the side of his nappy, or Nathan to wake and go full Hulk rage at not being asleep. I wait for Gemma to tell me I'm 'so embarrassing' or to ask for something really expensive so I know her lovely daughter act was all part of a ploy to get her hands on a Shein haul. But none of this happens. Apart from the increasingly stale smell of my own sweat and the fact my hair is stuck to my forehead, it is perfect.

I'm reluctant to break the spell, so I enjoy it for as long as I can, sitting in the lamplit room with my number one baby at my side and my smallest in my arms. But all good things must come to an end and eventually Gemma speaks.

'Mammy,' she says. 'I really love you, but you smell really bad. You need a shower.'

'I know, pet,' I say, kissing her on the top of the head. 'I'll get one now.'

I decide in that moment that not only will I go to the hotel with Paul, but I *want* to go to the hotel with him. Not just to, as Cat would say, 'get dat ass', but because we really do have something good going on, and it will do us no harm to remember that.

I know how tonight has made me feel. Like I'm starting to really know who I am – to remember the Tara that I was afraid had disappeared. This is a chance for Paul and me to remember the fun, cool, silly Paul and Tara that we used to be. The pre-*Gogglebox* couple. The walking-home-from-town-sharing-a-bag-of-chips couple, not giving a damn if it was bucketing with rain. The can't-keep-our-hands-off-each-other couple. I'd moved my body in ways tonight that I'd forgotten were possible. Maybe I can bring some of that energy to the night away with Paul. For the first time since I'd made the fuck-it list, I'm starting to feel really, truly, honestly excited about it.

Paul Gallagher, you're not going to know what hit you.

30

Blonde is the new pink

I haven't told Paul that I've booked the entire day off work and not just the afternoon. That may seem a bad way to start a romantic getaway, but I want to surprise him and to do that, I need to get some time to myself without him knowing.

I get up as usual and we both get the kids ready for school. Gemma seems a little sullen but when I ask if anything is bothering her, she shakes her head and tells me it's just Friday and she's tired and she has double geography to get through. Gemma and I share a disinterest in geography, preferring to learn about people and places instead of rocks and rivers. There's no scandal in a rock. No secret affairs, wars started, people beheaded or any such drama. Absolutely zero craic to be had.

'I know school is tough these days,' I tell her, 'But it's almost the weekend and, bonus, your dad and I won't be here tonight. You won't be stuck in with boring old me. You'll have your BFF Cat to entertain you.'

That makes her smile. 'I'd forgotten about that,' she says. 'I love Cat. I wonder if she'll bring some of her make-up over like last time. She does winged eyeliner like a boss. I've been begging her to teach me.'

'I'm sure she will,' I say, making a mental note to message Cat and remind her to do just that. 'I know what you two are like. She'll have you spoiled rotten the moment the boys are in bed.'

'She was messaging me during the week to see if I'd help do a Shein order,' Gemma says, as if she is the grown-up and Cat the clueless teen. I happen to know that Cat knows her way around every online shopping giant and could order up a storm blindfolded and with one arm tied behind her back. I know she's doing this purely for Gemma and I love her for it.

I envy their closeness sometimes because I know that Gemma can find it easier to confide in Cat than in me, but then I remind myself that I'm incredibly lucky to have direct access to my daughter's confidante. If there is anything I need to know, Cat will tell me. Unless of course, they're both keeping secrets from me, which is entirely possible but . . . naw . . . they wouldn't. Would they?

Anyway, the news of Cat coming to stay has the desired effect of sending Gemma into school with a smile on her face.

I drop Jax off at our childminder's and Nathan to school with the ever-lovely Miss Rose. Rather than hang about to see if there is a 'Mrs Gallagher, can I have a quick word?' I race back to my car so that I can make my early-morning hair appointment.

289

As much as I have enjoyed having hair the colour of candy-floss, it doesn't feel like the real me; more like the me I thought I wanted to be who had to change everything to be happy. I know I sound almost a boke-in-a-bucket sickening dick, but I've realized being cool has nothing whatsoever to do with my hair colour. Feeling comfortable in my own skin is more important. So I'm doing it. I'm going back to blonde. And for the purpose of this romantic getaway, I'm also getting some extensions clipped in so that I look extra gorgeous.

While my hair is being coloured, I'll also be getting a gel nail manicure. And when all that is done, I'll go home, get our bag packed, get everything ready for the kids, and slip into something sexy for our drive to Donegal. I'm going to remind Paul of all the things he loves about me, and that includes the fully made-up, big-haired, nude-lipsticked bombshell version of me.

Walking out of the salon a couple of hours later, my extensions catching in the wind, my make-up professionally applied, my nails a decadent, trampy red, I stick my Beyoncé playlist on my phone, pop my earbuds in and I'm halfway back to the car when I realize I'm giving it the full 'Crazy in Love' swagger as I walk. As a wee old man walking his dog looks at me with what might be fear in his eyes, I realize I've also been singing along. Loudly.

Dear reader, I cannot sing.

'Jesus, you've gone full Sandy,' Paul exclaims, his eyes wide as I totter down the stairs in three-inch heels wondering how under God I ever managed to wear three-inch heels all day, every day before. I feel like a five-year-old tripping around the house in her mammy's shoes. But Paul clearly doesn't notice that I am in mortal fear of falling and breaking my neck as he smiles up at me.

'Tell me about it, stud,' I purr back, and he laughs. I can't help but smile: how lovely is it to be compared to the sexy female lead in *Grease* as opposed to the beauty school dropout? I'm not quite full biker-babe Sandy, but I do have a little of her vibe about me. I'm wearing new leather-look skinny jeans, which are more forgiving than you'd think, nice and stretchy. I'd feared they might cause me to break into a fierce sweat and I'd find myself like Ross in the episode of *Friends*; the last thing I wanted on this romantic getaway was to arrive with a sweaty arse.

Thankfully, these trousers have more of a sexy, naughty-night-away vibe and appear to be breathable. I treated myself to a leopard-print, pussy-bow-neck blouse which skims in all the right places, and finished off the look with my high-heeled boots. The mirror shows me a woman who is sophisticated and alluring. There are no snotters wiped on my top. No sticky handprints on my trousers. There is no half-done make-up because of the kids interrupting or Gemma having borrowed my foundation/mascara/lipstick and destroyed it. I look hot. No – I look HAWT.

'I like the blonde,' Paul says. 'Not that you didn't suit the pink, but this . . .'

'. . . Is more me?'

He nods.

By now I'm at the bottom of the stairs and Paul takes the bag from me, but not before pulling me into a hug. 'I've a feeling I'm woefully underdressed now,' he says, but he isn't. Paul's wearing his relaxed dark jeans, a crisp white T-shirt that I'm pretty sure is new, and a rather fetching dark green utility jacket. If I'm not mistaken those are some shit-hot brand-new white trainers on his feet too. He smells fresh from his shower, a mixture of his aftershave and shower gel. His hair has been freshly trimmed into submission – a short back and sides, with just enough length on the top for a bit of boy band-esque movement. I'm not the only person who looks HAWT.

The boy has made an effort. But he doesn't have to do a Danny Zuko for me to think he is gorgeous. All he has to do is smile at the me the way he did when I walked down the stairs and I'm a goner.

Looking at him, there's a fizz of something right in the pit of my stomach. It's a mixture of lust, of hope and of excitement, that I've not felt in so long.

'Kid-free night!' I say cheerfully, playing it cool.

'Let's get this orgy started!' he cheers back. 'I've checked and the hotel has Channel 4 on each TV, so let's get proper Friday-night crazy and watch *Gogglebox*.'

'Away and shite. There will be no *Gogglebox*. We've a night to ourselves. I say we live it up like we used to and get wild.'

'Whoa, that could be interesting. I hope you've packed the Deep Heat, ibuprofen and comfy shoes,' he says with a smile.

'What kind of kinkery is that?' I ask, laughing. 'Because I'm not having Deep Heat anywhere near my bits.'

'For tomorrow, my love,' he says. 'I don't know if we can still party like it's 1999, but I know for sure that we can't recover that way. We have to take our hangovers seriously now – head them off at the pass. Drink our pints of water. Have the Deep Heat at hand to tackle the muscle strain.'

'Muscle strain?' I say, my eyebrow (perfectly plucked and shaped) raised.

'If you're lucky.' He grins.

As we get into the car, he reaches across and gives my hand a reassuring squeeze. No words are needed. This is our shorthand.

As Paul pulls the car into reverse and we leave behind our ordinary lives, I feel emboldened enough to place my hand on his thigh, perhaps a smidge higher than is decent, and give his leg a wee squeeze. 'I love you, Mr Gallagher,' I say.

'Do you really?' he asks, and I'm about to tell him to stop being so silly when I realize he's not messing.

'Of course I do,' I say. 'Why would you think I don't?'

I watch as he takes a deep breath, his eyes always forward on the road. 'Because you've wanted to change so much. I don't know if it's a premature midlife crisis, or you're regretting settling down so young, but for the first time since we got together, I have no idea what you're thinking.'

31

My name is Tara and I am a shitty wife

We've sat in silence for half the journey now because I didn't trust myself to speak in case I started to cry, and every time Paul even tried to say more, I raised my hand to signal to him 'not now'.

'Just concentrate on driving,' I managed to say, knowing full well that Paul is not a huge fan of driving on unfamiliar roads.

I've gone full grief journey: denial (What does he mean, 'I've changed'? Don't we all, isn't that a part of ageing?); anger (How bloody well dare he, I am a RIDE and he's lucky I put so much effort in); bargaining (Maybe I could give him a bit of time away from the kids once a week? He might not mind so much if I get my night out with Rebel Mums and he gets to go bowling with the lads); depression (This is it. He's going to leave me. He's going to leave me and shack up with some bloody twenty-two-year-old with perky tits and no kids. Me and the babies will be feral within the week). Right now I'm hovering somewhere near acceptance. Maybe . . . maybe I was throwing the baby out with the bathwater with all these changes at once. Maybe there's a middle ground where I get to feel like a whole person again, but I'm still in the loving bosom of my family. At the end of the day, I'm still me, and I still love him and my family madly.

I pull up my big-girl pants. If I don't get him to talk about this now, while we're still in the car, it's going to leak all over our fun night away like a bad smell. I swallow down the lump in my throat and replay what he said, and for the first time I recognize the fear in the tone he used. Before, when we've danced around this topic, I felt criticized and judged even. But maybe that's not what was driving him at all.

'You—' I cough; my voice has gone all croaky. I clear my throat. 'You actually believe that any part of me would want to walk away from us, and our family and our life?' I ask. He shrugs in response.

'I don't know,' he says. 'But we went from rubbing along nicely together to you suddenly changing as much as you could as quickly as you could.'

'That wasn't about us,' I say. 'Well, it mostly wasn't about us. If you want me to be honest . . .' I look away, blinking, glad all of a sudden that we're not doing this with eye contact. 'Paul, I felt I was letting you down. I'm hardly the toned and youthful woman you fell in love with.'

He snorts. 'Tara, you are ridiculous. You absolutely are the woman I fell in love with. When I look at you, I still see her, but I also see the gorgeous woman you are now.'

I snort. 'Oh aye, I'm a pure ride when I'm in my onesie with my bed socks on and my hair in a messy bun, curled on the sofa watching TV and not being able to hold in my farts.'

'Well, call me a fool for love then, but I still fancy you,' he says. 'I probably fancy you even more now than ever before.'

'You are so full of shite!' I laugh and there's a slight shake to it. How does he expect me to believe that he fancies me more now? I've extra wobbly bits, stretchmarks, crow's feet, a less than well-groomed appearance approximately 80 per cent of the time. He has seen me in labour, mooing like a cow as I pushed our children into the world. He has seen me covered in vomit – my own and the kids. He has seen me have a complete breakdown when utterly exhausted after Jax was born. I hadn't slept in two full weeks and I looked like Gollum from *Lord of the Rings*, all wide bloodshot eyes and skin the colour of a dead foot. Even more than that, he has seen me having this little crisis of mine over the last few weeks and behaving like a madwoman.

'I am not full of shite,' he says, 'because I'm not lying. I always did like an older woman,' he says with a smirk.

'Less of the older,' I respond, smacking his leg. But now we are both laughing.

'Seriously though, Tara. You know how you meet someone and you don't really think too much about their looks at first but then you get to know them and you start to see that they are really, truly gorgeous?'

'You didn't think too much about my looks at first?' I ask.

'Let me finish, woman!' He laughs. 'Well, imagine how

extreme that gets when you meet someone and you are blown away by how great they look from the very first moment and then, the more you get to know them, the more your opinion of their gorgeousness grows.'

'I look like Wurzel Gummidge most of the time,' I sniff.

'Not to me, you don't,' he says. 'Look, I know you. I've seen you through your best and worst times. I've seen the person you are. I've seen you at your most vulnerable. You're my best friend, Tara and there isn't a woman on the planet I'd rather spend my life with.'

I do love compliments, but in my thirty-six years on this planet I haven't figured out how to accept one graciously, not even from Paul. It's the law that I have to respond with a joke or a self-deprecating comment. 'Not even Scarlett Johansson?' I ask.

'Aye, true enough. I forgot about her. You'd be binned if she showed up. Wouldn't even have to think about it. But apart from her, you're the only one for me.' He smiles, eyes on the road but seeing something else. Seeing me.

'Oh Paul. I'm sorry if you ever thought I doubted us,' I say with a gulp. 'I just forgot who I was for a while. With Gemma turning thirteen, and the staff at work looking increasingly like they've not long left primary school, and that bloody promotion pushing me to the sidelines, I was starting to feel irrelevant. I didn't think I'd be the kind of mammy who loses it as their wains starts to grow up.'

'But you've always been that kind of mammy, Tara,' he says. 'Remember how you sobbed for two full hours when you bought Gemma her first pair of shoes because, in your words, "she can walk away from me now"? Or how you cheered like an absolute hallion when Nathan delivered his line as narrator number fourteen in the nativity play? You'd have thought he'd won an Oscar the way you cried with pride. You've given our kids everything – you still do. But let me tell you something: Gemma still needs you. Maybe even more than she did before, just in a different way.'

'She doesn't need me to teach her dance routines,' I sniff, and while I'm trying to sound light-hearted I can feel tears prick my eyes anew. I will not cry. I will not ruin the first proper make-up look I've done in years. No way.

'But you have a whole new group of friends who do want that from you,' he says. 'You don't have to be everything to everyone. And you never know, Nathan or Jax may well develop a Steps obsession in their later childhood. There is still hope.'

I sniff again, underestimating the amount of snot that appears to be running down my nose as I try to hold in my tears. It makes a very undignified and slightly nauseating slurping sound.

'I've never wanted you more,' Paul says. And here's the thing: even though this is a joke and he's trying to make me laugh, I believe him.

Lord, this man is in trouble as soon as we get to the hotel. Dat DILF ass is mine.

32

Take your too-tight trousers and leave

'Do you hear that?' Paul asks.

We're lying in a state of post-coital bliss, a bit sweaty and breathless and my make-up is definitely fucked, as am I, but I could not give two hoots.

'What?' I ask him. All I can hear is the sound of our breathing as we try to recover from a session so energetic I'm starting to realize all those spin classes are doing me the world of good. My thigh muscles are weapons of mass destruction now, able to pin a thirty-seven-year-old mechanic to a bed with one squeeze.

'Silence,' he says. 'Absolute silence. No babies crying. No music blasting from a teenager's bedroom. No *Paw Patrol* theme tune, no fucking Cocomelon. I've got to be honest with you, Tara, I can't take Chase and Rubble seriously any more after that sneaky quickie we had with their voices echoing around the house.'

'We had to keep the boys entertained in some way,' I say. 'Although I do sometimes get a bit horny when I hear that bloody song.'

'Doo doo-doo, doo doo-doo, doo doo doo doo doo-doo,' Paul sings, and he laughs.

'Don't pretend you don't know the words, Paul Gallagher. I'd say we both know them inside out and upside down by this stage.'

'Upside down could be fun,' he says with a sexy smirk, and I laugh.

'I think we'd need to build up to that one.'

We lie together in silence for a moment or two until Paul speaks again. 'I know we had our big heart-to-heart earlier about how you're feeling, but can I ask you, Tara – do you still fancy me? I know you've been working hard, and dealing with the kids, and your training and all, but I started to worry that the reason we didn't seem to be sneaking off mid *Paw Patrol*, or any other time for that matter, was because you'd . . .'

'. . . stopped fancying you?' I say, with a small, sad smile.

He nods.

Urgh, in all my thinking about *me*, I forgot to think about *us* and as a result poor Paul has been doubting himself. I can't believe I've been so stupid as to not think he might have been struggling too.

'Well, if the last half hour tells you anything, it's that I absolutely haven't,' I say, stroking my fingers up and down his chest.

'Well, I can see that now,' he laughs. 'But it worried me. I thought maybe you'd want to trade me in for a younger, fitter model. One without a dad bod and greying hair. And then that young fellah started at work with you and . . .'

'Luke?' I say incredulously, even though at first I did find him physically attractive and I was sure he fancied me too. 'Sure I'm almost old enough to be his mammy! He looks good, but he's not a patch on you, dad bod and all. I prefer to think of you as "lived in", and I like a bit of lived in.'

'What, like a comfy pair of shoes or a well-worn jumper?' he asks.

'Yeah, kinda. But sexier, obviously. You've always been sexy to me – more so now, in fact,' I say.

'And yet you couldn't believe that I still fancy the arse off *you* now?' he says, taking my hand in his and kissing it.

'Aye, but that's different,' I say. 'Your body hasn't been ravaged by three pregnancies.'

'Dear Jesus, woman! You know they were my babies, don't you? Or at least I really hope they were my babies, because if I've changed all those shitty nappies and it wasn't even my responsibility, I'm going to be raging.'

'Of course they're your babies. That's obvious. See that stubborn, mischievous, wreck-the-house streak that runs through them all? That's pure Gallagher blood right there. Obviously, they get their smarts and their gorgeousness from me.'

'Aye, did I tell you that Jax decided to hand me a poo yesterday. An actual poo nugget. In my hand. Told me he'd dropped it,' Paul says. 'Are those the smarts you're talking about?'

It takes less effort than I feared to reapply my make-up and fix my hair. There was something quite sexy about the tousled fresh-out-of-bed look anyway. Or maybe it was just that long since we had proper sex – the kind where you can make as much noise as you want, get wild without fear of a child walking in and seeing your boobs in mid-flight, and do it without hiding under the covers in darkness while both fighting the urge to have a sleep instead.

My body had forgotten it could do the things that it just very much did. It had also forgotten how much I could enjoy those same things. *And* I enjoyed them three times. I now feel languid and sensual, and I'm sure I have the glow of a very bold woman about me. I don't care; I love being bold. I loved taking control, enjoying my own body as much as his. I loved that I could make a grown man moan with pleasure. It was empowering. I was a total bloody goddess. So much air cleared just by giving each other some time and attention.

After my shower I slip on the new fancy underwear I'd bought so soon after Gemma's birthday, and a slinky black pencil dress that hugs in all the right places and skims over all the less than right places. Glancing in the mirror, I see a complete MILF staring back at me. It gives me a certain swagger, a confidence as I descend to the hotel lobby and enter the hotel bar, where I'll sip a cold glass of rosé wine while I wait for Paul to come and join me.

He urged me to head on downstairs while he finished his shower and got dressed. Said it would give the whole evening a more 'date night' vibe and I have to admit it does feel nice to sit, relaxing with a glass of wine while I wait for him.

I'm halfway down my drink, watching the condensation roll down the glass while replaying some of the afternoon's more memorable events when I hear a male voice beside me.

'Something, or is it someone, has you in a good mood,' in a posh South Dublin accent.

I look up to see a handsome older gentleman, a bit Clooney-esque around the eyes and with that same Clooney cheeky smile. He's dressed in what I can instantly spot is a very expensive suit. Money doesn't buy class though. It's one of those very expensive but very tightly cut suits that leaves nothing to the imagination. The sight of his meat and two veg squished into his crotch is almost enough to put me off my wine.

I smile a response but don't engage. He's probably making small talk while he waits for the barman to arrive to take his order.

'I'm here on business,' he says as he hoists himself up on the barstool beside me. 'You don't mind if I sit here?' he asks, not waiting for a reply. By the look of him I imagine he's used to being fawned over. If I ignore him, will he get the hint and get lost?

'Yeah,' he continues as if I've engaged fully with him. 'I do a bit of investing, you know. Property. Dublin's a bit of night-mare market at the moment. All those young ones snapping up property at the cheaper end of the market, thinking they'll channel Dermot Bannon or George Clarke and transform their pad into a luxury home. Most of them haven't a notion and end up almost bankrupting themselves. That's where I step in. I love a bargain!'

He either hasn't copped on to the fact I'm ignoring him and making no effort to hide my look of disgust, or he doesn't care. He's a man who likes the sound of his own voice and is talking absolute shite at colossal speed. Every woman in the universe has met one or ten of those in her lifetime. I nod and sneak a glance at the door, hoping that my knight in shining armour is finished preening in our room and will come to rescue me.

'Can I buy you a drink?' Mr Loves Himself asks me as the barman arrives.

'I'm good, thanks,' I tell him.

'Ah now, it's a Friday night. You're sitting at a bar looking, if you don't mind me saying so, stunning. Are you telling me you really don't want a drink? Ah c'mon. Sure you're more than halfway down that glass and a wee top-up will set you up nicely for the night.'

'Honestly,' I tell him, keeping my tone even. 'I'm grand as I am.'

'Oh God,' he says with a sneery smile. 'You're not one of them feminists, are you? Would it kill you to take a drink from a man?'

Even the barman has started to look awkward at this stage. 'Sir, perhaps the lady is happy in her own company,' he says.

'Or playing hard to get,' Mr Loves Himself says with a laugh. 'I know the type.'

Now, I'm not sure if it's the half glass of rosé wine I've had, or the deep sense of satisfaction and confidence running through my body after an afternoon of incredible sex with a man who loves me, or if it's that I am just sick, sore and tired of men talking to women as if we are stupid (Hi there, Mr Handley! Actually, hi there almost every male boss I've ever had the misfortune to work for) but something in me clicks. I'm not going to sit here and wait for Paul to arrive to give the very polite signal to this creep that I'm not available. I don't need to be rescued by another man staking his claim (although I do love it when Paul does a bit of claim-staking).

'Listen, mister, I don't know you or anything about you apart from the fact you are a self-obsessed gobshite who thinks he's entitled to anything he sets his eyes on. But you seem to have made an assumption that I'm happy to spend time in your company just because I'm sitting alone at a bar on a Friday night. I am able to decide who I want to spend my time with and it's not you, nor would it ever be you.'

He starts to splutter and cough, rage behind his eyes. I put my hand up to silence him. 'I'm not done,' I say. 'I am indeed a feminist. The reason I am such a fervent feminist is because men like you exist, who don't know how to take no for an answer, no matter how politely it's said, and then try to gaslight the hell out of women by saying we're playing hard to get. I didn't come here to play, and certainly not with you. So do me a favour, and saunter on.'

There's a vein twitching above his right eyebrow. His face has turned puce. He has gone beyond angry, but I don't care. All my ears hear is the approving roar of a thousand raging women.

'Ugly bitch,' he spits, losing all semblance of cool. 'It's a free country last time I looked, and I can sit anywhere I like.'

'That's true,' I say, lifting my wine glass. I've spotted a booth by the window, which is what I was really hoping for anyway. 'As can I.'

As I take my seat, I see a tall, rotund and fierce-looking security man arrive at Mr Loves Himself's side, clearly telling him in no uncertain terms he has to leave and if he doesn't leave of his own accord he will be forcibly removed.

I resist the urge to shout 'Yeet that sweaty motherfucka into the street' after him, but God do I enjoy the moment.

When the bar has been cleared of vermin, I see Paul standing inside the door, looking positively edible. And his trousers are not cutting off circulation to his genitals. What's sexiest of all, though, is the look on his face. It's love. And lust. And admiration. It's everything I could ever have wanted to see in his face, and maybe I'd stopped looking for.

'So,' he says, leaning over to kiss my cheek as he slides in beside me. 'That was incredible.'

'I can be a proper boss bish when I want,' I tell him.

'Oh I know. And I love it,' he says, and he pulls me in for

a full-on snog – in public! As if we're teenagers or in our twenties, not respectable parents of three children.

When we come up for air (in the interests of public decency) I look at him. 'We don't need to go and eat dinner, do we?'

'I'm sure they do room service,' he says with a smile.

'Perfect,' I say, grabbing his hand and pulling him out of the bar and towards the lifts.

33

Shake it off

'You two are so embarrassing! Oh. My. God! I'm gonny be sick!' Gemma is making fake vomit noises as Paul and I look at each other like love-struck teenagers while we do the dishes – stopping every few items for a wee kiss, or a hug or just a smile.

It's sickening, I know. If I was watching anyone else behave in this fashion, I'd probably be making the old 'fingers down the throat' gesture myself. But I don't care. I'm enjoying it. This is a new honeymoon phase – and even better than our actual honeymoon phase, when Paul got the shits in the Maldives and I spent a full week feeling a mixture of deep sympathy and disgust at the noises and smells my husband's human body could emit.

Ever since we went away for that night and talked things through, it's like the world has found equilibrium again. I no longer worry if the Gen Zs are judging me at work.

They're young and immature. Thirty-six (and maybe mother-hood) will come to them too some day and give them a wake-up call. I'm continuing to do my job so well that no one can dare complain about me not pulling my weight, but not so well that I'm picking up the slack that Luke, poor sod, keeps dropping. And do you know what, it's not his fault he got the job. Yes, he mined me for information and that was a definite sneaky bastard thing to do but again, like the Gen Zs, he's young. He's been brought up in the internet age, where it seems to be OK to do whatever you need to do to succeed. He's a young man being told by his boss that he's the dog's bollocks – did I really expect he would stop and say, 'Whoa! Hang on there, Mr Handley. We both know that Tara is infinitely more suitable for this job due to her years of experience and leadership on past projects'? Did I really think Mr Handley would see beyond the habit of a lifetime and give the promotion to someone without a penis?

I'm not taking it lying down though. I'm playing the long game and not letting myself get tied up in knots about whether or not I was ever good enough for the promotion. I know I was. I still am. Luke is starting to flounder and it will only be a matter of time before the wheels come off. I've made sure to keep a sneaky eye on things – so when they come looking for my help I shall have my glorious moment in the sunshine.

That said, ToteTech aren't the only game in town and if they don't appreciate experience and talent then I'm sure there are others who will. I've been brushing up my CV and putting a few very discreet feelers out. I've even, quite subtly, been encouraging the Gen Zs to think beyond the walls of misogyny central.

Of course, our night away hasn't fixed everything in our lives. Despite doing her best impression of behaving like her usual self with frequent 'oh my God's and 'you are so embarrassing's, Gemma isn't fooling me. She's not herself. For one, she is still more clingy than normal to me and her daddy, which, while lovely in a way, is worrying. When I ask her about school she shrugs or says 'was OK' and then the great silence descends once again. She hasn't been nearly coming through the ceiling doing TikTok dances all day every day, and the usual 'I said/Mia said' monologue is still missing from our daily conversation. I'm not sure how to tackle it, or if I should let her find her way, but it causes me physical pain to see her unhappy. It's one thing to mess with mama, but mess with my babies and you might as well be taking a knife directly to my heart. And if you're going to do that, I'm going to come after you. I just need to figure out how.

'Ach Gemma,' I say to her, after I've playfully smacked Paul on the arse with tea-towel. 'Is it not lovely to see your mammy and daddy so in love after all these years?'

'Erm, I don't think so,' she says. 'Do you not think you two are a bit, well, old for that carry-on?'

'I didn't realize there was an age limit,' Paul says with a grin.

'I don't think it's very appropriate to be carrying on like that in front of the children,' Gemma sniffs.

'Dear child of mine,' I laugh. 'It's hardly as if we're having sex on the kitchen counters!'

At the very mention of the word sex, Gemma has her hands clamped to her ears and is loudly shouting, 'I can't hear you, I can't hear you', which amuses both Nathan and Jax so much that they decide to join in and soon there is a cacophony of disgruntled children dancing around the kitchen. Me though? All I can do is laugh.

It's week three of the Rebel Mums' dance class and we are definitely getting into our stride. In fact, it's going so well that Eva has asked me, on behalf of the mums, if I'll take on the role of 'Dance Teacher' permanently. I, as you can imagine, very graciously accepted the proposal. (Imagine the scene, me, crying: 'Serious? Are you actually serious? Youse want me to teach it? All the time? Not Linda? But seriously though?')

All day the WhatsApp group has been buzzing with messages from the other women, curious about what song we might be dancing to tonight. Thursdays have become red-letter days for us and everyone has thrown themselves behind it. We're all walking around like boss bishes, shimmying while doing the school run, or the shopping or the laundry.

There was mention of buying leotards and high heels to pull off our 'Single Ladies' look properly, but thankfully we agreed that none of us will ever look quite like the single ladies in the Beyoncé video and that leotards are modern-day vagina wedgie devices that make wearing a thong feel like lying down in soft, fluffy blankets.

We have discussed dancing in heels though – with more and more women feeling brave enough to show up with some of their finest going-out shoes and trying to dance in them. Somewhere between your mid and late twenties the hell that is dancing all night in strappy, vertiginous, pointy-toed shoes becomes one of the fucks women no longer give. I can't pinpoint when it first happened for me, but I can tell you that the first time I slipped off my heels at a wedding and danced the night away barefoot with all the other barefooted women I felt as if I had been reborn.

And yet, here we are, talking about slipping our feet into some beautiful heels to sashay around a dance room. I blame *Strictly Come Dancing*. Next thing you know, we'll be putting in a bulk order for sequins, chiffon and fake tan.

I'm dancing in the kitchen with Nathan, Jax on my hip, when Paul comes in from work, a smile on his face as he sees us.

'Daddy, we're dancing!' Nathan shouts enthusiastically. 'Look, Mammy taught me how to do a twerk.' He turns his back on Paul and somehow manages to shake every part of his body except his butt, and yet he is so delighted with himself that Paul cheers anyway, before whispering to me, 'You taught the child to twerk?'

'Ach, sure it's only a bit of fun,' I laugh. 'We've been having a proper old school disco here.'

'Only a bit of fun, you say,' Paul laughs. 'I wonder if you'll think the same when Miss Rose calls you back for one of her friendly chats.'

Shite! I wonder if it's too late to remove 'twerk' from Nathan's vocabulary?

I'm pulling my new wick-the-sweat-away vest on in my bedroom when the door opens and a sad-faced Gemma walks in and throws herself, in a manner befitting Scarlett O'Hara, onto the bed. I wouldn't be surprised if I heard a big 'Oh fiddle-dee-dee' from her in a Deep South accent.

'You OK, love?' I ask.

'Hmmmmghhhmm,' she grunts, which seems to be an increasingly common response to any question these days. I lift my sports jacket from the bed and start putting it on, only to be met with an almighty sigh followed by another 'hmmmmghhmmm'.

'Gemma, love. Is there something you want to talk about?' I look at the clock. I need to leave in five minutes if I'm to have a hope of getting to the class on time. I know I am a mammy first and all, but I do wish my beloved eldest would cut to the chase.

'Nah, not really,' she says, and I nod as I lift a towel to throw it into my sports bag. Maybe she just needed to say hello or 'hmmmmmghhmmmm' and now that need is met?

'OK, love,' I say. 'If you're sure, I'd best be off to the Rebel Mums . . .'

'Aye, I'm sure,' she says, and in the future I know I'll look back at this moment and realize that this was my time to run.

But I don't. I pause. And my beautiful girl starts to speak. 'It's just that, Mammy, you know how Mia has been a real bitch and all?' She pauses to look at me when she says the word bitch, as if she's worried I'll admonish her for it – but given that I do indeed believe her friend has behaved appallingly, I keep my mouth shut.

'Well, it seems that Sorcha doesn't want to be her friend any more – says she is too vanilla for her gang. And I feel like I should be happy to see Mia left without friends, but I'm not. I feel sorry for her.'

My heart swells. 'Well, that proves you're a good person who gives people second chances.'

'Aye, but I don't know if I want to be her friend again. Or maybe I do, but I don't like how she behaved. You don't do that to friends,' she says, and even though she's only thirteen, I'm impressed that my daughter seems to have a handle on what don't-be-a-dick behaviour is already.

'Well, pet, I can't make that call for you. I'm not going to tell you to stay away from her. I'm not overly happy about what she did, but I want to be really clear here – none of my annoyance is about that stupid video of me. Aye, I was a wee bit embarrassed to begin with, but trust me, love, getting my ass stuck on a slide is pretty far down the list of embarrassing things I've done in my lifetime. What I don't like is how she wouldn't take the video down, even though you were getting ribbed for it.'

Gemma chews her lip. 'I think . . . Sorcha's a bully and Mia was afraid to speak up to her.'

I think of the mouthy girl in McDonalds. Sorcha does seem to have a very domineering personality.

'Does Mia want to be friends with you again?' I ask. Gemma turns her phone towards me and I see a stream of 'Pls can we be friends' messages from Mia and lots of 'I'm sorri!' messages. Ignoring the spelling travesty, I sit down on the edge of the bed.

'And you think Mia really is sorry?' I ask.

'I do, Mammy,' Gemma says, and it's clear that she so wants this. She needs this. She hasn't known how to exist in school without her wee bestie. But as her mammy, I'm also scared that her wee bestie could hurt her again. And, if I'm being completely honest, I'm a wee bit ragin' at Mia for being so rude about me when all I've ever done is feed her pizza, let her sleep over and listen to her and Gemma screeching along to Little Mix on a loop.

'Right,' I say, brushing myself off. 'You want to do this?'

Gemma looks at me, a little confused. 'Do what?'

'Make this right with Mia?'

'I think I do, Mammy,' Gemma says.

I glance at the time. I'm definitely going to be late now, but if I ask them to do a wee warm-up or two it won't be too bad. 'Get changed into your sportswear,' I tell Gemma. 'Text Mia and tell her to get changed and that I'll pick her up in ten minutes.'

'But you have your Rebel Mums class?' Gemma says.

'I do. And I've decided that tonight we're dancing to Taylor Swift. And so are you and Mia.'

Gemma's eyes widen. I'm not sure if it's terror or disgust,

but there's only one way to tackle this misnomer that I'm uncool – and that's to remind the girls of just how bloody cool I really am.

Laters haters.

34

I've found my tribe

Mia's face is more than a bit sheepish as she walks out of her front door towards my car. I contemplate giving her a really hard time but I'm going rise above it. For now. The hard time will come in the community hall when she's twerking with a bunch of oldies. It's about time this little madam, and my own little madam too, realized that older doesn't mean 'fit for nothing' or 'past it'. Quite the opposite, in fact. We're in our prime, even if we do make a grunting noise when we stand up.

'Mrs Gallagher,' Mia says, her eyes downcast. The glow off her face would heat a small house for a week.

'Jesus, Mia. You've never called me Mrs Gallagher in your life, don't be starting now. I'm Tara, and well you know it.'

'Tara,' she says and still her eyes don't meet mine. 'I wanted to say sorry for, like, the video and all. And for hurting Gemma's feelings – I didn't really mean it.' I can hear a break in her voice. Eugh, the last thing I want is for the little madam to cry; however much I want to teach her a lesson, I don't want to actually break her.

'Yes, well, I appreciate the apology, Mia. Hopefully you and Gemma will be able to rebuild your friendship and we can forget all about this. But if you are under any illusion whatsoever that I am not cool, then you're in for a shock. Trying to hang out with my daughter and her friends doesn't make me not cool. Caring about you all doesn't make me not cool. It definitely doesn't make me not cool to take Nathan to the park and make an absolute tit of myself getting stuck on a slide.'

'I . . . I know, Tara. I'm sorry.'

I hear Gemma make her 'hhmmmmgghhhmmm' noise in the background which I'm now interpreting as 'oh for feck's sake Ma, enough now. Let's get going.'

Ah, nature is healing.

'Ermmm, Tara, before we go can I ask you a favour?' Mia's voice is shaky and quieter than normal. When I look at her I see she's turned a shade of red darker than any ever seen on this planet before.

'What is it?' I ask.

'Well, you see, I told my mammy what you were doing and she asked me to ask you if she could come along and give it a go as well?'

Well, my inner Mr Burns steeples his fingers in glee: this is the perfect way to let Mia know that you don't, under any circumstances, fuck with a mammy in her thirties who has had enough of being disrespected by teenage girls who thought JoJo Bows were a legitimate fashion statement.

'Of course,' I grin. 'The more, the merrier!'

I watch as she gives a wave to the front door where her mother – a very lovely and usually shy woman called Kerry – is standing in full activewear, with a sports bottle of water in one hand and her handbag in the other.

'This is so exciting,' Kerry says as she gets into the car beside me. 'Mia was telling me about this class and I thought, well, I just thought fair play to you, Tara. I wish I had half your guts – the way you go out there and do what you want to do. You were always like that. I admire it so much. The confidence you had on stage when we were teenagers! You lit the place up, and I always thought it was a wee shame you never kept it up after school, but here you are now.'

I only vaguely remember Kerry from school. I'd be lying if I said otherwise. She was two years above me, and if she is shy now, she was positively paralysed with fear any time anyone so much as glanced in her direction back then. Obviously our paths have crossed many times over the course of the girls' friendship, but we've never actually spent a lot of time in each other's company. If she's impressed by me, I'm hella impressed by her. Imagine pushing that shyness aside and being prepared to let loose in a dance class?

'Sure here we both are,' I grin.

'I've a few stragglers with me tonight,' I say, as we arrive to the Rebel Mums. This is a safe space for mammies to have

319

fun and, if necessary, rant about the wee crotch goblins we love and gave birth to, so I did message Eva before we left the house to give her the heads-up.

The Rebel Mums are well versed in slide-arse-gate and on how Gemma has been coping afterwards and, thankfully, Eva declared it absolute genius to make Mia take part in the class. It won't do Gemma any harm to see how bloody class you are at this either, she'd texted.

Gemma and Mia are still looking terrified, but clinging to each other in that nervous giggly way teenage girls do. Kerry, on the other hand, looks as if she might throw up.

I take her hand and lead her to the centre of the group. 'Ladies, this is Kerry. She's Mia's mammy and she has never done anything like this in her life but she's very excited and I think she could really enjoy what we're doing.'

Kerry's eyes flicker briefly from the group to the floor and back again. I can feel her trembling beside me and I wonder why I never took the time to get to know her better; she could do with some fun, and some friends.

'You're very welcome,' Jacinta grins. 'It's all a bit of fun really.'

Kerry gives a nervous smile. 'I love your shoes,' she says, eyes fixed on Jacinta's bedazzled Latin dance pumps. That of course endears her to even more to Jacinta, who grins widely.

'Thank you. I love them too. I wish I could wear them everywhere – the school run, Tesco, visiting the in-laws – but they're proper dance shoes, you know. With special soles.' Jacinta loves nothing more than telling people about her proper dance shoes. She says they make her feel graceful and sexy in a way she hasn't in years.

'So you know Tara because of your daughter then?' Oonagh asks.

Kerry nods. 'Well, I knew her at her school, or knew of her at school, years ago. We weren't in the same year group, but I used to love watching her in the school shows, dancing and singing and all. I think we all thought she'd be pure famous one day. Like Nadine Coyle or something.'

Ah Nadine Coyle – the Derry girl the same age as me who has been living my dream life all these years. Fronting an internationally successful girl band, touring the world: there isn't a woman in Derry who hasn't felt a pang of jealousy towards the local girl done good.

Out of the corner of my eye, Gemma's eyes widen. She knows who Nadine Coyle is and maybe she's shocked to see her mum compared even in passing to such a stunning sultry songstress.

'Well. She's pure famous to us now,' Oonagh crows. 'And not just because of that video of her getting stuck on the slide.'

There's a moment of awkward tumbleweed sweeping through the room, silence before Oonagh slams her hand over her mouth. 'Oh God, I wasn't supposed to mention . . . sorry, ladies.'

Mia has turned the colour of what my mother would have called 'boiled blooter'. To this day I have no idea what blooter is, boiled or not, but I do know it has the same colour as someone very close to boking.

There's a snort from Eva, who is clearly doing her best not to pee herself laughing, and it breaks any tension. I can't help but laugh too and soon it has spread around the room. Even Mia has managed to break into a wobbly smile.

I clap my hands to get everyone started.

'C'mon now, ladies, pull it together. We're going to do something a little different this class. But first I want to show Gemma and Mia how the mammies do it.'

The girls and Kerry skitter over to the side, the mammies get into formation, and I set the track to play. That fizz is there, right in the pit of my stomach. The fizz I've been missing. We might only be dancing in front of my daughter, her best friend and her best friend's mammy, but we are dancing in front of an audience.

Closing my eyes as the music starts, I channel my inner Beyoncé, begging her not to fail me now. We start to move.

It's not perfect. It's very far from perfect if the truth be told, but it's fun and we have the best craic and by the end of it my heart is pounding with a mixture of pride and happiness and joy at being able to laugh at myself a little too. Looking around, those feelings are reflected on the faces of the other Rebel Mums, some of whom are now holding each other up with helpless laughter. But there's really only one face I want to see right now and I look directly at my daughter, who is applauding widely and cheering.

'Mammy, you're class!' she shouts. 'That was so cool.'

I want to punch the air with joy and relief and happiness. Yesssssssss! My daughter thinks I'm cool!

35

Hello, boss bish speaking, how can I help?

It's been over a month since the fuck-it list was created and a whole lot has happened in those few weeks. I'm in a much happier place as I slip into a pair of jeans and a floaty white shirt (French tuck done, cheers *Queer Eye*), ready to go meet Cat and Amanda for lunch. My painted toenails peep from my strappy tan-coloured sandals and my hair is back to its bouncy blonde.

I've managed to extricate myself from the bosom of my family without Jax or Nathan smearing any foodstuff or bodily excretions on my top, and Gemma even loaned me her lip balm, which gave my lips a tingling feeling and makes them look a little pouty. (Not sucker-fish pouty, more a kind of just-kissed pouty.)

Paul has given me a free pass to stay out as long as I want and has given me a free pass from dinner and bathtime duties later. Bring on the day-drinking – mama has the day off! In return for my husband's amazing husbanding, I've okayed a weekend away with the lads for him. Gemma has already promised to be a help. I mean, she's thirteen, she negotiated a sizeable Shein haul for her 'help', but it's in the bag, thank God. In fact, I breathed a bit of a sigh of relief, now that she's back to extortion, rolling her eyes dramatically and 'hhhhhg-gghmmm-ing' more than ever. Order has been restored to our world.

Yes, this is definitely going to be a much lighter lunch than my mini-breakdown last time we were here. I will *not* drink one too many cocktails and sob about my advancing years and my children's rejection of me.

Walking along the quay by the River Foyle in Derry, the sun is shining; I could be an ad for sanitary products, or shampoo or face cream or something. If someone were to rollerblade past me right now singing about being 'shaped for confidence' I wouldn't bat an eyelid.

I feel very much the millennial mum. Ready to chat with my girls and fill them in on all the goss. I arrive at the café to see Amanda is already there. And not only that, my brows inch upwards, she looks as if she has been dragged through a hedge backwards. She looks, dare I say it, haunted. She looks, if I'm not very much mistaken, like a *normal* mammy and not her usual brand of super perfect and polished mammy. There is already one empty cocktail glass in front of her and she is halfway down a second pink-coloured drink.

'Ehh, are you OK, Amanda?' I ask as I greet her with a hug.

She gives me a thumbs up as she sits back down and takes a long drink of her cocktail. 'I just need a moment,' she says, taking a few gulping breaths to calm her breathing. A bell tinkles over the door and Cat walks over to join us, glancing at Amanda, and then mouthing 'what the fuck?' at me. All I can do is shrug.

'She needs a minute,' I say.

'Well, I'll use that minute to order some drinks for us. Amanda, are you ready for another one?' The thumbs up gesture reappears and Cat nods. 'Tara, the usual? A French Martini?'

Maybe it's the fact that I've not eaten anything today, but I'm not quite up for a proper drink yet. 'Actually, I think I'll have a coffee first.'

'Have I entered the Twilight Zone?' Cat asks. 'Have you two hallions swapped bodies or something?'

I shake my head. 'Nope. I just feel like a caffeine hit.' It's quite amusing to see Cat walk away muttering to herself about never understanding other people. She's usually so completely self-assured that I'd be lying if I said I didn't get a perverse sense of joy from it. It's very rare that anyone rattles Cat's cage – so rare in fact that I'm focused on trying to think of the last time when I feel a hand clamp mine.

I look up and Amanda has a fairly wild-eyed gaze about her. 'You knew, didn't you?' she accuses, and she is staring at me with such intensity that I wonder if I did indeed know – even though I have absolutely no idea what she's talking about.

'Knew what?'

'That I was being a smug, self-righteous mammy and that one day – ONE DAY – it would inevitably bite me square in the arse.'

Well, she's not wrong but she's my friend and it was more that she was just better at being a mammy than me, plus a wee bit judgey. She takes my hesitation as permission to continue.

'We didn't have the terrible twos, or the trying threes, or the fucking fours. I'm going to say this, Tara, I was sure that the rest of you' – she gestures around the café – 'were all exaggerating. I mean, I've seen kids kick off, I'm not stupid. But I thought maybe I was doing it right. God knows, I couldn't have done more for my girls if I tried. I mean I haven't actually shared a bed with just my husband in six fucking years! But I was fooling myself, wasn't I? The day was always going to come when my darling children would turn into cheeky, messy, mischievous little shites and pull the fucking rug right out from under me, and I'd be left trying to explain to a crying mother why my daughters had seen fit to cut her daughter's hair with play scissors while the teacher's back was turned. I didn't even think those damn things could cut hair!'

I open my mouth to say something, but Amanda is not done yet. 'So I'm there, in the classroom talking to this distraught mammy who is now having to consider cutting her daughter's hair into a crop two weeks before she was due to be flower girl at her auntie's wedding. I'm apologizing profusely and saying I don't know what's got into the girls and this is very unlike them, when their teacher gently informs me they've been increasingly disruptive over the course of the last few months and, get this, there are a few children in the school – like primary seven children, practically bloody adults – who are scared of them.

'And then the mammy of the shorn-headed child nods and asks me with a very straight face if I've ever seen *The Shining*, 'cos . . .' and her voice is shaking at this point, her head bowed . . . ''cos my twins would fit right in.'

Now I want to be very clear about this. I did not intend to laugh, but before I know it, I have snorted – like a pig – and I can't hide my mirth. I feel awful. Here is one of my long-time, long-term besties, clearly beside herself at her children's segue into behaving like real children and not Stepford children, and I am laughing.

'Oh, Amanda, I'm so sorry for laughing,' I say, and she looks at me, stricken. 'But can I be real with you for a minute? I am so, completely and utterly delighted to hear that the girls are finally doing what all children do and making you wonder why in the name of all that is holy you decided to have them in the first place.'

'But my girls don't do that,' she protests as Cat joins us again, drinks in hand and I give her an abridged version of what Amanda just told me. It's comforting that Cat snorts as well.

'They're kids, Amanda. Kids can be wee shites. I'm not even a mammy and I know that. It's part of the reason I know being a mammy is not for me. There isn't a perfectly behaved, never-put-a-foot-wrong child on this planet – and if there is I'd be waiting for the moment they show themselves to be a full-blooded sociopath.'

'It's true,' I say. 'And look, your parents did everything for you and you still had some memorable moments growing up, if I recall correctly. Didn't you let all the rabbits out of their cages at Kelly's pet shop? And decide to cut the hair of all your Barbies, leaving them looking like skinheads and then crying when that look didn't suit their princess dress vibe?'

Amanda nods.

'I'm quite relieved now,' Cat says. 'I don't have to put them on a watch list or worry they'll turn into serial killers.'

'I'm mortified!' Amanda wails.

'You get used to it,' I tell her, rubbing her hand. 'Trust me. Miss Rose had me explain to her this week what twerking was and suggested it wasn't a dance move I should be teaching my five-year-old.'

It's Amanda's turn to snort, and soon that snorting turns into a full-bellied laugh, a clinking of cups and glasses and a welcoming of her to the 'Shitty Sixes' – it's going to be fun.

Three hours later and I'm home, my sides sore from laughing, my tummy full of the most delicious food and my heart feeling even fuller.

'Do I need to break out the pints of water, basin and darkened room?' Paul asks as I walk into the living room. He is sitting on the floor, ostensibly playing Lego with the boys, but they are glued to the TV and Paul has constructed a very intricate spaceship that is definitely not designed to be put together by young children.

'Nope,' I say. 'I'm sober as a judge. Which means I've had a couple, but I'm a judge so I'll get away with it,' I say.

'You'd a free pass and you only had a couple?' he asks.

'Yeah, we were too busy talking. You'll never believe the craic about Amanda and the perfect twins. But I didn't really feel like drinking. Maybe I'm faulty or something?' I laugh.

'I'm sure you'll be well recovered for a wee glass of something later. I was thinking we could order in, just the two of us. Gemma is staying over at Mia's. If we get the boys to bed early we could make a night of it. Catch up on *Gogglebox*, if you know what I mean?'

Gemma hasn't cracked our sexy-time code yet, which is a blessing because the last thing I need is my thirteen-year-old acting all Aunt Lydia on me. Or launching into 'Oh. My. God. You two are so dis-gust-in!' if we do more than breathe in the same room.

'I don't think I could eat another bite,' I say, 'but I'm definitely open to catching up with *Gogglebox*.'

'Mammy, can I have a drink?' Nathan wakes from his TV-watching trance.

'My hungry,' Jax chimes in.

'I'm hungry too,' Nathan says. 'Can I have food too, please? Chicken nuggets and wobbles and wed sauce and binegar on top.'

'Nuggets and wed sauce,' Jax repeats, clapping his hands with excitement.

Paul makes to get up and start on tea, but I wave him back down.

'Sit you down and finish making your spaceship, I'll do the tea.'

'It's a *Star Wars* X-Wing, not just any wee spaceship,' he smiles. 'But I'll let you away with not knowing the intricacies, this time.'

There is something so very lovely about Saturday afternoons with my family around me. (I realize I'm sounding like a bit of a sickener here, but I've had two French Martinis and at least three good orgasms this week and life is pretty damn fantastic.)

The icing on the cake arrives in the form of a panicked WhatsApp message at ten past nine. The boys are in bed. Paul and I are curled on the sofa and there is an open box of Maltesers in front of me. We've not reached the hot sex part of the evening yet, but I'm feeling chilled as we tell Netflix that yes, we are still watching *The Office* and let it play on.

I fumble for my phone. 'Probably Gemma,' I say. 'Or Cat, wanting to dissect everything that was said over brunch. If it's her, I'll tell her I'll be in touch tomorrow.'

'Cool,' Paul says, and takes a long drink from his beer.

But it is not Cat. And nor is it Gemma. It's not Amanda, or Kerry, or Eva. It's not my mother, who is morally opposed to sending text messages when people 'could just have the manners to pick up the phone and call each other'.

It's Luke. And he is in meltdown.

Work emergency. I really need your help before I fuck this up entirely. I'm in over my head, Tara. SOS.

I show the message to Paul, who snorts. 'He sounds pretty freaked out.'

'He is,' I reply. 'Should I call him straight back or let him stew for a few minutes?'

'Tara Gallagher, are you being a minx?' Paul asks, arching an eyebrow.

'Let's just say, I saw this coming. Obviously Handley should've seen it coming too, but he was too busy residing up his own hole to notice.'

Paul snorts again. 'I love it when you get all devious,' he says.

'Yeah, but I don't think I can leave the poor pet hanging on too long. That message is pretty desperate.'

'Go, wife of mine, and do what you need to do,' Paul says, and I walk through to the kitchen while dialling Luke's number. When he answers, he is breathless and clearly distressed. I sort of feel sorry for him.

'Oh Tara. Thank you so much for calling back. I am ready for the hills. I really think I've messed this up and I'm going to lose my job and . . .'

'Luke,' I say, 'breathe. Then tell me what is wrong.'

He takes a few slow, shuddering breaths until he is able to speak in distinct words and not just a jumble of words all rammed together.

'The Wilson pitch . . .' he says.

'Yes?' I know it. I've spent the last week collating relevant data, market shares, demographics, target demographics, potential growth markets, market research . . . It has been full on. I've kept a few files on the side, because Luke's approach didn't seem to be as meticulous as mine. I've not been intending to sink him, merely looking to illustrate my point.

'I was working on some spreadsheets, and I don't quite know what I did, but I seem to have fucked up the figures. Everything's jumbled and for some reasons the numbers are all backwards like some sort of satanic code. I've spent the last hour trying to fix them and only making it worse. My stupid computer won't revert to a previous draft, and then Peter Wilson sends me an email on a Saturday night asking me to look specifically into the – and these are his words not mine – yummy-mummy market and I googled that and now my brain hurts, I need eye bleach for some of the more interesting search results and how am I supposed to know what a yummy mummy wants? And then that's when I thought of you—'

'So, you see me merely as a mummy-type figure?' I ask. Fuck's sake. My professional experience is being undermined in favour of my 'one uterus, careful owner, no time wasters, please' status, *again*.

'No!' he says. 'Well, yes, obviously you are a mother and you have insider knowledge of what really makes the parenting pound zing. But more that you know how to get to the heart of the data, and we both know you can hone in on gaps in the market better than I can.'

I smile. Oh this is kind of glorious.

'And,' I say, 'I know how to make those numbers read the right way around again. I also have copies of all the raw data and a few spreadsheets I've been working on myself.'

I sound like a smug bitch but that is because, at this precise moment, I am feeling incredibly smug. I've always known how picky Peter Wilson is. I've known he likes to throw in curveballs at the last minute and that he is no respecter of anybody's time but his own. I've dealt with him, and men like him, my whole career, and I always come prepared.

'Luke, it's Saturday night. Take a breath. Have a beer, or a glass of wine, or a cup of Horlicks. Do what you need to de-stress. We can meet at the office tomorrow morning and work this all out. It's fine. Honest. We've got this.'

I hear an audible sigh of relief and perhaps the smallest of sobs. 'Tara, thank you so much. You've no idea . . . It's totally different doing this job than learning about this job, and I'm sorry if I was ever a prick. I'll make sure Mr Handley knows it was you who pulled me, and us, out of this hole. I swear.'

He doesn't go so far as to offer to throw himself on his sword and get Handley to offer me the job instead, but the last few weeks have taught me that it's OK to be happy with my lot. For now. There's still those other job applications, after all, and right now, I want the time to be a mammy. To be a friend. To be a dance teacher. And to be a little bit slutty with my gorgeous husband on a Saturday night.

I end the call with Luke, unzip my onesie to expose a flash of lacy bra, and sashay back into the living room to seduce the man I love.

'Paul, I think this just might have been one of the best days of my life, and it's about to get better . . .'

Epilogue

New phone, who dis?

Four weeks later

Gemma is going to kill me. I never thought this day would come, when I was actually terrified of my own daughter. But here it is. The fear is real.

I'm not sure when I first noticed that something was up. Looking back, that day – the day I declared the best day of my life – might have been a clue. I'd been super emotional, but in a good way. I was embracing my inner Oprah and being grateful for everything.

Nah.

I had smashed the preparation for the pitch for Mr Wilson, and Luke and I co-presented it. Of course we won the contract and I won the praise for my unique ideas and insight. But despite nailing the pitch, I'd felt edgy the whole day. Not a panic attack or my usual anxiety. Not quite sick. But something was off. I was a little light-headed and woozy from time to time. I put it down to nerves, and lack of sleep. Jax had decided to starfish in our bed the previous night and I'd been woken several times with a foot in my mouth, or ear, or eye.

It's surprising how easy it was to push it to the back of my mind, though. Things have been so busy. Work has been full on with the new contract, and then my exercise classes have zapped a lot of my energy. OK, I need to be honest: I dropped most of them. I still go to spin because I'll be damned if I let it beat me. And I quite enjoy yoga. (No one ever really tells you that yoga does wonders for keeping your bowels moving smoothly, eradicating the need for any vegetable smoothies.)

And the kids have been distracting me, too. Nathan has started at football. He's incredibly bad at it, but he loves it and he has enthusiasm. Paul is proud as punch and has even offered his services as a coach. Jax is pure ragin' he isn't old enough to join in yet, so we let him have his own ball to kick out the edge of the field while the big boys play.

The Rebel Mums still meet for our dance class, and yes, we finally talked ourselves into performing at the fundraiser for the hospice in a few weeks. Maybe, I told myself, that's what had me out of sorts. It's a few weeks away, but I've broken apart and rebuilt my choreography ten times already and, truth be told, my sanity. But no. I love it. I really love it, and it's one of the best things I've ever done.

Besides, even nerves don't cause sore boobs with nipples so tender that you want to scream if someone so much as breathes within ten foot of them. And last time I checked, nerves aren't terribly well known for making your period go AWOL.

'She's going to kill us, isn't she?' I say, as I sit in a very undignified manner and pee on a stick over the toilet. Paul is perched on the edge of the bath looking like he might pass out.

'Let's wait and see what the test says before we worry,' he says. 'It might be a false alarm.'

'But if it isn't?' I ask him.

'Then yes, our thirteen-year-old is going to kill us. 'Cos this is totally dis-gust-in,' he squeaks, in a perfect impersonation of her favourite catchphrase.

'Jesus, Mary and the wee donkey,' I say. 'This wasn't in the plan, pet.'

'Well, neither was Gemma, and she worked out OK,' he says.

'We're in a really good place,' I say. 'Will this change everything?'

He shrugs. 'None of our kids have changed anything for the worse,' he says. 'We'll cope, Tara. If we survive Gemma's reaction, we'll cope. How long do we have to wait for the result?'

'Coupla minutes,' I say as I pull my trousers up and wash my hands before taking a seat beside Paul on the edge of the bath.

'Was that trip away that did it,' he says.

'Hmmm,' I answer, but I'm not really listening. My mind is filled with images of tiny babies and the way they snuggle up on your shoulder and how their wee bums fit in the palm of your hands. A scary 'your baby will shit themselves inside out just before you are due to leave the house' thought pops up, but I push it away. If the test is positive, then we'll cope and we'll make the most of it. And I'll need my friends, and the Rebel Mums, more than ever.

I take a deep breath. 'I'm scared to look,' I tell Paul.

'Me too,' he laughs. 'But we have to do it. That plaster needs ripping off.'

I nod and reach for the plastic wand, turning it over to see the word 'Pregnant' across the digital screen.

'Yup,' I say, even though I feel a wee kernel of hope bud inside me. 'We're dead. Maybe we should move house and not tell Gemma where we've gone. Change our phones. Or just ghost her? You know "new phone, who dis?" – that kinda thing.'

'It'll be grand,' Paul says, putting his hand on mine. 'We'll be grand.'

A Glossary of Derry/Irish speak

Clattered: completely covered in, a huge mess, a Very Bad Thing.

Boke: vomit, can be a verb or a noun. Also a Very Bad Thing.

Crabbit: Ulster/Scots word – grumpy and argumentative. Certainly Not a Good Thing.

Dootsy: old fashioned and not in a cool, vintage aesthetic way. Definitely not a look people aspire to. If dootsy were a decade, it would be the 80s.

Take your oil/Take my oil: the Derry equivalent on putting on your big girl (or boy) pants and dealing with the consequences of your own actions.

Eejit: a fool but often used as a term of endearment.

Scunnered: in Derry this means 'fed up'. Belfast people will try and tell you the word is 'scundered' and means fed up and/or embarrassed. Belfast people are wrong. It's best you know that.

Pure: in Derry, adding 'pure' in front of anything indicates a passionate kinship with the state or emotion you are experiencing.

Wains (can also be spelled weans): children.

Up the Foyle in a bubble: the Foyle is the River Foyle, a fast flowing river which runs through the heart of Derry separating the Cityside from the Waterside. 'Up the Foyle in a bubble' is comparable to 'Up the Lagan in a bubble' which you may have seen used in 'Line of Duty'. It means naïve and without gumption. However, it is believed the saying originated in Derry and those Belfast ones stole it.

Up your hole, with a big jam roll: a rather lyrical way of telling someone to stick their ideas and/or opinions up their own arse.

Hallion: similar to hellion except more Northern Irish. A messer, lacking in social graces.

Youse/yousins: plural of 'you', used in direct speech.

Acknowledgements

Thanks to the wonderful Martha Ashby and the entire team at HarperCollins for this incredible opportunity and their continued guidance and support.

To my fellow Boss Bish, Claire Allan, for her long hours of support, even through Covid, and for keeping me in line.

To my mother Mary for embedding the love of books and creativity into my bones and always having my back.

To Ava for always reminding me that even though I'm not cool, I'm still her best friend.

To Alfie for always making me laugh and feel loved a hundred times a day.

To Mark for supporting my mid-life crisis/career change.

To the Mammy Banter followers who have embraced my madness as creative comedy and supported me throughout this journey.

You are all absolute rides.